W9-CLE-097

A RIB, HE THOUGHT . . .
I JUST LOST A RIB

The air of Mars whimpered and then screamed as the aeroshell started to burn. Kane's Valium calm vaporized and he was sure he was going to die. He'd looked at death before, sometimes gone out of his way to see it, but he'd never had so little control over the outcome. He felt as if he'd been thrown out of a helicopter with a mountain tied to his back. His vision narrowed to a gray, viscous tube and he prayed he wouldn't have to take manual control of the ship, because he couldn't lift his arms back up to the keyboard.

"FRONTERA is hard-edged and colorful and relentless, and altogether a compelling read. Shiner paints his picture of the day after tomorrow with a gritty realism that makes you believe every minute of it."

George R. R. Martin

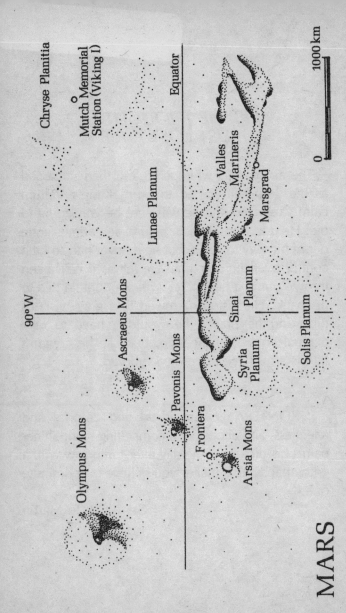

MARS

Olympus Mons

Ascraeus Mons

90°W

Pavonis Mons

Frontera

Arsia Mons

Chryse Planitia

Mutch Memorial
Station (Viking I)

Equator

Lunae Planum

Valles
Marineris

Marsgrad

Sinai
Planum

Syria
Planum

Solis Planum

0   1000 km

LEWIS SHINER

FRONTERA

A BAEN BOOK

FRONTERA

A Baen Book

Baen Enterprises
8-10 W. 36th Street
New York, N.Y. 10018

First Baen printing, August 1984

ISBN: 0-671-55899-4

Cover art by Vincent Di Fate.

Printed in the United States of America

Distributed by
Simon & Schuster
Mass Merchandise Sales Company
1230 Avenue of the Americas
New York, N.Y. 10020

Map by Lewis Shiner

For E.

I am deeply grateful to William Gibson, Edith Shiner, and Bruce Sterling, for making me see what it was I really wanted to do. Thanks also to my editor, Betsy Mitchell, and to the many other friends who contributed time and suggestions, including Ellen Datlow and the Turkey Citizens.

With less than five minutes left, Kane tugged nervously at his shoulder harness and tried to remember gravity. The feel of his arms dragging by his sides, the blood pooling in his legs, his head jerking forward in fatigue—it all seemed distant, clumsy, irrelevant.

"You've gone soft, Kane," Lena whispered, but her eyes were afraid of him. She locked her cleats into the gridded floor, peeled the plastic sheath from a hypo, and pushed 15 milligrams of Valium into his left arm. "You look like shit. You're about nine-tenths crazy and you haven't got any muscle tone at all. I don't think you're going to make it."

"Four minutes," Takahashi said.

"I'll make it," Kane said.

Not just gravity, he thought, but eight G's, wrenching, crushing, suffocating him while the ship threw off 10,000 feet per second of velocity by diving into the thin atmosphere of Mars. The ship's computer would sail them through a narrow, invisible corridor, balancing air drag against the strength of their reinforced carbon-carbon aeroshell, slowing them just enough to put them into a high, elliptical orbit around the planet and not send them crashing into the frozen martian wastes.

All because the corporation didn't have the booster stages to slow them down any other way.

He knew Lena had put him off, not caring if she

had time to give him the shot, not caring if his muscles had the elasticity to ride out the re-entry. Reese had been first, of course: the senior astronaut, the father figure. Then she'd taken care of Takahashi and after that herself, floating where Kane could see her, easing the needle into the soft flesh of her thigh.

In the first weeks of the mission she and Kane had struggled through a brief, sweaty affair; it ended when Lena, fingers stiffening in orgasm, drew blood from Kane's chest and triggered his defensive reflexes. Kane's erection had vanished and his hands had closed around her wrist and neck in a killing grip.

Within a second he was in control again, but Lena had panicked. Nerves, he'd explained, but she was already dressing, afraid to take her eyes off him. The next day they'd both started taking sex suppressants.

Kane had gone off them two days ago, hoping to clarify his muddled thoughts and desires. Now he found himself remembering her thin, angular body, the bones like negative shadows under the darkness of her skin, her breath moving against the underside of his jaw.

"Three minutes," Takahashi said. "Kane, you'd better punch in."

Kane's CRT swam with concentric circles, the ship's path projected onto the vortex of Mars's gravity well. He reached for the bank of knobs and switches in front of him, as familiar now as the M-37 he'd carried in North Africa, and hit control-C on the keyboard. At least once a week for the last nine months he'd been strapped to this couch or one of the others, working through endless computer simulations of the landing.

He remembered the morning he'd drifted in to find Reese buckled into one of the slings, jacked out of his skull on psilocybin, banging his massive fists into the control panel, and screaming, "We're crashing, oh jesus, we're crashing!" They had been six months out of Earth at the time, weightless, drifting, lights rheostatted down to save the fuel cells. Plague-carrying buboes on Reese's neck would have been no more terrifying than his hysteria. Kane had fled from it, back to the wedge-shaped coffin of his quarters, and spent two days in a tranquilized fog.

And now, he thought. Were they really braking for orbit? Or was this just another simulation? If he turned this switch would it fire a braking rocket or would it just force a branch in the computer's program?

He remembered childhood nightmares of sitting in the back seat of a moving, driverless car.

"One minute," Takahashi said.

The Valium washed over him like a lullaby. The blinking time display slowed as he watched and the muscles in his shoulders and neck began to loosen.

An attitude jet, fired by the computer, went off with a noise like a machine-gun burst. Kane's heart stammered for a second, then recovered as his brain identified the sound.

And then he was falling.

The air of Mars whimpered and then screamed as the aeroshell started to burn. Kane's Valium calm vaporized and he was sure he was going to die. He'd looked at death before, sometimes gone out of his way to see it, but he'd never had so little control over the outcome. He felt as if he'd been thrown out of a helicopter with a mountain tied to his back. His vision narrowed to a gray, viscous tube and he prayed he wouldn't have to take manual control of the ship, because he couldn't lift his arms back up to the keyboard.

One minute, he thought. I only have to take this for sixty seconds. He tried to see the time readout on his CRT but his eyes refused to focus.

The screaming turned into a metal icepick, driving into Kane's ears. He fought for air, imagining his windpipe collapsing like a soda straw. His lungs burned and he tasted blood.

He kept waiting for it to be over and the pressure kept getting worse. He felt thumbs gouging his eyes, blood pumping into his feet like water into balloons. And then something stabbed him in the chest.

A rib. I just lost a rib.

He felt the second one break. At first it was just the pressure, focused, inexorable, bearing down over his heart. Then he felt the muscles ripping and the sudden jerk as the bone snapped and bent inward. The pain knifed through his chest and for a long moment his own scream melted inaudibly into the shriek of the burning shield.

The G forces pushed the broken bones deeper into his flesh. He wanted to pass out but the pain was too intense. He could visualize the points of the ribs, the claws of some giant roc from mythology, digging deep into his heart. Killing him.

And for nothing, he thought. For a rescue mission that's ten years too late and too screwed up to do any good anyway. A broken-down ship full of losers, raving across forty million miles to add their dead, burned bodies to the corpses of the martian colonists.

He was convinced that something had gone wrong. The computers had lost control and the ship was obviously dropping straight out of the sky like a meteor. The deceleration had gone on an impossibly long time, could only end in blazing ruin.

And then the pressure fell away and the gray tunnel closed down into darkness.

When he opened his eyes again, the CRT showed that two minutes had elapsed since orbital insertion. They were weightless and the air was stale and flatulent. Above the time hack an irregular blue egg, dotted with four or five major craters, filled the screen.

Deimos, Kane thought. They were alive, then. In orbit around Mars.

He sucked a careful breath through the hot bands of pain around his chest. He could hear the ship creaking softly as it cooled, the rattle of an off-balance fan in the vent over his head.

"Kane?" Lena's voice. He managed a grunt in reply.

"Keep still," she told him.

He knew that. They weren't even supposed to try to move for two hours. "Broke something," he managed. "Ribs."

"Oh christ. Any blood? From the lungs, I mean?"

He wasn't sure. He had blood in his throat, but it could have been from his nose, which was still blowing a fine red mist when he exhaled.

He couldn't seem to sustain any serious interest in the source of the bleeding. It was nothing compared to the shrapnel fragment that opened the back of his skull near Dongola and left him nearly helpless between bouts of surgery. Now he was tired of complications, of moods, of dealing with Lena. He felt like a coiled spring that had been carrying a maximum load for nine months, the strain building beyond all tolerance levels, the coils starting to fray and shift out of line.

"Don't worry about it," he said. "I can manage."

"I'll get to you when I can," Lena said. "Anybody else?"

"I'm all right," Takahashi said. "Reese is still out." Of course Takahashi had come through, Kane thought. Three to five hours every day at the treadmill and the bicycle and the rowing machine had kept him precision-tuned, lean and rippling with health. Kane thought him deranged, obsessive, a robot programmed for masochism. Takahashi had been spit out of the factories of the New Japan, gleaming and flawless, blaming his ancestors' suffering on their excessive spirituality.

"Like Reese," Takahashi had said once, three months out of Earth, bent over the rowing machine, his muscles flowing like sine waves down his arms. It was the only image Kane had of him from the entire outward flight: there in the wardroom, the air alive with pinpoint dots of his sweat. "All that *Ch'an* crap of his," he had said. "Zen. Looking for illumination or cosmic purpose in *this*. It's a job. It's work. That's all there is to it."

And now his hands were moving over the keyboard in swift, precise gestures while Kane lay hostile and broken. "Is somebody going to call Houston?" Takahashi asked.

"Go ahead," Lena told him. "You're in command."

"You want to tell him about Kane?"

Him, Kane noticed. It wasn't Houston they were talking about anymore, it was Morgan. Morgan: Chairman of the Board of Pulsystems, economic king of Houston, the man who had bought all this slightly used hardware from the foundering U.S. government.

"No," Kane said. "I'll be okay. Just leave me the fuck out of it." It wasn't that he was worried about Morgan delaying the mission. It was just all the history between the two of them, between him and Morgan. Morgan had raised him since Kane's father died, ostensibly the benevolent uncle, in fact a ruthless business rival, more concerned with the block of stock that Kane had inherited than with the boy himself.

Kane worked for Morgan, had fought for him in North Africa, but their private struggle had never let up.

Takahashi's fingers kept rattling on his console as he dictated a mechanical report: "Orbital insertion at 1823 Zulu . . ."

Kane let his eyes drift back to the bright husk of Deimos on his CRT, cold, malformed, impassive. Mars was Ares to the Greeks, the god of war and mindless brutality, running red with blood. They hated him, and they hated his bastard sons, Deimos and Phobos, Fear and Terror. Mars had sired them on Aphrodite and they followed him like vultures over the battlefields to burn and mutilate the dead and dying.

He'd come to know the Greeks better than he'd wanted to five impossibly long years ago, studying mythology at Rice University. They'd read meaning into everything they saw, humanized an inanimate universe with bloodthirsty zeal. What did they know, Kane wondered, that we don't?

As Takahashi droned on, Kane drifted in and out of a hazy, painful sleep. When the beeping of an incoming transmission woke him, he saw that he'd lost another half hour.

The cratered oval of Deimos faded into Morgan's face, the two images nightmarishly superimposed for an instant. Morgan's hair, dyed unnaturally black, stood straight out from the back of his head where his fingers had repeatedly pushed it. His face was webbed with deep lines and his mouth couldn't seem to hold a smile. It was early afternoon in Houston, but he had obviously been up the entire night before.

"Our telemetry says you have a successful Mars insertion," he said. The 18-minute time delay each way gave him the awkwardness of someone speaking into a telephone recorder. "Congratulations, uh, a little late." Behind him Kane could see five or six white-shirted techs at their consoles in the trench in Mission Control. The picture flickered and Morgan seemed to shift his attention back from something just beyond the camera. "Nothing really to say to except we're all proud of you here, and we're hoping for good luck ahead, an operable lander, and a safe touchdown."

The screen flickered again and Kane felt a chill. Subliminals. The son-of-a-bitch was putting subliminals in the broadcast. He jerked his eyes away from the screen and looked around, but no one else seemed to have noticed it. What was Morgan up to? What the hell was going on?

"I, uh, guess that's it for now. We'll be back in touch after we hear from you." Kane heard him clear his throat, then saw the screen darken at the edge of his vision.

Morgan had, Kane thought, a lot to be worried about. The lander, for one thing. There hadn't been a complete Mars Excursion Module left anywhere on Earth or in orbit; and even if there had been, there weren't enough propellant stages to get it to Mars. Morgan had been willing to gamble that at least one of the abandoned landers on Deimos could be refitted. If not, it meant a nine-month trip back to Earth, empty-handed, and Kane didn't think they'd make it without at least one murder or suicide.

Whatever their individual strengths, they didn't seem to be able to function as a unit. Takahashi was distant and patronizing; he seemed always to be taking mental notes of the crew's behavior, comparing them against some hypothetical limits of social and biological disrhythm. Kane felt he'd been singled out for the worst of it. He suspected paranoia on his own part, but couldn't convince himself.

Lena considered the trip out just another nine wasted months to be added to the five years she'd spent looking for a chance to practice medicine again. She'd been the first to lose interest in the NASA regime of exercise and simulations; her moods shifted unpredictably within a narrow range of emotions. The one constant, since that early incident, seemed to be her fear and distrust of Kane.

If anyone could have pulled them together it should have been Reese. Even Takahashi had been a little awed by him at first. They all carried the image in their memories of Reese planting the American flag on Mars, back when there had still been an America, back when Mars had seemed like something important to everybody, if only because the Russians had gotten there first.

For Kane the memories had been even more potent, of adolescent weekends at NASA's Johnson Space Center, Morgan's privilege as a major government contractor buying Kane a ride in the shuttle trainer, a front-row seat inside Mission Control, lunch at the Central Cafeteria with the astronauts. Reese had seemed more than human then, a transcendant being who had actually touched an alien world.

Because of that Kane had expected some kind of spiritual leadership from him, a moral center that failed to materialize. Instead Reese had spent most of the nine months in his triangular sleeping area, floating in a lotus position, his circled thumb-and-forefingers just touching his knees. He never talked about his own reasons for going back to Mars, or why, at age 60, he was willing to risk aerobraking and NASA's antique hardware for a man like Morgan, whom he clearly disliked.

Kane's own motives were nearly as difficult for him to put into words. At one time being part of the Mars expedition seemed an obvious career move, a theatrical gesture to regain some of the momentum he'd lost after the war. The timing was right; he was unmarried and uninvolved, the doctors had cleared him, and his position in Labor Relations at Pulsystems was far from crucial.

Now it seemed a mistake, a costly retreat from the front line of the business, something near to professional suicide—or even a literal one.

North Africa had been the beginning, his head wound the sharp dividing line that separated him from the obvious and natural course his life had been following. He was lucky to be alive at all, they told him, said the headaches and the dizziness and the occasional failure of a motor nerve were minor side effects of a brain lesion that should have been fatal. He'd been unconscious for a month and had been kept in a private ward at the Pulsystems clinic for over a year.

What he couldn't understand was the atrophy of his ambition, his sudden inability to reach a threshold of drive and desire that would bring him into the highest echelon of the company. His intelligence was unimpaired; his memory was perfect, frighteningly so at times. Yet in the three years that he'd been back at work he'd hesitated over the smallest decisions, unable to focus his thoughts, intimidated by the endless chain of consequences that each one provoked.

And in those years Morgan had seemed to lose interest in him, had become cool, preoccupied, indifferent. Before the war, before the wound, there had been a moment, an instant, when Kane had seen fear in Morgan's eyes, fear of what Kane was becoming, of his growing power in the company, of the physical strength and competence he'd developed in basic training.

But not since. Even when Morgan had first suggested that Mars mission it was offhand, as if he didn't care whether Kane went or not. Kane himself had brought it up the second time, and pursued it.

And so, he thought, this was where it had brought him. Lying on a canvas sling, a sack of raw nerve endings and sublimated combat training, knowing that if they couldn't come up with a working lander, if they had to turn around for another endless, horizonless, destinationless trip, he would be the first to crack.

He closed his eyes again.

Sometime during the two hours it took them to catch up to Deimos, Reese recovered. He said he was unhurt, but to Kane his voice sounded old and strained.

Kane himself had developed a savage headache that burned the backs of his eyes and seemed to be deforming his skull. He'd had others like it over the past three years, but this was the worst yet. When he managed to find a few minutes of sleep, he was assailed by vivid dreams of a blue ocean and a hot wooden deck beneath his feet, the smells of salt and sunlight, a high murmuring of voices.

The gentle tug of braking rockets finally brought him back. The gravity of the tiny moon was negligible, less than a thousandth that of Earth, and Takahashi had to guide them in with dozens of tiny course adjustments, more of a docking maneuver than a landing.

Deimos occupied barely six cubic miles, and as they drifted toward the surface Kane was reminded of the garbage dumps on the outskirts of Houston.

With the exception of a melted patch near the domes and tunnels of the base, the entire visible surface was littered with cast-off technology. Propellant tanks, some empty, some fully charged, lay around like oversized soup cans. Abandoned shelter halves were scattered randomly among plastic bags, tripods, and scraps of crumpled foil. The conical outline of one complete lander and the ruins of a second were visible from the ship, the exposed metal sparkling cleanly in the faint sunlight.

The ship bumped to a stop. For the first time in nine months he was actually at rest compared to another object in the universe, but to Kane the change was imperceptible. It could have been no more than another trick of perspective, another elaborate simulation.

Lena moved him gingerly to Health Maintenance while Reese and Takahashi started closing down the ship. The sickbay was not designed for even the minimal gravity of Deimos and Kane had to lean against a suddenly vertical wall while Lena took X-rays and taped his ribs.

"It's not serious," she said. "Comparatively. You're going to be in a lot of pain, but it should heal up cleanly enough. I'd give you something for it if you didn't still have all that Valium in your system."

"Right," Kane said. His voice had turned scratchy and his face glowed with a light fever. He had become excruciatingly aware of the structure of his chest, of the muscular contractions that raised his ribs as he inhaled, the flattening of his diaphragm, the abrupt collapse as his breath spurted out again.

Lena pulled herself back up to the Command

Center and a moment later Reese and Takahashi came down the same ladder, carrying their suits. Reese's face was the color of dirty concrete and he lagged behind as Takahashi disappeared below the level of the deck.

"You all right?" Reese asked.

Kane nodded. "You?"

"Sure."

"You look like hell, Reese. Angina?"

"Maybe a little."

"Get Lena to—"

"No. I'm fine, goddammit. I'm fine."

"At least rest a minute."

"There's no time. I have to know if that lander is going to work. It's important."

"To Morgan, yeah."

"It's important to me," Reese said. "Just leave it at that for now, okay?"

"Sure," Kane said.

Reese dropped through the hatch. Kane worked his fingers nervously, feeling the tension again. The walls of the ship constricted him, seemed to be pressing in on his ribs. His head was all right now and the chest pain was nothing he couldn't handle. If he didn't get out of the ship he might explode.

Fuck it, he thought. If Reese can keep going, so can I.

He poked his head into the Command Center and said, "I'm going out." He had to raise his voice to get it to carry in the low pressure of the ship.

"You're crazy," Lena said. She seemed to be pushing him away from her with the intensity of her stare.

"That's right," Kane said. He let himself fall through the center of the ship, braking himself against the gentle pull of the moon with open hands on the sides of the ladder. There was a way to breathe, he was sure, that wouldn't hurt so badly. He just had to find it, that was all.

Takahashi was already in the airlock by the time Kane got to the quarters level. Reese was tightening the straps of his Portable Life Support System and reaching for his helmet. The atmosphere of the ship was pure oxygen, so they could use standard shuttle suits at 4 psi and not worry about nitrogen bubbles and the bends.

Kane pulled the lower torso of a suit over his trousers and then squatted and stood up inside the upper half, which was still racked to the wall. Raising his arms brought a new onslaught of pain, but Lena had said it wasn't that serious and he chose to believe her.

"Are you sure you're up to this?" Reese asked, still holding his helmet.

"Yeah," Kane said. He put on his black rubber gloves and locked the metal wrist-rings.

"Do something for me?"

"Like what?"

"See if you can get into the base. Takahashi and I can check out the lander by ourselves."

"And if I can?"

"Just wait there for me. All right?"

"Sure."

Reese's head disappeared under the helmet as the airlock light went green. Kane closed the hatch after him and got into his own PLSS and helmet and waited while Reese cycled through.

Finally he was sealed into the narrow cylinder of the lock. The controls were clustered on a small box, painted off-white like every other inch of the room. Each switch was protected by an aluminum cap on a chain, and Kane screwed them back in place as he finished.

The hatch opened and he fell gently to the surface of Deimos, his legs flexing slightly to take up his momentum, then straightening to send him halfway back into the lock.

He lowered himself more carefully and looked around.

Outside the burned, pavement-colored slab where they'd landed, the entire surface of the moon was pocked with craters, some of them smaller than Kane's thumbnail, some even fresher than the oldest footprints, whose familiar wide bars overlapped each other in a heavy crosshatching. His visor cut down the glare of the sun on the metal and the white powder of the surface, but made the black of the shadows impenetrable.

Lena's voice cut into the silence. "Kane, uh, we're showing the hatch still open . . ."

Kane slammed the hatch and moved away from the ship. The drastically foreshortened horizon gave him the feeling that he was standing in a low spot in some terrestrial desert; at the same time the ground seemed to slope away from him, confusing his spatial perceptions.

He took a few cautious steps toward the airlock of the base, then had trouble controlling his forward momentum. With a good run, he thought, he could probably jump into orbit.

Puffs of dust hung around his feet with every

step. Even in the negligible gravity the dust seemed
to be weighing down his feet. After-effects of the
aerobraking, he realized. According to the book,
none of them should even be moving around yet,
let alone trying to work.

He made it to the base entrance, a half-buried
section of corrugated pipe that led to a cluster of
metal and durofoam structures that looked as solidly built as a child's treehouse.

He held on to the hatch valve to get his breath,
then looked back toward the ship.

Mars filled the sky.

For an instant he felt he was falling into the
vast dark side of the planet. He groped behind
him, found the edge of the steel tunnel, and clung
to it.

He hung by his feet and hands over a brilliant
yellow and white and orange crescent, suspended
in absolute black. On the right-hand tip Kane could
see the Argyre Planitia, white with frost; to the
left was the great inflamed wound of the Valles
Marineris, torn from the upper right edge down to
the center of the crescent, disappearing into the
dawn along the Tharsis Ridge. Ascreus Mons, the
only one of the Tharsis volcanos touched by the
rising sun, trailed a thick plume of ice crystals
down toward the west. The Lunae and Chryse plains
glowed ghostly white against the orange of the
surrounding high ridges.

If Kane stood there long enough, the sun would
reach Pavonis and the third volcano, Arsia Mons.
He wondered if the ruins of the base would be
visible from this far away, if the great foil mirrors
would catch the sunlight. He could point to the

spot where they'd be, there, just northeast of Arsia Mons, toward Pavonis, still in darkness.

The speakers in his helmet buzzed and Reese said, "We're inside. We've got power and the pressure's coming up . . . looks good."

"Oh, man," Lena said. "Oh, man. I'm just starting to figure out how scared I've been."

"Don't break out any champagne," Reese said. "There's a ways still to go."

Kane himself felt the first stirrings of relief, the easing of a knot of tension in his stomach that had been there so long he'd lost his awareness of it.

He turned his back on Mars and concentrated on the mechanics of the hatch. The station's power was on standby and none of the automatic controls functioned. He finally found the manual release set into the recessed spokes of the cover, the flat of the handle barely wide enough to grip with his fingertips. The lever resisted the strength of his hands, but he finally forced the toe of his boot into the opening and threw the mass of his body against it.

The hatch swung open and Kane scrambled to hold on to the lip of the tunnel above it.

Just a few more minutes, he thought, and I can go sleep this off. The light on his chest pack revealed the standard switches inside the airlock, with an additional set for bringing the main power on line. He ran through the sequence, and a moment later the caged bulb overhead came to life.

"Reese," he said. "I've got power up in here, too. Now what?"

"Go on in," Reese said. "Check it out."

"What's going on?" Takahashi broke in. "Kane? Where are you? Are you inside the base?"

Kane lied without stopping to think about it, instinctively protecting Reese. "Morgan wanted to know if it was still habitable."

"He didn't say anything to me about it."

"Come off it, Takahashi," Kane said. "What difference does it make who he told?"

Takahashi let the silence drag on for a few seconds, and then said, "All right. But be careful. And you can make your report to me, and I'll pass it on. Understood?"

"Sure," Kane said.

The telltales for internal pressure all showed green, so Kane gave his helmet a quarter-turn and pulled it off. With the servos operating, the inner hatch swung open easily and Kane stepped inside.

The auxiliary generators had kept the air above freezing, but only slightly. Kane's breath puffed out in thick clouds and it took a second or two for the smell to penetrate. When it did, he fumbled his helmet back into the collar and turned the PLSS up to high.

Beneath the odors of rot and decay had been a dry, alkaline smell like moldy bread. As he coughed the last of the foul air out of his lungs he saw that it *was* mold, thick and bluish gray, growing up to shoulder height on the foam walls. Oily water dripped from the ceiling and pooled on the floor, which felt spongy under Kane's feet.

He slogged through the tunnel and crossed a bulkhead into the Control Center. At first glance the damage didn't seem so bad, but Kane found rust on the chrome surfaces and greenish corrosion on the solder points. He brought up the drives on the main computer and tried booting an operating system, but nothing came up on the lead CRT. It could have been anything from ROM failure to bad cabling, and Kane didn't see the value of trying to pinpoint it.

The astrometry processor, attached to a wire grid telescope on the far side of the moon, was still running, its red map lights still winking into new patterns as Kane watched. The gauges on the little fusion pile were stable as well, and with a little work the place could be used again. But it would be a long time before the smell was gone.

Kane turned back to the astrometry unit. It was one of Pulsystems's most sophisticated computers, designed to measure the universe with a combination of light, radio, and neutrino detectors, so sensitive that it could calculate the motion of planets around nearby stars.

As a teenager he'd seen it being tested in the basement of the company's downtown Houston office, encased in glittering black aluminum and plastic, promising answers to questions that no one had even thought of asking. Now it lay in the ruins of a deserted outpost, part of another era. Kane felt like a Goth at the sack of Rome, watching his stream of piss wash the delicate paints from a piece of Grecian marble.

No, he thought, not as bad as that. The fact that he was standing there at all proved that it hadn't been completely forgotten, that the riots and hunger and brutality of the last ten years might be no more than a temporary setback. Now that the worst of it was over, the human race had a genuine chance to start fresh, to make a blind, quantum leap into an unimaginable future.

Maybe it was already happening; maybe this expedition of Morgan's would be the first step. For once Morgan might have seen past his anachronistic squabbling over the division of the world's spoils, but Kane found it hard to believe. For Morgan, self-interest was everything, and sooner or later Kane expected to find the short-term payoff that Morgan was counting on.

A shame, Kane thought. Once he'd seen himself as the answer to Morgan's greed, a new program for a new age, but now he wondered if he had the conviction to bring it off.

He was pulling a clogged filter from the ventilator when Reese broke in on the radio. "I'm in the airlock. How bad is it?"

"Not good. Leave your helmet on."

A few seconds later Reese came through the bulkhead. Kane noticed the gray stains on his suit where surface dust had turned to mud in the hallway. Reese clicked his radio off and waited for Kane to do the same. Then he crouched in front of the astrometry unit and pulled a diskette out of the drive.

Kane stood next to him so they could touch helmets. "What the fuck are you doing, man?"

"I need this."

"That's the map, isn't it?" Kane asked.

"Yeah," Reese said. "It's the map." For twelve years the processor had been updating and refining the state vectors of every object it could perceive, storing not only position but direction and speed of relative motion.

"What for?"

"I can't tell you that. Maybe later, but I can't tell you right now."

"Okay, Reese. If that's how you want it."

"I didn't take this, okay? We looked around and then went back outside."

"Sure, Reese. Whatever you say, man." He pulled away and turned his radio back on. "The place needs some work."

Reese switched on. "Too much to do anything about it now. Let's get back to the ship." Reese slipped the diskette into a zip pocket on his thigh. "The lander looks tight. The computer came right up and it seems to think it's okay. There's nothing it can't check out better than we can anyway."

"A piece of luck, then," Kane said. "We were about due for some."

"Not luck," Reese said. "It's a good piece of hardware. Takahashi's gassing it up right now and we're going to go ahead and get out of here."

"Suits me," Kane said, grateful not to have to spend another night in the Mission Module. It's happening, he thought. In a few hours he would be on Mars.

"Get your stuff together," Reese told him, "and take it on over to the lander. Bring Lena with you. We should be ready to lift inside an hour."

He nodded, not caring that Reese couldn't see it, and stayed behind to shut off the lights. Before he left he put a fresh diskette into the astrometry processor and reloaded its program.

Just in case, he thought, shutting the outer hatch of the base. In case we're back this way some time.

Back inside the ship, he hung his helmet on the wall outside the airlock and wore the rest of his suit into his quarters. Dirty clothes were slotted into neoprene knobs along the wall and he wadded them into his fist, wondering what he should bother to bring. Somewhere in his overhead locker was a duffel bag that he'd unloaded when he first came aboard and hadn't looked at since. He pulled it out and tore open the velcro fasteners.

A Colt .38 Police Positive, huge, steel-blue, and menacing, tumbled out of the bag.

It spun end over end as it drifted toward the gridded floor, bounced once and hung there, the hammer snagged in a metal hexagon. The barrel of the gun slowly wobbled in a parabola and then stopped, the muzzle pointed accusingly at Kane's chest. He jammed his palms into his temples and held on as a yellow beam of pain arced through his skull.

"No," he said out loud. It had to be a hallucination. It was the same gun he'd found in Houston, hidden underneath his cot in the Project Management Building. But he'd gotten rid of it then, put it in a dumpster or something . . . hadn't he?

Tiny hemispheres of sweat clung to his forehead. He bent over and touched the steel, its hardness palpable even through his thick gloves. Not an illusion, then. But he had no memory of packing it, would in fact have been insane to bring a gun into this fragile tin can of a ship. . . .

"Kane?" Takahashi's voice came from just outside the cubicle. "We're closing the ship," he said in Japanese. "Hurry up. *Isoide kudasai!*" The polite form, Kane noticed, but his use of Japanese instead of English was uncharacteristically rude.

Kane's hand closed over the pistol barrel, shoved it into the duffel bag, and pushed a layer of clothes in over it. "Yeah, okay, for christ's sake. *Kite!* I'm coming."

His hands shook. He felt an eerie, disembodied compulsion urging him to bring the gun along; at the same time he was terrified of bringing it, wanted somehow to break the chain of events already forming around it.

He had no time left to decide. Takahashi was already suspicious and irritable, might take it on himself to search Kane's quarters. Nearly frantic, Kane stuffed the rest of his clothes into the bag and ducked into the hallway to put on his helmet. He could see Takahashi's feet through the open gridwork of the floor above him, making a last pass through the ship.

He cycled through the airlock and followed Lena's retreating suit toward the MEM.

Without conscious intent, his eyes moved upward for another look at Mars. The sunrise had reached Pavonis Mons, just to the north and east of the colony. Frontera.

It had been ten years since the last ship had left there for Earth. Fifty-seven colonists ignored the recall order from the collapsing U.S. government. For two years messages trickled out sporadically: grim stories of nitrogen shortfalls, radiation-induced cancers, famine, and suicide. One of the last told of the failure of the Russian settlement at Marsgrad, on Candor Mesa in the Valles Marineris. The survivors had arrived at Frontera over a period of weeks, starving, crippled, irradiated; and no one knew how long they'd last.

Then the messages had stopped altogether. NASA's last official act had been the launch of a final shuttle, deploying a lightsail vehicle full of medicine, electronic components, food, and chemicals. But a solar flare had scrambled the drone's guidance system and sent it hurtling off into the asteroid belt.

The sight of the decaying Deimos base had turned Kane's imagination loose, conjuring endless hideous details of the disaster on Mars; cryptic, desperate messages typed into video terminals, slaughtered livestock, tiny deformed skeletons.

Sleep, he thought. Just get through these next few minutes and sleep.

The entry module was only a little larger than the old Apollo spacecraft Kane had seen at NASA, but with its fuel tanks and conical shielding the descent vehicle stood over thirty feet tall. Reese, who had obviously taken over for Takahashi, was uncoupling the FLOX hose that led to the tank of fluorine/liquid oxygen built into the base's refinery complex. He held up one thumb and Kane managed to acknowledge him with a wave of the hand.

A ramp led up inside the cowling, and from there Kane climbed three rungs to the open cockpit. He stowed his duffel under the canvas slings and then crawled in next to Lena. She didn't ask how he was and he didn't volunteer any conversation. It was enough just to close his eyes for a few minutes.

His nerves kept him from falling completely asleep. As Reese and Takahashi strapped themselves in, he gave up and opened his eyes again. He waited in cold silence while Lena and Takahashi ran through the pre-flight checklist, and then, with no more than a sort of throat-clearing *"de wa,"* Takahashi lifted them gently off Deimos's surface and turned them toward the "high gate," the point where they would hit the martian atmosphere.

Kane forced himself to focus on the *pranayama* exercises Reese had taught him, separating his breathing into outgoing, incoming, and the long *kumbhaka* between them.

The shielded bottom of the capsule brushed the outer layers of the atmosphere and the screaming started again. Kane opened his eyes to columns of data scrolling down the screen in front of him. The capsule bucked as the braking rockets fired and Kane ground his teeth together. No more than two G's this time, Kane told himself. It's almost over.

Within a minute or two Kane could feel the pressure easing. As the MEM hit terminal velocity the gravity stabilized at Mars normal and the module began to fall straight toward the caldera of Arsia Mons.

When the soft, female voice came through his helmet speakers, Kane was too startled to manage a reaction.

"This is Frontera Base. Since you're obviously not going to turn around and go home, why don't you set down southeast, repeat, southeast of the dome. We'll send somebody out for you."

"Reese?" Lena said. "Reese, did you hear that?"

Jesus fucking christ, Kane thought.

They're alive.

• • •

With a whine like a muezzin's call to prayer, the eastern mirror opened to the light of the martian dawn.

After twelve years I should be used to it, Molly thought, holding a pillow over her ears against the noise; able to sleep right through it.

She rolled onto her left side and watched a rectangle of muted light crawl across Curtis's smooth, depilated scalp. He slept flat on his back, the breath rasping quietly in his open mouth. Nothing bothered him, not noises in the night or bad dreams or life-and-death decisions. She could remember when she used to admire him for it.

She tried to go back to sleep but it was no use; she felt alternately like she was waiting for Christmas morning or for a final exam. It had been this way since they first picked up the signals from Reese's ship, and today was the worst. Today they would be landing.

The phone rang and Molly got noiselessly out of bed to pick it up. "Yes?"

"They're coming in." The awkward Slavic consonants told her it was Blok, on night duty at the monitors.

"And the others?"

"At least another day away. No signals."

"All right." She looked down, saw that she had instinctively covered her breasts with one arm, as

33

if she could feel a stranger's eyes on her. It's starting, she thought. Already they're an alien presence, already they're changing things, and they haven't even landed yet. "I'll be right there," she said, and put the phone back on the table.

She got into her T-shirt and her last, worn pair of jeans from the night before. Blue used to be my favorite color, she thought, and now look. No oceans, the sky a sickly green on a clear day, and these jeans faded nearly white. Maybe, she thought, maybe they brought new blue jeans with them, like the tourists used to take to Russia.

Sure they did. Blue jeans and French wines and *Vogue* magazines. They don't even fucking know we're alive.

She slid her feet into moccasins and debated, just for a second, waking Curtis and letting him deal with it. But they'd been over it and over it and there was nothing he could do that she couldn't. He'd be furious, of course, but he'd survive.

She closed the bedroom door behind her and took her mask and oxygen tank off the hook by the front door. She stifled a yawn behind the mask and stepped out into the warm CO_2 under the dome.

The clear plastic walls rose over her like the sides of a giant bottle buried in the sand. The components of the western mirror, like huge foil shades pulled down the curvature of the dome, scattered morning sunlight into the gardens below. To her left and right, durofoam living modules alternated with fields of crops in various stages of ripeness. The corn outside her bedroom window stood two meters tall, ready for harvest, and the fields behind her kitchen had just been sown with sugar beets.

She squatted for an instant on the dirt path, trying to really see the colony, to reduce it to some kind of single, simple image, but the vision eluded her. She had been here too long, become too bogged down in the details. She could only find distance through an effort of will, putting herself, for example, in Reese's position, coming in from above.

First there would be the volcano, leveling off to no more than a persistent slope of the rocky land. Then his eyes would find the dome, a cylindrical bubble half a kilometer long and over 200 meters wide, capped at the southern end by the main airlock and garage, and at the northern end by the greater thickness of the machine shops and the compressors and solar furnaces that mined the martian atmosphere.

Closer still and he could see the land under the dome divided into two chessboards, one due north of the other, with ten squares on a side instead of eight. What would have been the white squares held the houses, the living modules, one- and two-bedroom cottages sculpted from durofoam at the whim of the original occupant. The black squares were green, most of them anyway, planted with wheat or cotton or pineapples and not, thank god, with radishes anymore. In the beginning, radishes had been the only crop that would grow in the salty martian soil, and they had always tasted to Molly of failure.

Between the two chessboards lay the inverted bowl of the Center, bracketed by the animal pens where the colony's goats and chickens fought for their few centimeters of space. The Center was the only two-story building under the dome. Some well-intentioned planner back on Earth had meant for it to be the focus of the colony's bustling social life, a shopping mall in space complete with video theaters, a bar, a gym, and a row of shops where the docile colonists were supposed to sell their handicrafts to each other.

The problem was the colony's social life didn't bustle, and the one thing most of them wanted was a little privacy, a little time completely alone.

Molly herself was not immune to the feeling; as she looked around she felt crowded, constricted by the half-dozen people around her, just off the late shift at the Industrial Complex, or watching the sunrise from a bench along the wall of the dome, or still drunk from the night before and wandering aimlessly. Arctic syndrome, the psychologists called it: the sense of lost privacy that came from the knowledge that there was nowhere else to go, no chance to get away from the structures of the society, except in the confines of a rigid pressure suit.

Or, of course, in one of the isolation tanks.

They'd started building them two years after the break with Earth, heavy cellulose coffins made of processed leaves and stalks. The upper floor of the Center, with its Nautilus machines and ping pong tables and basketball hoops, had been walled off down the middle and the tanks lined up and filled with ten-percent magnesium sulfide solution.

Molly had tried a few hours in the warm darkness, but she couldn't deal with the disorientation afterward, the luminescent colors and undulating walls. She wanted a solid reality, unlike the others, like Curtis, who couldn't get enough time in isolation, who claimed it purified and crystallized their thoughts.

As far as she could tell, it had only made Curtis stranger.

She stood up and shuffled toward the Center, ignoring the people she passed. The years had taught them a kind of Japanese politeness that retreated from physical existence, that tried not to intrude with meaningless conversation.

The concrete walls of the Center were a dirty reddish-gray, cast from martian sand mixed with salty contaminants from the fields. A long time ago somebody had painted *Tharsis Hilton* across the front of the building. Molly went through the double doors just under the faded letters and pulled her mask down around her neck.

Astronomy was the first office on the left. The walls inside were covered with printouts, charts, and notes thumbtacked directly to the durofoam. Dirt and shreds of paper had been ground into the carpet beyond the saturation point.

Blok didn't look up as she sat in the swivel chair next to his. "They came through the high gate about two minutes ago. They're headed right for us."

His eyes were bloodshot over his heavy mustache and stubbled chin. Many of the Russians from Marsgrad had hair all the way down their backs, the men growing thick beards and the women experimenting with permanents and peroxide. But Blok had kept his hair short and his chin shaved, almost as if he expected the Party to check in with him any day.

Molly patched in a microphone, then hesitated. She had too many questions: what were they after, how had Morgan talked Reese into working for him, what condition were they in, how long were they planning to leach off the colony's meager resources? Static popped on the line, making her jump. Say something, she thought.

She switched the mike on, gave them landing instructions, then pulled the plug. The rest could wait.

"Get sickbay mobilized, will you?" she asked Blok, rubbing her forehead, trying to plan the contingencies. "We'll probably need some stretchers to bring them in, depending on how beat up they are."

"This is the biggest thing that's happened in eight or ten years," Blok said, his hands stretched like talons. "Don't you even care?"

"I care," she said. "I care so much I hope they burn up on re-entry, even with Reese on board. We don't need them, not any more. Haven't you thought it through? They want something from us, and they're coming here to get it. Whatever it is." She was a poor liar, she knew, and she was afraid Blok would see through her, through to her knowledge of the machine in the cave, the thing the Earthmen wanted. "Can't you see that? Do you think this is going to be some kind of high school reunion or something?"

"I just want things to be different," Blok said. "I don't even care *how*, any more. I'm sick of that plastic sky overhead, of goat meat and goat milk and goat cheese, sick of wearing a mask everytime I go out of my own house—"

"They're not going to change any of that. What, do you think they're going to take you back to Earth with them? Forget it. You know better than that. Earth's gravity would kill you, cripple you at the very least. You've been here too long."

"You don't have to remind me."

"I'm sorry," Molly said, and she was. "I know how you feel. It's just . . . not the answer, that's all. It's going backwards, looking for help from Earth. We have to find our own way, by ourselves."

"Eight years ago, when I came in out of the desert, I might have believed that. I would have looked for a martian flag to wave and I would have waved it. But I don't believe it any more. I'm sorry."

How many others were like him, she wondered? Most of them seemed to feel the way she did: bitter, betrayed, abandoned. But was she just seeing what she wanted to see?

She stood up. "I have to go talk to the kids," she said.

"The kids," Blok said, nodding, knowing which kids she meant. And then, a little hesitantly, he added, "Good luck."

She shrugged, taking extra care not to slam the door on her way out. Diplomacy was a survival trait here, and she refused to let him know how much his attitude hurt and angered her. As far as she knew he'd never had any children of his own; afraid, probably, they'd turn out like Molly's daughter and so many of the others.

It was the risk you took when you got out from under the barriers of Earth's atmosphere and left yourself open to the hard radiation of space: the cosmic primaries, the solar flare protons, the solar X-rays, doses of ten to thirty rads a year. The dome cut out the worst here on Mars, but during solar maximum or heavy flares they had nowhere to hide.

The adults paid for it with cancer and miscarriages, and the kids paid for it with birth defects and the rarest, strangest price of all: genetic change.

Of the nearly fifty children born on Mars, the ones that made it all the way to term, most were perfectly normal. Of the fifteen or so who weren't, the damage was usually insignificant or easily correctable—a vestigial sixth toe, cleft palate, malfunctioning kidney.

Usually.

What Blok would never understand was what it felt like to carry a child for nine months and feed her with your breasts and diaper her and love her and still not be able to look at her without a shadow of fear and sadness and even, on the worst days, just the slightest trace of hatred. It changed you. Even though you were one of the top fraction of a percentile that had been judged stable enough to be here in the first place, let alone one of the tough ones who had stayed behind when the failures shipped back to Earth.

And then sometimes it seemed like leaving had been the only sane decision, that the rest of them were all crazy, from the borderline paranoids like Curtis with his shaved head and power obsessions to the extreme psychotics who were sent out to work the fields with their pre-frontal lobes chemically numbed.

She stopped and put one hand on a crumbling wall of durofoam that had once twisted and curved in an ornate imitation of the onion domes of Moscow. These had been the last living modules to go up, back before the last ship to Earth and the casualties of the next two years, before Curtis put things back together. And after those years the survivors had lost their desire for durofoam crystals and Mayan pyramids and giant, abstract igloos. They'd pulled back to the center, to the comfortable cottages and geodesics that, whether they wanted to admit it or not, reminded them of Earth.

Somebody had thrown a rock through the onion dome, maybe one of the Russians, maybe one of the normal kids who roamed the fields in packs, chafing at the limits of their existence. The morning condensation that fell from the inside of the dome, the local equivalent of rain, had started to rot the foam and nobody had bothered to stop it. The decay had been gradual enough that she hadn't really noticed it before, but she was still seeing things through the eyes of the Earthmen who would be coming in through the south locks. Through Reese's eyes.

Forget it, she thought. By the time they've recovered enough to notice our slums or our kids they're going to have other things to worry about.

A pack of maybe a half dozen five- to ten-year-old kids raced past her, following the dirt track around the inside walls of the dome. When they got bored enough they would work for a while with their parents, helping out in the fields or the machine shops, studying at night on computers. Healthy, normal kids, except for a tendency towards fat—the martian gravity never seemed to burn up the calories their appetites demanded—but Molly still found them strange. They had so little sense of history, such vague, contradictory notions of Earth that she wondered what they would pass on to their own children.

She crossed the track and shut herself in the changing room, put on a suit and went outside.

To her right the great volcano Arisa Mons climbed gently into the sunrise. In the clear morning she could see the lip of the caldera, twenty kilometers high and nearly a hundred kilometers away. She'd climbed it once; most of them had, at one time or another. It had taken her three days to reach the top, leaping over fissures in the rock with a recklessness unimaginable on Earth, climbing glacial sheets with only a rock hammer to support her, sliding down the shallower inclines on the hard plastic seat of her suit.

The effort had been worth it. In those three days she had literally walked into outer space. She had stood on a knob of ragged brown basalt at midday, the sun blazing down on her, and looked up to see a sky of unwinking stars overhead.

Curtis had been the first, of course, and he'd symbolized his conquest by draining his urine collection bag over the lip of the crater. That had been his "hero thing" in the tradition of the Antarctic explorers, and at least three of his subordinates had killed or crippled themselves trying to follow his example, skiing down a glacier or running naked between the garage and the air lock.

She knew some kind of pressure valve was necessary, but the adolescent macho tone of it all offended her. Their current fad was the "sapping expedition," where five or six of them would take off in jeeps and blow up underground ice deposits with lasers. Of course they were "releasing valuable volatiles" and "contributing to the density of the atmosphere," but she knew they did it just to watch the ground explode.

She started for the cave, watching a small pocket of ice glitter faintly from a rift high on the volcano's flank. Curtis had promised they would melt that ice and be swimming in it within their lifetimes, back when people had wanted to hear that kind of thing.

It could still happen, she thought. But it would be because of the kids, not Curtis.

The entrance to the cave was invisible from the locks, a few hundred meters up the rocky slope and concealed behind a lip of frozen lava, bright orange with iron oxides and silica. The airlock was a cylindrical unit pulled off one of the early mission modules, cemented in place with durofoam and painted to blend with the background. Molly and the other adults had to crawl on their hands and knees to get into the cave. The kids liked it that way.

As she pushed the inner hatch open, a large white rat scrambled past her into the lock. It took her a minute to corner it and carry it back into the cave, by which time she felt her temper beginning to unravel.

The room smelled of the lab animals they left running around, and looked even worse than it smelled. Reese, she thought, would not understand how it could have happened. The cave had been the first permanent habitation on Mars, used while Frontera was being built, and by all rights should have been some kind of monument.

But they'd needed a physics lab, one far enough away that an accident wouldn't take the entire dome with it. And maybe more importantly they'd needed a place for the kids that couldn't or wouldn't fit in, the deformed, the strange, the unwanted. Friction had been building since the first years of the settlement and the decision just seemed to happen, more and more of the kids spending the night in the lab, until a dozen or so of them were hardly home at all.

This morning they had the red lights on, barely illuminating the distant corners where the duro-foam floors and ceilings met the natural walls of the cave. The rats had dragged used computer paper across the floor for their nests, leaving what they didn't need in crumpled heaps. Children were sleeping on mattresses on the floor, in niches along the walls, some of them under the desks and tables in the front area of the huge room.

"Verb?" she said. The girl had been named Sarah, once, but five years ago the children had come up with their own names for each other and had stopped answering to the ones their parents had given them. "Verb, are you here?"

A head of close-cut blonde hair, just a little too large for the body it rested on, lifted itself from one of the desks. "Mom?"

"How's it coming?" Molly asked, hearing the unnatural cadence of stress in her voice.

"Okay. I've got some new math to show you."

Molly picked her way carefully to the desk. In a

distant corner one of the children gave a brief, strangled scream in its sleep and then went quiet.

On the girl's CRT screen Molly saw the calculation for quantum shifts in the apparent mass and charge of an electron in an electromagnetic field. In quantum mechanics the solution produced divergent integrals, but Verb's equation balanced.

There had been a time when Molly had to choose between the doctoral program at the University of Texas and a slot on one of the Mars missions. She opted for Mars because she thought it could give her science *and* adventure, and besides, grant money had dried up and universities, even state universities, were folding as fast as the steel mills. She couldn't have guessed that she was going to end up at the cutting edge of a new physical theory.

She watched the numbers scroll by. Like all the great ideas, she thought, the math was beautiful in itself, elegant, symmetrical, not just in the flow of logic but in the very patterns of the numbers.

"Look ma," Verb said, "no infinities."

Molly smiled at the obscure, ingrown humor, resisted an impulse to touch her daughter's hair. None of them liked to be touched, even by each other. Too much like sex, Molly thought, the imperfect chromosomal dance that had spawned them. "It's beautiful," Molly said. "It's almost there, isn't it?"

"Almost," the girl said.

It had better be, Molly thought. For the thousandth time she almost said it, almost let the words out: *Sarah, I have to talk to you.* But they wouldn't come. She'd waited too long, could not just blurt out the fact that her daughter was dying and that she had waited this long to tell her. Waited because she was afraid, waited because she'd kept hoping they were wrong, waited because she didn't want to interfere with the work.

She told herself it was for the girl's sake, that the work meant so much to her. But it meant as much to Molly, to all of them, because if Verb really could harness antimatter, if she really could build a working transporter, then all their lives depended on her.

Verb sat back, revealing the heavy, flat lines of her body, the stains on her dull yellow shift. "It's almost finished. All but a few of the transitions. I can see where it's going but I can't always ... can't quite see how to get there. Why don't you tell me what it is you're afraid of?"

The girl's startling intuition of quantum physics seemed to be part of some larger, more general empathy. She can't really read your mind, Molly told herself. She's just reading your emotions.

"Remember I told you about the ships from Earth?" It wasn't the whole truth, maybe not even half, but it was the reason she'd come. "One of them is about to land."

"Is it the one with Reese?"

"That's right. It's Reese." Molly crouched beside the desk, putting both hands on the arm of the girl's chair. "Listen. I know you don't care much about this kind of stuff. But it's very important to me and the rest of the grownups here. Okay? If the people from Earth find out what we're doing up here, they're going to try to take it away from us. It means people will get hurt, maybe even killed. So I want you to promise you won't talk to anybody about the transporter, or about the antimatter, or any of that stuff. Will you do that?"

The girl pushed the screen-erase key and the equations vanished into blackness.

"Please?"

"Is this for Curtis?" Verb said at last. Molly at least she would call "Mom" but her father was always "Curtis."

"No," Molly said. "It's for me. And for your friends. I don't want the Earth people to hurt your friends." Christ, Molly thought, this is low. Why not tell her they have long, forked tails and eat babies?

Verb pressed a function key, covering the screen with winking graphics. She stared at the shifting patterns as if she could read meaning in them, refusing to look at Molly. "All right. I won't break it to anybody. Do we have to come back to the dome?"

"That's up to you. Reese is probably going to want to see you, sooner or later, but we can work that out. When you do come . . ."

"Yeah, I get it. Don't say anything about the cave."

"Is that okay?"

"Yeah, sure, it's okay."

Molly stood up. It was the best she could hope for, really. "I'll let you talk to the others. You'll know how to explain it to them." She worked with three or four of them every day, a boy with an uncanny knack for integrated circuit design, a girl who could think in hexadecimal machine code, but she couldn't penetrate their rigid, exclusive culture.

"Sure." As Molly walked away she could hear the girl's fingers clicking over the keys again.

She made it outside without any rats or monkeys following her. As she rounded the jut of rock that cut her off from the base she saw the medics lining up at the south airlocks, stretchers ready.

The MEM was a bright flare to the east, coming in out of the sun. She hurried down the slope, taking long, floating strides, and stood next to Blok as the lander made its final descent, lost in billowing dust.

● ● ●

For Reese it had started in Mexico.

In the dead heat of the afternoon, even the birds had gone quiet. The swimming pool, deep blue and wide as a lake, threw blades of sunlight into Reese's eyes. He drained the last flat, salty swallow of *Bohemia* and dropped the bottle in the sand next to the others.

The Hotel Casino de la Selva was the end of the earth, the last place Reese ever expected to see. Some mornings he would walk down the Calle Carlos Fuero to the *baranca*, the steep-sided canyon full of garbage and blooming flowers that separated the eastern third of Cuernavaca from downtown.

He could get as far as the narrow bridge but he couldn't seem to cross it.

In the mornings he drank beer, at night mescal. Once a week he would buy a few magic mushrooms, *psilocybe cubensis*, from the kid who trucked in fresh vegetables from town. The mushroom changed the decaying pleasure palace into a fairyland, made sense of the vines and wild grasses growing over the jai-alai courts, the crumbling concrete heliports, the circular casino like a stranded alien spacecraft awash with dust and splintered furniture.

At night he could see Mars.

He was beyond remembering how many nights he'd spent in the hotel, beyond caring about the expense. The money he'd milked out of his days as a public hero was secure, all of it invested in the multinationals that had succeeded the big governments. Enough, he figured, to drink himself to death or to sobriety, and he didn't particularly care which it turned out to be.

Footsteps crunched toward him across the sandbox, the artificial beach that was no more preposterous than any other of the hotel's excesses. Reese, eyes closed, assumed it was the impassive waiter who seemed to be the only other inhabitant of the hotel. He extended his thumb and little finger in the time-honored Mexican signal for liquor and said, "*Otra, por favor.*"

"Reese?"

He forced his eyes open. A young American stood just out of arm's reach, wearing a collarless blue shirt, khaki pants, and mirrored sunglasses. The man's dark hair was razored within a quarter inch of his skull and he stood with the unconscious tension of the corporate mercenary.

"Jesus christ," Reese said, pushing himself to a higher center of gravity. "Kane? Is that you?"

"It's been a long time, Reese." The man did not offer his hand or relax his expression.

"Jesus christ." Reese felt addled and clownish, unprepared, a little frightened by Kane's lack of emotion. "What are you doing here? How did you find me?"

Kane shrugged. Smooth, Reese thought, professional. The last time Reese had seen him Kane had been no more than sixteen, still in high school, full of inarticulate wonder at being inside the restricted areas of NASA. With an effort Reese came up with other pieces of information, something about Kane's father dying in a car wreck and Morgan, the boy's uncle, adopting him. All of it seemed impossibly long ago.

"I'm here on business," Kane said. "I've got a proposition for you, if you want to listen to it." Reese noticed that Kane had nervously chewed at his lips, leaving dry flecks of skin protruding over raw, red welts.

"Okay," Reese said. "Just give me a second." He walked as steadily as he could to the edge of the pool and dove in. He swam the entire oversized length of it, and by the time he started back his lungs burned and his feet thrashed spasmodically at the water. Back at NASA he'd always had trouble with the weight limit because of his big bones and heavy build. Now he was just fat, out of shape.

Swim, he told himself, and he cupped his hands and dug his strokes in deep, put his head down and his ass up and pumped with his legs. When he got back to the edge of the pool he pushed himself up on his arms and swung his legs out and stood up.

"All right," he said. "Let's talk."

They moved into the bar. Reese had another *Bohemia* and Kane ordered Tehuacan water. "You remember Pulsystems," Kane said. "My uncle's company."

"Of course," Reese said. "I own a block of their stock. I consulted with them when they had the principal contract on the Mars hardware."

That was only part of it, and he didn't volunteer the rest. In fact he had worked in Pulsystems's downtown Houston office for a few months after the collapse of the government, looking for information. He'd used a phony identity to keep from attracting Morgan's attention; with a full beard and long hair he'd felt reasonably inconspicuous.

Houston had been the obvious step after Washington, where one job after another had disappeared as the government tried desperately to cut itself down to a size that its tiny budget could support. For two years he'd burrowed through the Washington underground, searching for tapes or transcripts or some kind of communication from the colonists that had stayed behind at Frontera.

He'd had no better luck in Houston, and after a few months he'd developed a paranoid fear of Morgan.

During his NASA days he'd thought Morgan a posturing fool, the sort of clown that gravitated to public office to feed his ego on privilege and publicity. He remembered Morgan's hearty back-slapping in the VIP lounge at Mission Control in Houston, the load of lapel pins he'd pressured one of the astronauts into taking to Mars and back, his endless posing for photographs with NASA celebrities.

But once inside Morgan's home ground Reese had seen another side to the man, a sense of destiny that he kept hidden from the rest of the world. From the moment Reese sat down at a terminal in a corner of the Quality Control department he was inundated with company propaganda: how Pulsystems fed the unemployed, rebuilt public roads, brought law and order back to the city. In all of it Reese saw a sort of messianic madness that had no regard for individual lives, only for image, cash projections, and the vindication of history.

What a wonderful piece of PR I would make for him, Reese had realized. Ex-astronaut brought low, rescued and sustained by the corporate dream. Within a few days of the thought he'd packed his clothes and moved on.

"Right," Kane said, "of course you know him. Well, when the government went under, Pulsystems was the major creditor against NASA. They bought off the other parties and ended up with the entire Johnson Space Center in Clear Lake, two shuttles, launch privileges at the Cape, and certain specific hardware already in orbit." Kane's mineral water came and he used it to wash down a small green pill. "That hardware includes a working Mars spacecraft."

Reese said, "Go on."

"Pulsystems is going to sponsor a Mars expedition. Chairman Morgan wants you to train the crew and direct the mission from Houston."

Reese set the beer bottle on the table, pushed it away. "They're all dead, you know."

"Sorry?"

"The colonists. Nobody's heard anything from them in over seven years."

"He's not expecting to find them alive. This is just the beginning. If this works out there'll be a space program again, with the companies sharing the expense and pooling the results. It could be a new age."

"Who's the crew supposed to be?"

"Me, for one. There's a doctor, and three pilots."

"So," Reese said. "After all these years. You

finally get your shot. How did you talk Morgan into it?"

"I work for him now. Foreign security."

, In other words, Reese thought, Morgan's corporate mercenaries. In the last days of the government the U.S. Army had become a parody, two officers for every enlisted man, obsolete weapons, no morale or fighting experience. The corporations had hired the best strategists and munitions people for their own use, protecting overseas investments from terrorists and rebel governments.

"You were in North Africa, then," Reese said.

Kane nodded.

Nobody in the States really understood what had happened there—at least no one outside the boards of directors of the companies involved. All anyone knew was that the Red Chinese had moved on the UN biotechnology lab in Luxor—Biotek Afrika—and the U.S. government hadn't been in any shape to stop them. Instead the multinational corporations and *zaibatsus* had sent their own troops, and when the shooting was over the corporations were in control, all over the world.

"Tell him it's no," Reese said. His stomach was jumping and his blood ran icy and thin. He forced himself to stand up, draining the rest of his beer for moral support. "I have to go along, or it's no. Tell him that."

"Reese."

He turned back.

"I've seen the mission profile. This isn't NASA. This is a stripped-down, high-risk, low-redundancy mission. Antique hardware, not even our own excursion module. Aerocapture. Do you think you could handle that?"

"Tell him," Reese said, and walked out.

Outside the sun smoldered and flowers ran riot over the guest cabins. Reese had never seen so many flowers in his life; Mexico seemed a nation of flowers, obsessed with them, drunk on their color and perfume.

Not like Mars, he thought. On Mars there were only edible flowers; no trees, no wood, no yards, no swimming pools.

He climbed two steps into his cabin, kicked off his damp bathing suit, and stood under the shower. When he finished he put on real clothes for the first time in days, black cotton pants and a black pullover shirt. In the mirror he saw jowls, puffy, sunken eyes.

The kid is right, he told himself. You'd never make it.

He took out his *I Ching* and the envelope with his three coins. They were copper pennies from the year he graduated high school, dark brown and corroded now from the acids in his fingers. He tried to focus his thoughts, failed, threw the coins anyway.

He built hexagram 34, the Power of the Great. Not, as he'd hoped, something obvious and straightfoward, like *Shêng*, Pushing Upward. The oracle was enigmatic, as always. The judgement, minimal, was merely "Perseverence furthers." The interpretation tantalized him with bits of relevance: "inner worth mounts with great force and comes to power . . . one may rely entirely on one's own power and forget to ask what is right . . . greatness and justice must be indissolubly united."

His change line in the third position gave him: "The inferior man works through power. The superior man does not act thus."

Morgan, Reese thought. It's trying to warn me about Morgan. And sure as hell, if he's involved with this, he's up to something. He put the book away, restless and uncomfortable, and stepped out into the blazing sunlight.

Without conscious thought his feet took him down the Calle Cuaglia to Carlos Fuera and across the *baranca*. His diaphragm hurt and his eyes burned, the first physical pain he could remember in weeks. Like the pain, he thought, when the blood starts moving again in a leg that's gone to sleep.

He crossed over to Avenida Morelos with its long, whitewashed, windowless walls and downhill to the Borda Gardens. Maximillian and Carlotta had used it for a summer retreat in the 1860's, but now it was just another elaborate ruin, a walled maze of garden paths, stagnant ponds, and crumbling outbuildings. For a while the government had charged admission, with a pretense of repairing it, but the charade was dropped when the *socialisticas* took over. Now that PEMEX was the de facto ruler of the country there was little interest at all in the past.

The gardens covered five or six city blocks, but only the immediate area near the entrance had been kept up. Towards the northwest the park disintegrated into dying trees and ruined fountains.

Another message, he thought, this one from my subconscious. A metaphor for Frontera, its gardens and fields and buildings all walled in by the dome. Like this now, gone, crumbling, ruined.

And yet, he thought. Perseverance furthers. "A movement in accord with heaven, producing great power." He bent his legs into a lotus, straining the shortened muscles. In front of him was a crumbling adobe wall, beyond that the hills of the city, and beyond that the pine-covered mountains. In time his mind began to clear and he sat for over an hour, feeling the sun move in the sky overhead.

From the gardens he took Lopez Rayon toward the zocalo, his sense of calm evaporting. He wanted to go back to the hotel and see if Kane had talked to Morgan. Instead he forced himself to keep walking, past the dilapidated theater and its endlessly recycled kung fu movies, past the steeply climbing streets and the tiled hotels.

Mirrored glasses winked at him from the shadows of *El Portal*, an open-fronted restaurant across from the *Hotel del Parque*. Kane sat calmly at a side table, watching, making no effort to attract Reese's attention. A clever piece of tradecraft, Reese knew, designed to work on his nerves, impress him with Kane's omniscience.

He sat down at Kane's table without speaking. Together they watched a party of Japanese tourists posing for pictures on the steps of the hotel across the street. Without looking at him, Kane said, "I talked to my uncle. He says it's your ass. You can kill yourself if you want to. Those were his words."

Reese stood up.

"Reese."

"Yeah?"

Kane took off his glasses, folded them carefully, and put them in his shirt pocket. His eyes were dark, emotionless. Reese wondered if he could trust someone with eyes as dark as that.

"When I was a kid," Kane said, and then looked down at the street. "When I was a kid it meant a lot to me that you did what you did. Showed me around. Talked to me. I used to think what it would have been like if you were my father."

"I hardly remember any of that."

"I suppose. But it doesn't matter. The thing is, if you insist on this, it's going to kill you. I don't want to be responsible for that."

Reese shook his head. "It's not your responsibility. Okay? It's something I want more than anything. More than anything. That means I take the risks I have to in order to get it."

Kane put his glasses back on. "Okay," he said.

Reese left him there. He was suddenly tired, and took a taxi back to the hotel to pack. In the nearly empty room he found the scrap of paper with his hexagram and followed the change line; the old yang would move to a yin, becoming *Kuei Mei*, the Marrying Maiden. It was, in a vague sort of way, supposed to be his future. "Undertakings bring misfortune. Nothing that would further." Too late now, he thought, dropping the book into his bag.

They caught an *Estrella de Oro* bus for the short ride to Mexico City; from there Kane had them booked on an evening flight to Houston.

Reese sat back in the plush red seat of the airliner, relaxed, watching the lights moving below him. It was almost, he thought, like checking into a hospital. He was no longer making decisions, had been relieved of responsibility for his own existence for the first time in eight years. He'd heard of ex-convicts who'd deliberately put themselves back in jail, and for a second he understood the logic.

The flight came in to Houston Intercontinental a little after ten P.M. Kane had left his car in the parking lot, a large V-8 gasoline-powered sedan. To Reese it seemed almost as cumbersome as the aircraft they'd just left. He sank helplessly into the heavily cushioned seats and flinched as Kane power-locked the doors.

He hadn't seen much of the city during his brief stint at Pulsystems, had not, in fact, spent any time there since his NASA days before his first Mars flight. The changes were sweeping and dramatic.

Kane drove them over a nearly deserted Gulf Freeway, avoiding gaping holes in the overpass and the worst of the broken chunks of pavement. Twice he swung off the freeway altogether and sped past collapsed interchanges. The barricades blocking the mounds of shattered concrete and twisted rebar were themselves falling apart, obviously temporary precautions that had become permanent.

"From the riots," Kane said as Reese turned to stare out the rear window. "There's probably a hundred people in each of those piles. Kids set off some bombs at rush hour. That was about the last rush hour Houston ever had."

"You were here then?"

"Hospital," Kane said. Reese raised an eyebrow but didn't want to press him. "It was right after North Africa. I was in the hospital a couple of months."

Reese's memories superimposed themselves on the dark screen of the city: streetlights that burned all night long, the brilliant, tangled geometrics of the Houston skyline at night, the hundreds of thousands of cars—now rusting and abandoned at the edges of the expressway.

Reese could see no details once they passed through the deserted downtown, only a few ragged pines and collapsing tilt-wall warehouses blurred by the speed of their relative motion. They passed South Houston and the old white-on-green signs for NASA shot by with increasing frequency. Finally, after nearly an hour in the car, they roared off at the NASA/Alvin exit and screamed left onto NASA Road 1. Kane's driving had the intensity of a compulsion, but with the scarcity of cars on the road it seemed harmless, almost childish.

Clear Lake City had virtually dried up and blown away. Reese remembered the long lines of convenience stores and gas stations, burger joints and boutiques that had lined the highway. Hardly a pane of glass had survived.

Finally they swung left into the Johnson Space Center, past the paint-flecked Saturn V shell, then right past Visitor's Parking and into the restricted lot behind Building One, the Project Management Building. At nine stories it was the tallest in a matched set of concrete-and-smoked-glass boxes scattered over the 1600 acres of the complex.

"No security?" Reese asked.

"Surveillance," Kane said. "They know we're here."

Kane released the locking mechanism and Reese got out of the car. A breeze from the lake, a few hundred yards to his right, touched his face and rustled the high grass all around them.

"The place has gone to hell," Kane said. "But cut grass doesn't launch a shuttle." He brought Reese's bag around from the trunk and Reese took it absently. How long had it been? Nine years since he left Mars, and they didn't even debrief him when he got back from that one. A year on Mars and almost another year getting there, so that made it eleven. . . .

It had all happened so suddenly. He hadn't had time to prepare himself, to anticipate these sudden attacks of memory. He wanted a bath and a drink and a chance to meditate.

Kane unlocked the door of the building and led the way to the elevators. At the top floor they got off and Kane pointed to the end of the hall. "The last office on the left has been fixed up for you. There's a shower in the bathroom next door, refrigerator and hot plate in the room."

"That's it?"

"That's it. Somebody will call us in the morning for a briefing."

Reese tried the door of the room, found it unlocked. The air inside was stifling. He flicked on a light and went straight to the window, letting in more thick, humid air. It wasn't until he threw his suitcase on the bed that he noticed the man in the far corner of the room.

"Hello, Reese," Morgan said. He sat slouched in an armchair, legs stretched out in front of him, and Reese saw with some relief that he wasn't going to offer to shake hands. He looked just as Reese had remembered him, over six feet tall with the physique of a drugstore cowboy: broad shoulders, no hips, and a convex stomach with a belt cinched underneath. His dyed hair shone like black patent leather.

"So," Reese said, "you're the welcoming committee?"

"We need to talk."

The furniture, Reese noted, was plain but comfortable. A double bed, chest of drawers, and a portable closet. He took a stack of shirts out of his suitcase. "Then let's talk."

"I want you to know I'm serious about this. We have all the hardware we need and I've got a lot of the old Mission Control people back on board. We can pull this off."

"Maybe you can. The question is why you want to bother. You don't think they're still alive up there, do you?"

Morgan stood up and walked over to the window, hands at his waist, theatrically straightening his back. After a long moment he said, "No. It wouldn't be realistic to expect to find any survivors. But there's reasons enough to put a mission together without any of that. Hell, man, the climatology alone paid for that first Mars mission, paid for it when they broke that drought in the Midwest. Look at history, look what happened to the Chinese when they shut themselves off back in the 15th century. If a company the size of Pulsystems stops growing and stops taking chances, it dies in its tracks. Christ, Reese, I don't have to tell *you* how important it is to have a space program."

Reese finished unpacking and closed up the suitcase. "Only if you intend to keep it going," he said. "And that's a hell of an investment for one company to take on."

"What if I told you," Morgan said, "that I'm prepared to take that risk? Things have been pretty stable for almost five years now. The corporations have pretty much divided up the world and it's back to business as usual. Somebody needs to make a gesture, to take the lead, to try something new. What if I told you that once things got rolling, other corporations will want in, that the momentum will take us . . . well, as far as we want to go."

I'd say, Reese thought, that you were lying.

"There's another reason," Morgan said, sitting down in the armchair again, twisting sideways and throwing both legs over the arm. "The Russians seem to be over their hard times as well. It looks as though Aeroflot is going to be trying for Mars too."

"Another space race? Come on, Morgan. Nationalism is finished. Aeroflot is just another *zaibatsu*; they've got branches all over the world, just like you do."

"But they're Russians, Reese. The people running that company all grew up under the Soviet, they all played war games in grade school where Americans were the bad guys. The first generation to grow up without nationalism is just barely out of its diapers. Don't forget that. Don't underestimate the old factionalism. They beat us to Mars before and I don't plan to let it happen again."

Reese stretched out on the bed. "Whatever you say."

"You sound awfully skeptical, Reese. Especially for a man who insisted he get to go along. The same man who was so desperate for information that he went to work for me under a false name five years ago."

Shit, Reese thought.

"I didn't find out till you'd already disappeared again," Morgan said. "But I must say, it hurt my feelings. I wish you'd just talked to me."

"Look, Morgan. I don't trust you. We've got what they call an adversary relationship. I'm going to be trying to get your people to Mars, and you're going to be trying to make money. Anything else you say is just a smokescreen, just so much bullshit. I don't see any point in our trying to be friends, or your trying to sway me with a lot of outmoded politics and noble-sounding rationalizations."

"If that's the way you want it, Reese, that's okay with me. I've always admired you, and I would like to have your respect. But I can't force you to be my friend and I'm not going to try."

The hell of it is, Reese thought, he's probably sincere. Whatever view he has of himself, whatever he sees when he looks in the mirror, is probably a lot like the way he sees me. As if we were brother pioneers or some such shit.

"I'm a little tired," Reese said, the closest he could come to an apology. "Let's just put the personalities aside for now. What can you tell me about the crew? How long have I got?"

Morgan cleared his throat. "Kane didn't tell you?"

"No."

"Um. There's a bit of pressure, because of the Russians, you see. I'm afraid you've only got six weeks."

"Six *weeks?*"

"I'm afraid so."

"No way," Reese said. "It's impossible."

Morgan leaned forward, his eyes glittering. "I

don't like that word, Reese. If we're going to be working together, you'll find it's to your advantage not to tell me something's impossible. Ever. Do you understand?"

Reese nodded, almost involuntarily. The force of the man's will was frightening, almost psychotic. He thought of Kane's driving, wondering if the entire family was unstable.

"Fine," Morgan said, relaxing again. "NASA used to train mission specialists for the shuttle in five weeks. And my people are in top condition, all of them with pilot experience. Most of the lander training can be done with the on-board computers in simulator mode anyway, give them something to do on the trip out. Now if you're worried about not getting yourself in shape in that amount of time, that's no problem. You can pull out any time you want."

He is not, Reese thought, the clown he played for so many years. It was not just intensity that Morgan shared with Kane but an aura of danger, the dark, flat, predator's eyes that were alert for the slightest weakness in their prey.

"I can handle it," Reese said.

Morgan stood up, smiling, and stopped by the door. "Sleep on it. I'm sure you'll come through for me."

In fact Reese cleared his mind and let himself sleep deeply and well. The phone woke him at 8:15 and he did a hundred situps before he got dressed.

At breakfast Kane introduced him to Lena, Takahashi, and the other two pilots: Walker, a thirtyish woman with hooded brown eyes and leonine hair, and Phut, a slight Vietnamese who took

Reese's hand with barely repressed hostility. Five of them, Reese thought, and only five places on the ship. I'm putting one of them out of a job.

Theirs was the only occupied table in the long, sunlit room and Morgan's absence allowed Reese to eat in relaxed silence. As soon as he comfortably could, he excused himself and wandered through the room, ending up at the souvenir counter. Between the T-shirts and the plastic shuttles was a small hologram unit. Reese switched it on and saw himself in miniature, planting the American flag in the rusty soil where the Frontera dome would be built.

That morning he put them on the wheel.

The centrifuge had a building to itself, the Flight Acceleration Facility, just north of Building 5 and its Link Shuttle Trainer. Even after all these years he still felt nauseated at the sight of the curved gray walls and the radial concrete struts across the roof. He thought of the Hotel Casino de la Selva as his footsteps echoed across the dusty, slick-trowled floor under the fifty-foot arm of the centrifuge.

He remembered the techs talking about some trainee who'd ridden the wheel "eyeballs out," lying on his belly, hemorrhaging all the capillaries in both eyes, turning the whites bright red for a month. He remembered his first sight of an Apollo spacecraft, how amazed he'd been by the sheer, clumsy, mechanical weight of switches and latches and levers and knobs. Then, as now, the very idea of space travel seemed ludicrous, beyond the capability of the equipment.

But the power plant started and the centrifuge turned, and one by one he took them up to five G's and let Lena watch their signs. Then it was Lena's turn and then it was his, and he had to climb into the gondola and let Kane control the wheel, thinking, I can't be afraid of him, I have to learn to trust him, I have to learn to trust them all.

And after all, it was only five G's, not even enough to bring out the purple splotches of petichiae on his back. He remembered the breathing technique, filling his lungs and just sipping air off the top, not letting his chest muscles relax. And then it was over, almost before it started.

Easy, he thought, no problem. But he knew that it didn't get hard until it got over eight G's, and he knew that ten G's were going to be very hard indeed.

In the afternoon he left them with Takahashi for a full workout and tried to round up the material he would need for the classroom work. Six weeks seemed so pathetically short to teach them upper atmosphere physics, flight mechanics, guidance and navigation, systems and hardware, not to mention some kind of hands-on simulation and escape and contingency drills.

Which left the flight out for all of the lander instruction and simulations, training on the onboard medical and science equipment, preparation and rehearsal of the Mars surface excursions, as well as diagnostics, housekeeping, communications and exercise.

So many things, he thought, so many ways to go wrong.

After supper he took them to the auditorium in the Visitor's Center and ran them the films he'd been able to find, keeping the volume low, correcting the affable announcer's voice on the soundtrack when he had to. Around eight o'clock Morgan took a seat in the back row and stayed for the remaining two hours.

In the flickering light of the projector Reese watched the recruits. Kane and Takahashi were both impassive, Lena very serious-looking, and only Walker seemed openly enthusiastic. Phut was restless, bored, and seemed to fall asleep a little after nine.

When the others had left, Reese sat back in a red-plush chair, one seat away from Morgan, and closed his eyes.

"Well?" Morgan said.

"Where did you find these guys?"

"What's wrong with them?"

"Walker and Takahashi seem okay. But Lena doesn't know a goddamn thing outside her specialty, Kane is probably a borderline psychotic, and Phut thinks I'm here to do him out of his job, which in a way I guess I am. What happened to the NASA people? They can't all be too old."

"The best ones I need for my shuttle pilots. Don't forget, you can't even get to the spacecraft without a shuttle ride. And the short-range economy is going to be in Earth orbit for a while."

"So these are the dregs, in other words."

"As a matter of fact, Takahashi is a pretty high-ranking officer of this company, and the oldest son of the head of the Tokyo office. His loyalty is impeccable, and he's one of my strongest and smartest people. Kane is family, and there is nothing wrong with his mind. He and Phut both showed great loyalty and courage in the war, and they're two of the best helicopter pilots in Texas. Lena and Walker are strong, capable, bright, and physically fit."

"But the risks involved . . ."

"We've been over that. You said we were in an adversary position, and this is an example. Some of the decisions you're unhappy about may be company decisions, which is to say decisions made in a larger framework than the one you're responsible for. Those are the kind of decisions you're just going to have to live with."

"Even if it jeopardizes the mission?"

"I'm sure you'll manage," Morgan said. "I have every confidence in you."

On the third day Reese took them to 15 G's. Phut's trachea blocked with vomit and Lena had to clear it with her finger and give him mouth-to-mouth. Morgan had been watching from the doorway, lurking, Reese thought, just like he did in the old days.

"I'm washing him out," Reese said, and Morgan only nodded.

Phut's dismissal seemed to break the tension in the crew and for the first time Reese began to think they might make it. That afternoon he let them on the Mars Mission Module in Building Five. Reese had asked Morgan to have it fixed and Morgan had done so, quietly and invisibly, taking away the blue painted exterior stairs that the tourists had used, stripping out the plastic sheets that sealed off the Command Center, patching the cutaway sections of the hull.

Reese watched them crawling through the four hideously familiar levels, quarters at the bottom, then Wardroom, Health Maintenance, and Command, each just twelve feet in diameter, knowing how soon they would all learn to detest the sight of the light-brown walls, the gridded metal floors. Reese had spent three years of his life, nine months at a time, in various duplicates of the Mission Module, and still at least three or four times a month he had claustrophobic, slow-motion dreams of drifting between the levels.

At the end of the second week, exhausted by the fourteen-hour days, Reese gave them the evening off. They could only learn so much, he told himself, and even Takahashi was starting to show signs of stress, confusing his right and left hands while running the shuttle trainer, questioning the relevance of graviton theory in the classroom.

He was collapsed sideways across his bed when Kane knocked on his door. "I'm going in to town," he said. "You want to come along?" He was back behind his mirror shades, as close to relaxed as Reese had seen him in the last two weeks, wearing a loose cotton-knit pullover and fatigue pants.

"Sure," Reese said impulsively. "What are we doing?"

"Bringing in some stuff from the downtown office. Maybe get a bite to eat while we're down there."

They took the elevator to the roof where a late-model four-seat helicopter was moored.

"You fly these?" Kane asked, and Reese shook his head. "It's nice," Kane said. "A real power trip. Planes just go fast. This'll do anything you want it to."

Kane took them up smoothly into the fading sunlight. Gray, four-lane highways squared the JSC;

just beyond it Clear Lake's muddy water picked up muted blues from the sky. As Kane heeled the copter over, Reese could finally see what happened to Clear Lake City. The residential areas were mostly burned to the ground, and the storefronts were glassless and hollow.

"I didn't know the riots spread this far," Reese shouted, over the thudding of the rotors.

"Used to be a rich neighborhood. That's all it took. Somebody finally figured out that nobody gave a shit if the people who were starving just burned down their own houses. This piece of work got them a lot of attention, but no food. By that time the government didn't have any money to give them."

"What's the population now?"

"Nobody knows for sure. Probably around a million five or so."

"Jesus."

"A lot of that's because of people moving out to Smithville and LaGrange and getting the hell away from here. There's farmland out there and cattle and it's a lot easier to get by. I mean, a million people didn't die here. A lot, but less than a million."

Kane tilted the rotors into the wind and the copter shot forward, making for the cluster of reflective-glassed buildings to the north and west. Underneath them flowed a procession of warehouses, factories, and swamps, all of them flanked by scraggly pines and scrub brush.

"Looks like Morgan's the only corporation in town."

"There's others," Kane said. "The worst part

was currency—nobody wanted dollars and we had to get changed over to an electronic transfer system before things could get rolling again. Of course we make the computers to handle those transfers."

The "we" surprised Reese, giving him a sudden insight into Kane's character. Kane might be the only one of the crew, he realized, who saw Pulsystems as more than just Morgan.

"A lot of these places," Kane went on, waving his hand, "belong to the majors now. They'll be up and running again in a couple years."

The industrial wasteland gave way to poorer neighborhoods, the hulks of rusting cars cluttering the streets or sitting up on blocks in front yards, icons of an obsolete god. A few trash fires smouldered weakly, spreading a faint haze through the evening and blurring the knots of people on the corners who drank from refillable beer bottles and leaned against light poles that had lost any other usefulness.

On the average, Reese knew, less than half of them had jobs and the rest collected what Pulsystems and the other major corporations euphemistically called a "pension," paid out of a fund that all the corporations supported. During his days on the line at Pulsystems Reese had heard one management trainee refer to it as the "riot prevention tax."

The result was a supposedly temporary phase of cable TV addiction that would eventually give way to a new age of cottage industry and informed consumerism. Reese did not expect the new age in his lifetime, not on Earth. The entire planet seemed in decay and he wanted away from it, back into space where he belonged.

As they began to thread their way into downtown Houston through the jungle of gold- and blue- and brown-tinted glass, Reese noticed that only the smaller buildings were missing panes, that the largest were clean and intact. Kane brought the helicopter down onto a yellow-painted target on the roof of one of the nearly identical towers in the center of the city.

Reese waited while Kane called the elevator, using both a laser key and a combination typed into the elevator console. When they finally got inside they dropped to the second floor at about three G's of acceleration.

Morgan's office seemed cluttered and lived-in, with no sign of imposed aesthetics. The wooden desk was old and stained, while the chair behind it was a modern sculpture of chrome and steel. One set of bookshelves had been built into the wall while another was bolted together from perforated metal.

The paneled walls were hung with framed photographs, most of them the obvious shots of Morgan with assorted celebrities; a few of them, though, showed a clear mountain stream with a cabin in the background. They seemed to go with a shelf of books on fly-fishing. The other shelves held bound printouts, self-help books from Machiavelli to Dale Carnegie, biographies of astronauts, the usual dictionaries and references. Most of the books were paperbacks, with broken spines and dogeared pages, victims of hard use.

Kane dropped into the desk chair and propped his feet on the oversized blotter. "He's got another office, all steel and glass. That's where he culti-vates the image."

Reese noticed that the early photographs of Mor-gan showed him in a somber suit and short hair. "Morgan's not even from Texas, is he?" he asked.

"That's right. Born in Detroit. The accent comes and goes, you probably noticed that. All part of the protective coloring."

Reese sat by the door, trying to reconcile this image of Kane with the others: the eager teenager, the detached mercenary, the makeshift astronaut. "It's funny," Reese said. "You look like you belong here."

"I'm the crown prince," Kane said, with an irony that Reese couldn't quite believe in. "I was brought up to do just this. Sit behind this desk."

"Instead you're going to Mars."

"Yeah, well. The crown prince is out of favor at the moment. I could use a few points with the Board. I could use *something*." He pushed a button that brought a console up from the desk top. He punched in a complex sequence of numbers and a moment later a large portion of the wall to Reese's left swung out into the office. "*Et voilá*," Kane said.

The three inside walls of the vault held three further doors. Kane stood inside the cubicle and entered another combination, opening one of the doors to a thin cloud of steam. Slipping one hand into an insulated mitten, he pulled out a small gray cylinder labeled "Cryogenic Material" in red letters. He put the cylinder into an insulated car-rier that looked like an ordinary briefcase, then resealed both doors.

"This'll keep for a couple of hours," Kane said. "Can I buy you a beer?"

"Sure. What's in there?"

"Christ knows. Something Morgan wants. I didn't even bother to ask him—he would have lied to me anyway."

They took the elevator down to the basement and followed signs saying "To The Tunnels." They came out in a tiled, fluorescent-lit underground mall full of travel agencies and boutiques.

Reese had to hurry to keep up with Kane's natural pace. "Is it safe to be carrying that around?"

"No," Kane said.

Reese shook his head. "I'm sorry. I don't get it."

"It's simple, man. This is Morgan's shit. If something happens to it, I don't really care. He should have sent one of his goddamned couriers after it if he was that worried. Not me."

Kane seemed nearly irrational on the subject of Morgan and Reese decided to let it go. In fact he could see too many similarities between them, from their chameleon qualities to their flat, deadly eyes.

The bar Kane took them to was aboveground, converted from a parking garage. A ramp at one end led to a crude cement patch; the low ceiling and huge floorspace made Reese feel disoriented and out of proportion. An autosynth at the far end of the club played neowebern at high volume, the repetitious, atonal phrases adding to his unease. Most of the other customers were young, poor, and faddishly dressed in *hiparis* or full Arab drag, complete with black-rimmed sunglasses.

Kane ordered sushi and Tsing-Tao beer for both of them, talking easily about the woman who owned the bar and the details of its renovation. Reese watched the tension in Kane's fingers as he raised his glass, the pressure of his ankle that held the briefcase against a leg of the table.

When the fish came, Reese couldn't eat it, repelled by the oily sheen of the skin on a piece of tuna belly, the insectile curl of the shrimp. Kane speared the pieces with a recklessness that seemed exaggerated, inappropriate; but it was only when he finished eating, as Kane paid with his plastic Pulsystems ID and they stepped outside, that Reese understood.

Night had transformed the city. Here in the heart of the business district there were streetlights, but they only deepened the shadows on the high, tan walls of concrete. People were moving in the darkness with carnivorous stealth and Reese could feel their attention concentrating on the two of them, on the briefcase in Kane's hand, the potent symbol of affluence and oppression. Reese loosened his shoulders reflexively, clearing his mind and speeding his pulse rate.

Something brushed him, knocking him off balance. He saw Kane spin halfway around, saw a shadow reaching for the briefcase, speared and flung away by a lightening movement of Kane's knee. Then the briefcase was in Reese's hands and Kane was using both of his, throwing the broken body of a teenaged boy into the wall. The boy hit face first and slowly slid to the ground.

"Kane?" Reese said. He held the briefcase with both hands, expecting another attack, waiting for the flash or snap of gunfire. Instead a blinding spotlight swept over them and stopped, freezing them in position.

"Hands straight up and away from your bodies. Drop that case."

Reese set the briefcase at his feet and then straightened slowly, still unable to see where the voice came from.

"ID?" it said, and Kane took out the same card he'd used in the bar, making careful, broad gestures.

As Reese went for his own NASA ID, Kane said, "Don't bother." He handed the bit of plastic to a bulky silhouette in the spotlight and said, "Kane. Pulsystems."

The cop did something with the card, then handed it crisply back. "Very good, sir. I'll take care of this for you. Are both of you okay?"

"Fine," Kane said. "Thanks."

On the elevator to the roof Reese asked, "Doesn't it scare you?"

"What?"

"The cop. How did he know you weren't just working over some innocent kid?"

"He didn't. But he works for us. It's not his job to ask us a lot of annoying questions." Kane's voice was flat, unemotional.

They got in the copter. Kane started the motor, then took his hands off the controls. They were shaking.

"Shit," he said.

"You okay?"

"Yeah," Kane said. "Fine. Shit. I hate this. I fucking asked for it, carrying something valuable around on the streets at night. Begging for trouble because my goddamn uncle pissed me off. Now that kid is dead, or worse, and it's my fault." He held his hands out in front of him until they were steady again. "It just pisses me off is all. I'm fine." He put the rotor in gear and they lifted off.

Reese saw that the entire evening had been meant as a humanizing gesture on Kane's part, an attempt to bridge some sort of gap between Reese and himself. But the attempted mugging had soured it and Reese could feel Kane's disappointment.

But I can't do it, Reese wanted to tell him. I can't be your father, I can't be responsible for what you are or for what you want to be.

For the next two weeks Reese pushed them harder than before. At night, before sleeping, he focused his mind on a memory of Earth from shuttle orbit, 115 miles up, the cities reduced to simple color and geometry.

Kane missed two days in the second week for an "unavoidable" medical checkup. Reese assumed it had something to do with the wound Kane had received in North Africa; his suspicions were borne out by a freshly shaved patch on the back of Kane's skull when he returned to training. "I'm clean," was all he would tell Reese about it. "Everything checked out okay." For a couple of days he seemed sluggish and a bit confused, but Reese didn't have time to worry about him.

With nine days left until the launch Reese could feel the tension starting to build in his chest, like the pressure that built up inside a rocket engine between ignition and the time they blew the bolts that held it onto the pad. It was *shakti*, spiritual thrust, and he felt it rushing out of him every time he'd gone up.

That was the night Walker came to him where he sat under the SIV-B, the third stage of the Saturn V booster, now rotting in drydock by the visitor's parking lot. He'd brought his last bottle of *Gusano Rojo* mescal, Red Worm brand, and even though the traditional worm floating near the bottom of the bottle was yellow, he remembered how the mescal could work on the brain's color map like a psychedelic drug, until the sky and the grass and the inside of his own eyelids turned flaming crimson.

He'd been remembering his early days in NASA, the parties in sprawling, tasteless mansions along Memorial Drive, the perfumed and tinted society wives with hairline surgical scars on the undersides of their breasts, the cable interviews and charity luncheons and expensive scotch in plastic motel glasses.

"You come out here a lot?" she asked him.

"Just restless," he said, and offered her the mescal.

"That's awful," she said, tasting it. "Like a bile-and-vodka cocktail."

He literally could not remember the last time he'd been alone with a woman. Even the professionals had avoided the Hotel Casino and its deserted bar, and before that he'd just been traveling aimlessly, by bus and train, hardly speaking to anybody. He felt a sudden, familiar stab of desire and chased it with the mescal.

"Were you looking for me?" Reese asked. "Or just passing by?" The words came out more dismissively than he'd intended, but he let them stand.

"Wandering. I don't sleep much; I'm out a lot at

night." She leaned back, her mane of dark hair catching the moonlight, tension bringing out the clean lines of the muscles in her neck. "I heard somebody over here and thought it might be you. So it seemed like a good chance to talk to you about something, something I didn't want Morgan to overhear."

"You don't think we're going to make it, is that it? I don't blame you. I feel that way myself about half the time."

"It's not that. It's something I found." Her eyes were nervous, her mouth a thin, hard line. "Like I said, I'm out a lot at night. There's a lot of history here, stuff Morgan keeps locked up, stuff I wanted to look at. Like the moon rocks over at the Lunar Receiving Lab, and that big padded room—"

"The anechoic chamber. Where they test the communication stuff."

"Yeah. And Mission Control. He's got some kind of recorder there, and it's still running."

"What?" Reese could still taste the bitter oiliness of the mescal, but his brain was suddenly clear.

"A tape recorder, it looks like. You want to see it?"

"Show me," Reese said.

She led him across the courtyard to Mission Control. She looked good, wearing loose trousers and a delta top that left her sides bare instead of the baggy coveralls from training, but Reese's heart was no longer in it. She hesitated at the corner of the north wing and Reese walked past her, eager to get inside.

"Wait!" she hissed at him, and he stopped.

"What's the—"

"Camera!" she whispered, and he looked up to see the eye of a video recorder sweeping toward him. He ducked back out of sight, wondering if he'd been quick enough.

"This way," Walker said, and took him around the side to a fire exit. She pulled a folding knife from her pants pocket and slid back the tongue of the lock. "Watch your step," she said. "It's dark in here."

Every fifty feet or so a single fluorescent light burned; fire regulations, Reese remembered. They took stairs to the second-floor mission operations room and Reese switched on a single bank of lights by the door.

The outlines of the continents were just visible on the darkened mission board, navy blue against a black-on-black grid. The rows of CRT's were gray-faced and silent, the film of dust on the floor hardly visible.

—Except, Reese noticed, where a path was worn through it, leading to the communications station at the back of the room. He hurried to the console, afraid to hope, staring at the frequency on the digital display, the band reserved for incoming broadcasts from Frontera Base, not sure if he was really seeing it or just imagining it so strongly that even his eyes were deceived.

"Do you know what it is?" Walker asked him. "What does it mean?"

"It means," Reese said, ejecting the cassette that was locked in the mechanism, already half recorded, "it means maybe, possibly, somebody is still alive up there." He put a fresh cassette into the receiver and fed the other one into a playback unit in the next console. He backed it up, pushed PLAY, listened to the tape shriek and squeal.

"From some satellite?" Walker asked.

"It's from Mars," Reese said. "From Frontera. It has to be. They're using some kind of high-speed dump." Reese found the dial that controlled the tape speed and spun it down from $1\frac{7}{8}$ to $\frac{5}{16}$ ips.

The scream dropped to a woman's voice: "need to change our schedule on the reply to fit with the new shifts up here . . ." Reese pushed the REWIND button and wound the tape all the way back. He knew the voice, the soft, breathless whisper. He shut his eyes and could see her face, lean and tanned, with hair a colorless shade between brown and blonde. "Dian," he said. She was one of the physicists working with Molly, with engineering expertise that let her turn abstract ideas into physical reality.

"You know her?"

"Yeah. She's one of them. They're *alive*, goddamnit, and Morgan knew about it!" He forced down his excitement and started the tape, pulling up a rolling armchair and easing down into it.

The tape ran for nearly fifteen minutes.

There were six different transmissions, probably boring to Morgan and barely comprehensible to Walker, who paced back and forth tirelessly while it played. But to Reese they were maddening glimpses of a world he'd given up for dead years before, enigmatic references that sent his imagination spinning. And the names—names he'd thought he'd never hear again.

"Molly's alive," he said. "I can't believe it."

"Who's she? Old girlfriend?"

"No," Reese said. "She's my daughter." He looked up at her quickly. "Jesus, that slipped right out, didn't it? It's not something I ever told anybody before. Except Molly. Her mother was married to somebody else."

Not just somebody else, of course, but to one of the other astronauts, compulsively unfaithful while Jenny, with her physics degree and her national recognition, her red-gold hair and freckled shoulders, had nothing left but an empty Houston apartment and a stable of quarterhorses in a pine forest outside Clear Lake.

That was where Molly had been conceived, on a red plaid blanket spread over pine needles, a thick Gulf mist dripping from the branches overhead, a week before Reese's first shuttle flight. Their hot, guilty desire had built through an afternoon of riding and gentle, brushing contact, culminating in the electric touch of her fingernails on his nipples, the smell of leather and horses still on them as he buried himself in her body, promising himself that this first time would be the last, not dreaming the promise would come true.

Jenny's husband had transferred out of NASA, and Reese found out about Jenny's pregnancy in a scrawled note on the bottom of their Christmas card, a note that told him the child was his. There was no return address.

It had taken him two years to find them again, another year of phone calls to persuade Jenny to let him see the child. In stolen meetings he had watched Molly grow up, a chubby little girl with calm eyes and an amused tolerance for the affec-

tion of this large, awkward man that her mother
watched on television. And through it all Jenny
had been cold, distant, with no more for him than
a tired smile or the gentle pressure of her arms
around his back.

Molly was thirteen when Jenny and her husband
died in the fire in the orbiting colony *Gerard K.
O'Neill*. He didn't see her again until she showed
up at NASA ten years later, transformed somehow
into graceful womanhood, applying for a slot on the
next colony ship to Mars.

Their first meeting was an uncomfortable mixture of Molly's childhood memories and Reese's
guilty search for traces of Jenny in her daughter.
But within days they found themselves locked in a
sudden, genuine friendship that surprised them
both. They'd flown to Mars together on that colony mission, a crowded, hectic nine months that
were the happiest Reese ever spent in space.

Curtis had been part of that mission, of course, a
younger, more dynamic Curtis, and Reese had
watched with more than a hint of jealousy as Molly
fell in love with him. Reese had been best man at
their wedding, only days before he had to return
to Earth.

Curtis's name was on the tape as well. Reese
rewound the cassette and started listening to it
again.

"Uh, listen," Walker said. "Shouldn't we be getting out of here?"

"This is unbelievable," Reese said. "Something's
going on, something really big."

The first message made guarded reference to it.
"Verb is toying around with some kind of matter

transporter. She's got a couple of the other kids working on it, and Molly and I are getting pieces for her out of the machine shop. I'd think it was a joke, but she's already accomplished so much . . ."

The second message didn't add anything, but the third said that Curtis was "getting suspicious." Dian went on to say, "The political situation up here is getting weird. Curtis is coming down on everybody, and we're now smuggling stuff up here from the machine shop. Molly doesn't want him to know what we've got going, and I think she's right."

Reese had never liked Curtis; he was too self-consciously good looking, too much like Jenny's husband. He didn't like the idea of Curtis being in a position of power at Frontera, was desperate to know what was happening there, who this Verb person was.

The next transmission had more details: ". . . she thinks it's really going to work. With enough information about the terminus she's going to be able to deliver anyplace within ten or twenty light years. If it works, it could be a way out of here for all of us . . ."

But by the next broadcast, a week later, something had gone wrong. Dian sounded drunk, despondent. "The first test was a flop and Verb doesn't seem as interested as she was . . . she doesn't care how much it means to the rest of us . . . christ, I want out of here. When are you going to start keeping up your end of this? Curtis would kill me if he knew I was leaking this stuff to you. I want a ship out of here . . ."

The tape had run into the last message, something about shift changes and a detailed description of the power panel for the transporter, when Morgan's voice came from the door.

"Heard enough?" he said. He flicked on the overheads and Reese blinked in surprise. "This is certainly cozy," Morgan went on. "Sneaking around in the dark, spying—"

"Cut the bullshit," Reese said. "They're alive. You've known all along and still you lied to me about it." Walker moved away from Reese, her frightened eyes fixed on Morgan.

"We've been over this, Reese," Morgan said. "That was a management decision."

"God *damn* it!" Reese shouted. "Those are my friends up there! It was just bad luck I was on rotation when the recall came or I'd still be with them, right now. And I wouldn't be putting up with your fucking counterplots and corporate images and lies."

"That's enough, Reese."

"It is fucking well *not* enough! I want to know what's going on. I want to know everything you can tell me about Frontera and what's happening up there. I want to know what this matter transporter is they were talking about."

"Or?" Morgan said.

Reese took a breath. "Or I'm finished here."

Morgan turned his head, a quick, predatory movement like a bird's or a lizard's. His eyes locked on Walker and she stepped forward. "Get the tape," he told her, and she ejected it from the deck. "Bring it," he said, and she did. Her helplessness made Reese feel a little sick.

"Think about it," Morgan said, one hand on the woman's upper arm. "If you walk out, the mission goes without you. You lose your last chance to get back to Mars, and all I lose are a few percentage points on the odds of this thing working." He turned to go, then stopped in the doorway.

"One more thing. You're now in possession of stolen information, whether you stay or not. The gold standard is dead, and we're on the data standard now. That means that what you've got is extremely valuable and if you try to pass it on to anybody, and I mean Kane or Lena or *anybody*, then you die. You and anybody you tell it to."

It had started in Mexico and it changed that night, changed the moment that Reese tried to bluff his way past Morgan and lost. He'd gone back to the mescal but been unable to finish it, its brutal anesthesia too much like the dark, slick edge of a long fall into nothingness.

Walker, of course, was gone the next day. Dead, brainwashed, or transferred; Reese would never know which. The four of them, Morgan said, would be perfectly adequate to fly the ship.

For the next eight days Reese worked them with cold precision, his brain shut down during the day, at night replaying the soft, breathless voice he'd heard on the tapes. "Ten or twenty light years," she'd said, "with enough information."

He slept badly. Faceless shadows dodged through his dreams while he flailed at gelatinous air. In the training sessions his concentration faltered and his reflexes turned erratic. On the last morning of instruction he crashed the MEM simulator, and as he walked away he could feel waves of doubt and hostility move through the crew.

But none of it mattered. That afternoon they took one of Morgan's private jets to Cocoa Beach, with Kane as co-pilot and Lena in the left seat, claiming it would help her nerves. Morgan had his own cabin in the rear of the plane and stayed in it for the entire flight; Takahashi slept, or at least pretended to. That left Reese to stare out the window by himself, watching the fertile soil of Earth turn under the plane, wondering if he would ever see it again.

At five the next morning they drove from the Sands Motel to the Cape, Reese in one car with Lena and Takahashi, Kane and Morgan alone in the second. By six o'clock they had changed to blue coveralls and were walking out to the shuttle on pad 39A.

The sky over the ocean was turning gray; overhead Reese could still see Vega and Altair. His stomach had the light, quivering feeling of hunger, excitement, and too little sleep. The Cape had barely changed, had been built to stand up under the exhaust of a Saturn V, and against its solidity he felt like a pretend astronaut, an astronaut who'd just spent the night in a motel, an astronaut who was being laughed at somewhere, by somebody, as he stopped at the foot of the service and access tower for a last look.

The orange shell of the shuttle's external tank seemed unlucky to him; the orange girders of the floodlit tower were harsh and jangling. He pushed past the others into the pad elevator and together they rode up to the white room, where Morgan's shuttle pilots were waiting.

Reese nodded to the pilots and they gave him a

thumbs-up signal and crawled through the small, square hatch into the orbiter. A technician fitted Reese with a soft white flight helmet, the dark ovals of the inset speakers protruding like cartoon ears. Then he swung into the middle deck of the ship.

The orbiter was designed for level flight and now, sitting on end on the launch pad, everything was on its side. Reese climbed awkwardly up to the flight deck and into one of the two seats in the back of the module, just in front of the on-orbit station. Takahashi, the mission commander, would take the other one, and Lena and Kane would ride out the take off from the middle deck. The gray-green nylon seat covers reminded Reese of army surplus air mattresses; the four separate seat belts and buckles were clumsy and oversized beyond any necessity.

He plugged in his headphones and they filled instantly with the jabbering of Morgan's imported technicians, flown in from Houston two weeks before, less than half of them with any real launch experience. He wanted to pull the plug out again, knew it instantly for a disturbed and dangerous impulse, yet still had to struggle to resist it.

Only the pilots had window seats. Through the front of the spacecraft Reese could see nothing but the reds and grays of the Florida dawn. He listened to the pilots move through the pre-flight check, relieved that he wasn't having to gamble on his own nerves and reflexes.

At T-minus three minutes they switched onto internal fuel tanks, and at minus two minutes they cleared the warning memory. At minus a minute twenty seconds they had flight pressure on the liquid hydrogen. Eyes closed, Reese followed them through the sequence from memory. At T minus 55 seconds the hydrogen igniters were armed and at minus 30 the hydraulics went on. Then the long count, and at minus five seconds the main engines ignited.

The ship began to vibrate, massive bolts holding to the pad while the pressure built to full thrust, 375 thousand pounds from each engine, and then the Solid Rocket Boosters cut in with five million more and then the bolts exploded and Reese felt the thrust begin to press him gently downward. The smoke from the exhaust, billowing up from the fire pits on either side of the pad, was just visible through the front windows, shimmering in the blazing heat.

The real view, Reese knew, was from the pursuit planes following them, planes that Morgan was sure to have laid on, to get the maximum publicity from his expense. They would be shooting footage now of the launch pad, falling away until it became a neat gray hexagon against the greenish-brown land and the distant blue of the sea. The long teardrop of flame from the boosters would be too bright to watch with the naked eye, but Morgan's cameras would be getting it all, probably piping it into the cable and onto TV screens around the world as soon as he decided they weren't going to be consumed in a humiliating fireball.

"Okay, *Enterprise*, we've got nominal performance."

Nominal being NASA-ese for letter-perfect, Reese thought. So far, so good.

"Roger. Main throttle at 104%. All three main engines go at throttle up."

The sky deepened into violet and at 30 miles the exhausted SRB's were blown away, spattering brown film across the windows. "Christ," the pilot complained, "where's the goddamned windshield wipers?" The other pilot laughed, but Reese had misplaced his sense of humor. He glanced over at Takahashi, who was staring ahead out the windows, impassive.

Eight minutes after launch the external tank fell away and the orbiter climbed the last few miles on the nitrogen and hydrazine in its own tanks. Night was falling across the Mediterranean below them and bright, unwinking stars rose over the crescent Earth.

"Holy christ," the first pilot said. Reese stripped the thick webbing away and floated out of his seat. The orbiter still flew on its back, the Earth directly overhead as Reese drifted up between the pilots' seats for a look.

Morgan's presence seemed to have stayed behind on the planet, dropped away with the pull of gravity. Though he knew it was a simpleminded and even dangerous illusion, Reese felt as if his perspective was intact for the first time since he left Mexico.

Lena and Kane rose through the hatch, Lena pale and unsteady. "Oh my God," she said, at the sight of the blue slice of planet over her head.

Kane strapped her in Reese's seat and gave her a pill to swallow. "Stay put," he said, "keep your eyes closed, and just concentrate on holding that down."

Space Adaptation Syndrome, NASA's fancy term for space sickness. Reese could already feel his own facial tissues swelling and his inner ear sending garbled signals to the brain. If Lena was the only one incapacitated they would be ahead of the percentages. But he couldn't do anything more for her than Kane already had, and at the moment he was more interested in the tracking signal from the Mars Mission Module, less than an hour downrange of their current position.

They spent a second long, frustrating hour as the novice pilot tried to dock with the MM. His instincts were useless; increased thrust moved them into a higher, slower orbit, and by dropping low enough to catch up they overshot, time and again. Reese finally went below decks and suited up to begin denitrogenating.

And then they were docked and Reese was finally through the airlock and out the open bay doors, strapped to an M509 maneuvering unit, rising into the shadow of the Mission Module. The fifth booster stage lay in the orbiter's payload bay; when it was in place the spacecraft would be nearly two hundred feet long, a tall, thin cylinder pointed into space. He squirted nitrogen from his jets and lifted to the top of the ship.

"Reese?" Kane said. "How does it look?"

"Fine," he said. "Listen, can you leave me alone for a minute?"

"Uh, sure."

Reese cut the radio off and watched the planet slowly turning beneath his feet. Looking down the ship gave him an eerie sense of perspective, as if it were a tower running all the way to the surface, flexing in the wind as the planet moved.

There it is, he thought. A fragile accident of a world, the one place in the solar system, maybe in the universe, that is truly hospitable to the human race. Could you turn your back on it for ever?

He touched his gloved index fingers to his thumbs, closed his eyes, and waited until he could feel the stillness all the way through his lungs and stomach and heart. Here he could feel a deeper, slower rhythm, a music inaudible on Earth.

One single world, no matter how rich or familiar, was not enough. He'd been stranded down there, rescued by circumstances he didn't fully understand. Before he would let himself be trapped there again he would risk anything.

Anything.

He opened his eyes and turned the radio on. "Let's go to work," he said.

The pilots fitted the final stage into position with the orbiter's manipulator arm. Lena, nearly recovered from her SAS, hovered outside with Takahashi and gave directions.

Meanwhile Kane and Reese opened the Mission Module to hard vacuum. Then they blasted the inside surface clean with nitrogen jets and pumped in a fresh atmosphere. The module still smelled faintly of rotting food. In time, Reese thought, the Sabatier units would clean it up, or they would just get used to it.

During the second day the abandoned Antaeus facility passed slowly overhead. Reese had spent three redundant weeks there after the first Mars landing, quarantined even though they'd been isolated for nearly ten months on the return trip. Later the station had been turned over to genetic engineers, then abandoned when the government fell.

There had been rumors, doubtlessly exaggerated, of some strange experiments in the station, and it gave Reese a momentary chill to see, through the orbiter's telescope, a light still burning in the lab.

That afternoon Takahashi pronounced the ship's computers functional and the four of them said their goodbyes to Morgan's pilots and watched the shuttle move slowly away. And then they stood in awkward silence in the Command Center of the Mission Module as the first stage ignited, building slowly to the one-G thrust that would ease them out of Earth orbit and into the long fall away from the sun.

For nearly a month Reese kept them on a tight NASA schedule of exercise, EVA, and simulations. He watched with twinges of misplaced desire as Lena and Kane dabbled in zero-G sex, then settled into quiet antipathy. And when the schedules began to break down he found himself unable to argue. He spent more time alone in his cabin, or struggling with his personal demons in the midnight, hallucinatory silence of the command center, leaving Takahashi to his fanatical exercise and quiet arrogance.

For Reese, familiarity reduced the trip to a few milestones: the passage of lunar orbit, shutdown of the last engine, the midpoint of the Hohmann ellipse; nothing else seemed real or significant. He had internalized the voice on the tape and he lost any desire to talk about it, even though he was no longer afraid of Morgan.

Only as they strapped themselves in for aero-braking did he realize that the time was coming when he would have to act, to try for the astrometry diskette on Deimos if he wanted it. There could be no second chance, no other way of giving the person named Verb "enough information about the terminus" for her to give him what he wanted.

And then he realized that his mind was already made up.

As the MEM sank toward the giant, striated flanks of Arsia Mons, he was a bullet that had been fired, mindless, unable to change his course. He watched the slow-falling dust as the lander bumped to a stop, his helmet seeming to find its own way into its socket, his legs taking him down the ladder after Takahashi. One of the colonists held out an arm to support him and he took it, watching the figure by the airlock door that held her hand to her throat in an achingly familiar gesture.

"Reese?" she said, and he nodded, let her help him inside and into a cot in sickbay. "Sleep," she said, and he felt the needle go into his arm, the warmth of Butorphenol spreading through his jaw and the underside of his tongue, taking the gravity away again.

Kane looked into the greasy water and saw himself reflected, from his worn boots and woolen trousers to the crude leather helmet on his head. A cold wind blew off the ocean, its breath whistling past him with a faint, chilling melody. He shivered and stepped carefully around the tidal pool, the rocks painful to his feet.

Through the fog a ship landed, its motion unaffected by the sea, drifting exactly to the shore and then pausing. Words were carved into the prow and he could barely make them out:

Thou man which shalt entir into thys shippe, beware that thou be in stedefaste beleve, for I am Faythe. And therefore beware how thou entirst but if thou be stedefaste, for and thou fayle therof I shall nat helpe the.

Caxton's Mallory, a distant part of his brain told him, but the words had no relevance to what he was seeing.

The ship rode low in the water, low enough that a dozen steps across the rotted pier took him onto its deck. He breathed the salt, stinking air and then climbed down creaking steps into the hold.

As his eyes adjusted to the darkness he made out a crude bed in one corner. On it lay a silver serving tray that held a silver goblet, a half-drawn broadsword etched with runes, and a long-bladed pike.

The sight of the objects filled him with terror.

He woke with a scream gurgling in his throat and his hands clutching at his face for a beard that wasn't there. Even when his conscious brain recognized the glazed walls of the martian sickbay, his body, down to the cellular level, felt displaced, disoriented.

He had never dreamed so intensely before, felt so clearly that he had been transported through time, or into some parallel universe.

A sharp spasm of hunger brought him to a sitting position. Gravity clung to him like mud and the effort of fighting it made him dizzy, nauseated. The pain in his ribs awoke with a dull throbbing and he touched his chest, finding a tight lattice of surgical tape.

He didn't hurt as badly as he thought he would, but then again, when he'd felt that second rib crack he'd thought he was going to die. He sat with his feet off the edge of the cot and drank a little water. Compared with the brownish, alkaline water of the ship it tasted impossibly sweet and pure.

As long as he kept still, both his stomach and ribs were all right. Turning his head slightly he could count twenty beds in the sickbay, all of them in use. Takahashi slept peacefully across the room; next to him Lena kicked and moaned softly. Reese was off to Kane's left, pale but breathing.

A row of windows above Lena and Takahashi's cots showed a twilit garden and squat, distant houses. The dazzling reddish light from overhead faded as Kane watched, giving way to the sudden martian night and the colorless glow of fluorescents.

Almost immediately he felt a slow, distant rumbling in the walls. He gripped the sides of the cot, afraid of a tremor, and then saw a silvery line rising slowly across the open section of the dome.

"They're just raising the mirror," a voice said, and Kane recognized it as the one that had come over his headphones. He turned slowly and saw a very tall, intense-looking woman standing behind him. She had tangled, dark blonde hair to her shoulders and the beginnings of intriguing lines around her eyes and mouth. Her scent, compounded of strong soap and mild exertion, alerted Kane on a primitive level. He felt a surge of almost impersonal longing, an upwelling of his imbalanced hormones.

"They close both sides at night. During the day one side is always open to the sun. Are you all right?"

"Okay, I guess," Kane said. As she moved, her breasts turned under her T-shirt in a way that wouldn't have been possible in Earth's gravity.

"Do you want to try and stand up?"

"Sure," he said. "Why not?" She helped him to his feet, carefully avoiding his ribs. She was an inch or so taller than Kane and had to bend her knees in order to slide one of his arms around her shoulders. The pleasure of touching her was muddled for him by vertigo and a sensation that his intestines were going to spill out of his body.

"My name is Molly," the woman said.

"Kane," he said.

"I know."

"The others . . . are they okay? How's Reese?"

"He's the worst off, but he'll get over it. He's been through this before."

They made it twice around the room. Only once, when he stumbled, did Kane have a serious vestibular problem. The worst part was seeing the faces of the other patients, most of them in their fifties and sixties, their sunken eyes, gray skin, hollow necks ringed with bowstring muscles.

He lay back down on his cot, exhausted, his shrunken heart hammering and his ribs aching dully. "These others," he said, with a limp gesture, "what's wrong with them?"

Molly's mouth stretched out into a hard line. "Cancer, most of them," she said. "We're what you call a high risk up here. The dome cuts out most of the hard radiation, but enough still gets through . . ." She trailed off, started again. "Get some rest. I'll come back with some broth or something in a little bit."

"Molly?"

"Yes?"

"You knew we were coming. We signaled you all the way here. There must have been broadcasts from Earth at least every couple of months for the last nine years. Why didn't you ever answer?"

She sat on the edge of the cot, one hip a distracting pressure against his leg. "Do you really need an answer to that? We didn't want you to come. You people, you and the Russians both, you pulled out and left us here and that was the end of it. You've been through your problems, apparently, or you wouldn't be here. Well, we've been through our problems too, only they're not the same. We don't want your help and we don't want to belong to anybody anymore."

"Well," Kane said. "At least I know where we stand."

"Don't get me wrong. I don't have anything against you personally, and I don't even care if you stay here for a week or two or whatever. But there are people here who *are* going to care. Curtis, for one, and he's the governor. Then there's about thirty people who survived the Marsgrad disaster. They wouldn't want to see anybody waving an American flag around here."

"Nobody's going to wave any flags, if that matters. There isn't even a U.S. anymore."

"We kind of figured that out. We got your broadcasts, saying you were a Pulsystems expedition. I've got nothing against corporatocracy myself, but nationalism doesn't die out overnight. We've seen that here, and we don't want it starting again."

Kane raised his hands, palm out. "Truce," he said. "As far as I knew, we were only coming here to sift through the ruins. Nobody's even told Morgan that there's anybody alive up here yet." He gave in to a yawn. "Besides, we're not really in any condition to overthrow your way of life."

"Granted," she said, and stood up. "I'll get you some soup."

After she left he sat propped up in bed, reluctant to let himself sleep again. What, he asked himself, could have been so frightening about the dream? As far as he could tell it was no more than a scene from Mallory's *Le Morte D'Arthur*, left over from his college mythology courses. Nothing particularly sinister in that. Yet he knew it wasn't the events, but the *consciousness* in the dream that had frozen him, a medieval terror of the gods and their instruments.

Takahashi woke, sat up, and took a few clumsy steps away from his bed. Kane watched him with a cold, grudging respect as he forced himself to walk, his face as immobile as during his interminable hours of exercise on the ship. Lena had opened her eyes, but lay quietly, making no effort to join him.

By the time Molly came back with a tray of food, Takahashi was already sitting at the long Formica table in the next room. Kane joined him under his own power, but both Lena and Reese needed help. Molly passed around bowls of steaming chicken broth and glasses of ice water. Kane took a long drink and then let go of the glass. He watched in embarrassment as it fell to the floor, spattering his trousers.

"Gravity," Reese said, with a weak, gray smile. "You'll get used to it."

Kane realized that his instincts were no longer trustworthy, had altered in free fall to the point that he was unsuited for the simplest behavior. He lifted a spoonful of soup, the muscles of his hand and arm unconsciously accelerating it as it rose, to keep it from wobbling off into space. No, he thought. He stopped his arm, watched a drop stretch downward from the spoon and fall gently into his lap.

The stock was rich with globules of yellow fat, and Kane's hunger won out over his feelings of clumsiness and shame. He bent over the bowl and slurped it up, amazed how the reduced swelling in his face was allowing him to taste things for the first time in months.

When he looked up again someone else had come into the room.

"Don't stand up," the man said, walking quickly to the table.

Kane stared at him, a slow, psychic tremor moving through his brain.

"I'm Curtis, and I'm the governor here. Reese, of course, I already know, but I look forward to meeting the rest of you. Welcome to Frontera."

Kane, paralyzed, heard something that was not quite a voice speak to him. It spoke inside his head, with the voice of authority. It said: "This man is your enemy."

The paralysis broke, and Kane let out a trembling sigh. He continued to stare at Curtis, as if fixing his image on a photographic plate in his memory: bald, shining head, short-sleeved dress shirt with threadbare collar and seams, forearms matted with black hair, the lower half of his face darkened by a half-day's growth of stubble.

Anybody, Kane thought, who shaves his head and doesn't think it's weird is kidding himself.

"I see you've all met my wife, Molly," Curtis said. "I hope she's taken care of your immediate needs." Kane did not miss the brief glance of resentment that Molly turned on her husband.

"Now," Curtis said. "I know you're all tired, but I'm sure you can see our position. We haven't had any coherent information from Earth in eight years. We don't know what's going on there, or what you people's intentions are." He knitted his hands together in front of him and waited, but none of them showed any inclination to answer. Kane looked down the table and saw his own hostility reflected in Reese's eyes.

Curtis was sitting next to Lena, and Kane watched his right hand move within a fraction of an inch of hers. "We monitored some of your broadcasts as you came in. Kane and Reese we knew about, but I don't know your name."

"Lena," she said.

Incredibly, to Kane, Curtis seemed to be taking up some sort of flirtation with Lena, within moments of having clearly branded Molly as his possession. Even more incredible was Lena's obvious interest. She must have gone off suppressants too.

"How about it?" he said to her. "What's the story?"

"Things on Earth," she said, a little awkwardly. "I guess they're okay. The big governments collapsed, and the corporations just sort of took up the slack . . ."

"At the same time? Russia and America both?"

"No," she said, "not quite. Russia was worse off, with crop failures and revolts in the provinces. They must have gone down first, but nobody knew about it. Everybody was so used to not hearing about them, we just didn't know. I guess the first time we really knew they were gone was during the North Africa thing. They would have sent troops, but obviously they didn't have any to send."

"North Africa thing?" Curtis said.

"Ask Kane about it." Lena said. "He was there."

"Kane?"

Kane shrugged. "Supposedly this UN group at

Biotek Afrika—that was a big lab in Luxor—had made some kind of breakthrough in implant wetware. Biological circuitry, that kind of shit, tied right into the nervous system. The Red Chinese were almost as bad off as the Russians, all their 'modernizations' didn't have enough public money behind them. So they made one last grab for world power and tried to take over the lab."

"And the U.S. sent troops?"

"The U.S. didn't have any troops," Kane said. "The corporations sent their own armies. That was when everybody figured out that the governments were gone. There was a lot of rioting and all that, and finally the big companies just stepped in. Started policing the cities, paying welfare, reopening the hospitals and all."

"What happened in Africa?"

"Nothing happened," Kane said. "Everybody came home."

He didn't want to talk about what had really happened, what it had really been like. It was still too soon, would always be too soon . . .

Kane had thirty men and women under his command, part of a total Pulsystems force of nearly five thousand, veterans of mercenary firefights from Taiwan to Ecuador, from the rescue of company personnel to the quelling of riots on company property. But this time it was different, this time they were moving into a combat theater already occupied by armed forces of the largest corporations on Earth. And none of them was really sure what they were doing there.

The decisions were all being made at computer consoles in air-conditioned offices halfway around

the world, while Kane and five thousand others
waited in tenuous pharmaceutical calm near the
drowned city of Wadi Halfa, exposed again now
since the Chinese sabotage of the Aswan High Dam.
Their Mylar tents glittered between the melted
mud bricks of the city like globs of mercury in a
shattered sand castle. The air stank of rotting cat-
fish and every day the enemy changed, from Hitachi
on Friday to a Russian steel combine on Sunday,
and still the only shots they had fired had been at
cancerous Nile crocodiles where they lay stupefied
in the sun.

When the order came to move it took them all
the way to Luxor, five thousand of them moving
downstream in anything they could commandeer
from inflatable Zodiacs to crumbling feluccas, even
a World War II landing craft that had been working as a ferry between the East and West Banks.

Just before dawn Kane spotted the helicopters
moving in from the west. He remembered wondering who they belonged to just before they opened
fire, catching a glimpse in the sudden, harsh light
of an exploding gasoline tank of the PEMEX logo,
the Mexican oil cartel, wondering if they even knew
who they were attacking, wondering if the raid
had been launched by operator error five thousand
miles away.

Less than seven hundred of them survived,
washed up at the Temple of Amen-Mut-Khonsu
just outside Luxor. Kane, in agony from a laser
burn across his left thigh, clutching his M-37 so
tightly he thought the plastic stock might shatter
in his hand, lay and stared at the high-water lines
on the columns of the temple, at the stylized beard

of Ramses II, shattered by a high-caliber bullet, at the compelling and unintelligible hieroglyphics stained muddy red by the rising sun.

Beyond the temple lay the fragrant, smoking ruins of the village where Biotek Afrika's cooks and day laborers had lived, their cauterized bodies now scattered over a square mile of DMZ. Beyond that lay the walls of the Biotek compound, breached by mortar fire and melted by beam weapons, manned by frightened Europeans in lab coats or street clothes, their M-16's and Ingrams chattering harmlessly into the dirt.

Kane waited for orders to come through the receiver clamped to the mastoid bone behind his ear, the sunlight burning into his leg, the tension building in him, desperate with the need to turn his fear and pain and confusion into the clean lines of laser fire and the purifying glow of thermite.

The sound of helicopters came to him there, freezing his blood. He could see the sickly green of their fuselages and knew they were the same PEMEX machines, knew that this time there was no escape, not inside this giant, roofless pachinko machine of ancient sandstone. He set his back against the swollen base of a column and raised his gun.

What had happened to their communications? What sense was he to make of his own death when it came to him like this, anonymously out of the sky? He waited for a shot but the chance never came.

Instead the copters veered wide around the Temple and began to rake the Biotek complex with withering fire. Kane rolled onto his elbows, blinking. He hadn't been mistaken, he could see the

PEMEX logo as the pilots swooped low over the burning buildings. A new deal then, another turn of the wheel.

In seconds the way was open. Kane's last memory was of standing sentry duty inside a white-tiled lab while one of Morgan's techs dumped the Biotek computers in a continuous high-speed transmission, aimed at a relay satellite that would bounce it on to Houston, while the air around him steamed with CO_2 from the chunks of dry ice that littered the floor, thrown out as the fragile living circuits were looted from the cryogenic vaults and stuffed into anything that would hold the cold.

He never saw the explosion that split his skull, remembered only a flash of light and nausea that existed outside of time, a memory still in reach as he sat there in the martian sickbay, staring at Curtis.

"I don't understand," Curtis said. "If nothing happened there, why was it so important?"

"It wasn't what happened in North Africa that was important," Takahashi said. "It was what happened afterwards. In point of fact a lot did come out of it—Pulsystems moved into a whole new field of technology, but that's not the main thing. The main thing is that North Africa showed the world where the real power lay."

"I didn't get your name," Curtis said.

"Takahashi. Vice president at Pulsystems. I'm in charge of this mission."

"Not Reese?"

"No," Reese said. "I'm just here for the ride. It's Morgan's mission, and Takahashi is Morgan's man."

"Then I guess I should be talking to you," Curtis

said. "You're obviously the one to tell me what this is all about."

Takahashi shrugged. "It's like Lena said. Things have stabilized with about 50 percent employment and a guaranteed income. The standard of living certainly isn't what it was fifteen or twenty years ago, but it's on the way up again. The worst is over and a company the size of Pulsystems has to look for new opportunities for growth. The NASA hardware was on hand and it was the decision of the Chairman that we would take the first steps toward reopening space."

"More than that," Lena said. "We had to see what had happened to you, to rescue any survivors—"

"You've come to save us," Curtis said.

"Sure," Reese said. "Why not? Don't you need saving?"

"As a matter of fact, no. But I would have thought a rescue mission would have at least two or three ships to bring back the rescuees. You didn't even bring any supplies or special medical equipment."

"We didn't know you were alive!" Lena said.

Kane put his spoon on the table. "You've already been through the ship, then."

Curtis ignored both of them. "In fact, you didn't even have enough propellant to slow yourselves down. We tracked you all the way through that aerobraking stunt. My guess is you didn't have enough stages for the ship. Which tells me that your man Morgan isn't building any new hardware, just using up the leftovers. Now tell me, does that sound like an ongoing space program to you?"

The worst part of this, Kane thought, is that he's right. Just what the hell *are* we doing here?

"As far as Chairman Morgan is concerned," Takahashi said, "he undertook the entire expense of this mission himself. If it's successful, he should be able to get funding from some of the other majors. When that happens there will be time for fabricating new hardware."

"And what," asked Curtis, "constitutes a successful mission?"

"We found a surviving colony up here," Reese said. "I'd call that a pretty big success in itself. Wouldn't you?"

Curtis stood up. "I'm sure you all need some rest." He looked at Lena. "We'll talk more later. If there's anything you need, just let me know." Kane wasn't sure if the offer was for Lena alone or extended to all of them. "Molly?" Curtis said. "Are you coming?"

"I'll be along," she said, and Curtis left.

She stood behind Reese and put one hand on his shoulder. "I'm sorry. He's gotten worse, hasn't he?"

"I never knew him all that well," Reese said, "but yeah, he seems to be losing whatever he had. Is he okay?"

"I don't know. He's changed. I don't think he ever meant to put himself in a position of power. But once he got there—it's like he can't do without it now."

"Of course he's got a point," Lena said. "This whole thing *is* suspicious. I mean, if Morgan somehow knew they were alive, it would explain why he was so desperate to get here. But why us? What does he expect us to do without ships to evacuate them or supplies or anything else?"

"Ask Morgan," Reese said. "I don't know." He took Molly's hand and held on to it.

Kane wondered if the warmth between Reese and Molly was the remnant of something sexual. It seemed unlikely; she would have been barely twenty the last time Reese saw her, less than half his age. Kane found himself resenting the intimacy, partially, he thought, from sexual attraction to Molly, partially because of the distance he still felt between himself and Reese. And then there was the overwhelming sense of alienation that Curtis had given him. He not only didn't belong here, but his connection with Morgan made him an object of suspicion and anger.

"You'd better get some rest," Molly said to Reese, squeezing his hand and letting it go. Then she turned and smiled at Kane. "Take care," she said. Kane nodded and watched her walk away.

"We have to get back to the ship," Kane said. "We need to tell Morgan what's happening." Reese shrugged.

"I'll go," Takahashi said. "I'm in the best shape for it, and it's my job." Kane didn't argue with him, and neither did Lena or Reese. "The question is, what are we going to tell him?"

"Tell him they don't want us," Kane said. "Tell him we might as well pull out."

"We don't know that," Reese said. "The only one we've really heard from is Curtis. He doesn't speak for the whole colony, regardless of what he thinks." He stood up, steadied himself for a moment on the edge of the table, then walked cautiously back to his cot.

"Lena?" Kane asked.

"I don't know. All I know is I don't want to go back on that ship again. Right now it feels like I never want to go, and I expect I'm going to feel that way for a while."

"I'll tell him we're okay," Takahashi said. "I'll say the colony's functional, I'll say we'll get back to him. If he wants any more than that I'll just tell him he'll have to wait."

"Sounds good to me," Kane said. He finished Reese's soup and drank most of his water. Nine months of zero-G had cost him a tenth of his blood plasma, and it had left him enormously thirsty.

On his way back to the cot he dialed the lights down to a pale glow. He was exhausted; whether he wanted to or not, he was going to have to sleep again. He closed his eyes, felt the soft texture of the darkness.

He couldn't remember having dreamed, wasn't sure if he'd actually been asleep or not. The hand shook him gently by the arm again and the voice whispered, "Kane?"

"Mmmm?"

"Quiet, now. Don't wake the others."

He blinked, focused on a tall, tanned woman with dust-colored hair. "Who are you?"

"Dian," she said, staring at him intently, as if the name should mean something to him. "You *are* Kane, right?"

"Uh-huh."

"Listen, we need to get on with this thing. I'm starting to get really paranoid."

"Paranoid?"

"Curtis is suspicious. We've got to move soon. And I for one want to get the hell out of here."

Kane was fully awake now. "Maybe there's some kind of misunderstanding here. Am I supposed to know you?"

The woman rocked back on her heels. Her eyebrows were so light that Kane had trouble reading her expression. "Okay," she said, tilting her head and raising one hand apologetically. "If that's the way you want to play it. It's your show. But for god's sake don't wait around too long, okay? Before this whole thing falls apart on us." She stood up smoothly, blending in with the shadows, and Kane was left with nothing but a faint afterimage on his retinas.

He got shakily to his feet and moved to the pile of belongings that they'd brought from the ship. His bag was in the middle, and as he lifted it he could feel the weight of the pistol inside. He carried it back to the cot and spread it open on the floor beneath his feet.

He was not hallucinating. Something was going on that no one had told him about; the gun, and Morgan's subliminals, and the woman named Dian were part of it. He took the pistol out, repelled by its dark gleam and oily scent, wrapped it in a dirty T-shirt, and stuffed it under the mattress of his cot. Curtis had searched the ship; apparently they hadn't gone through the bags yet but it only would be a matter of time before they did.

Kane lay back, conscious of the bulk of the gun against his left hip. The princess, he thought bitterly, and the pea.

Dian obviously had at least some of the story. In the morning he would get what he could from her.

For the moment he was too tired even to put his duffel away. He closed his eyes, drifted.

A cool breeze swept down out of the pines. He stood for a moment on the narrow path and savored the paradox of the sun's warmth and the air's chill. The Shinto temple stood only a few yards away, its long, low walls no more than a palisade of bamboo, the thatch of its roof brown and in need of replacement.

The name of the temple was Atsuta. He was here on the instructions of his dying father, stopping on his way east before confronting the Ainu aborigines who were said to be as fierce as the bears they raised from cubs and then strangled, smearing themselves with the blood, even drinking it. The impurity of it nauseated him.

With manicured, tattooed hands he removed his sandals and entered the temple. The air inside, musty and chill, made him draw his robe closed over the tattooed serpent that wound its way around his chest. He could feel the spirits of the *kami* moving through the ancient, gnarled trees around the temple, whispering to him in an indecipherable language.

He squatted in front of the shrine itself, a wooden box the size of a child's coffin, its shelves containing the heads of snakes, bottles of pink and scarlet dyes, and a crude painting of a waterfall. The shrine was dedicated to Susa-no-wo, god of the plains of the seas, born from the snot of Izanagi, the last of the first gods. He began to pray, as his father had instructed him.

The screeching of a hawk shattered his concentration. He looked, saw the hawk flying straight at him through the open door of the temple, wings back, talons extended. At the last possible moment the bird veered up and burst through the rotten thatch of the roof, releasing a cascade of ill-smelling straw.

A single shaft of light fell into the shrine.

He put out one hand and touched the dried yellow monkey skull that lay in the circle of light. He felt a latch click. The shrine trembled for an instant, and then a side panel fell away and a long, narrow object fell into his lap.

A sword.

He saw the eight-headed snake, as big around as a grown man, its fangs dripping venom, saw Susano-wo slashing the monster to pieces, saw him taking the sword, Kusa-nagi, from the tail of the snake.

He saw again the hold of the ship, the tray, the goblet, the pike.

He screamed.

● ● ●

By the time Molly got to the sickbay, they had Kane sedated and strapped to a gurney. The room stank of fatigue and worn tempers. Reese sat on the edge of his cot, head down, arms on his thighs; Lena and Takahashi were at the table, not looking at each other.

"What happened?" she asked.

"We don't know," Reese said. He looked bad, she thought, necrotic, hypoxic. He needed sleep, not another crisis. But then the same was true of them all. "He woke up screaming and couldn't seem to stop."

She picked up a used hypo from the table. "Valium?"

"I gave it to him," Lena said defensively. "It's out of my medical kit."

Molly nodded and stood next to Kane. Even with his eyes closed he had an intense, haunted look that attracted her. After ten years of the same faces, she thought, it's such a pleasure to see a new one.

She raised one eyelid. The pupil was dilated from the drug, but otherwise seemed to be responding normally to the light.

"Did he say anything?" she asked. "Anything articulate?"

"He said 'no' a lot," Lena offered. "And something like 'leave me alone' or 'get away' or something like that."

Takahashi helped her roll Kane into the next room and shift him over to the holo scanner platform. She sensed that he was indifferent to Kane's condition and was only demonstrating how well he'd recovered from the flight.

She noticed Lena watching her as she connected the intake and outtake lines of the blood processor to an artery and vein on the inside of Kane's thigh. Like a musician, Molly thought, watching somebody else on stage. "You want to start that for me?" she asked, nodding to the processor terminal.

"Sure," Lena said.

Molly brought up the scanner and typed in a series of commands.

"He's anemic," Lena said, watching the readings scroll up on the CRT. "The volume is low. Leucocytes up a little because of the ribs. As expected. But there's nothing else wrong here. No alkaloids, no other apparent hallucinogens."

Molly watched a diagram of Kane's body form on the scanner's CRT, white lines on black background. The image of the body began to rotate on the long axis, the major organs appearing in green as the scanner worked in, the cracked ribs surrounded by the bright blue of damaged tissue.

"What's that?" Reese asked from behind.

"Where?"

"There. At the back of the skull. That yellow patch."

Molly called up an enlargement of the head and froze the posterior view. A small, flat rectangle of yellow was attached to the back of the right temporal lobe. "Jesus christ," Molly said.

Lena came over to look. "What is it?"

"I don't know."

"A tumor?" Reese suggested.

Molly shook her head. "Cancer cells are un-differentiated. This system shows them in red."

"What else could it be?" he asked.

"Um," Lena said. "You want a guess?"

"Go," Molly said. "We're listening."

"What Kane said tonight about North Africa. He said nothing happened, that they all just came back. I don't think that's the way it was."

"What do you mean?" Molly said.

Lena looked over at Takahashi. He was staring back at her coldly, impassively. "I heard rumors. They said before Biotek Afrika burned that Morgan's people got what they were after. Implant wetware. Biological circuitry. Supposedly Pulsystems now has working organic ROM's."

"ROM's?" Molly said. "You mean there's programming in that thing?"

"I told you it was just a guess. But look where it is. Kane's right-handed, so that's the mirror image of Wernicke's area in his left brain, his prime language center. The two lobes are connected, here, through the anterior commissures. So programming inserted where that thing is, in a basically unused part of the brain, would go straight over to the language center."

"And then?" Reese asked.

"Well . . . stimulating that area of the right brain in supposed to cause hallucinations. Voices. People hear their dead parents talking to them."

"Morgan," Reese said.

"You—" Lena broke off, then started again. "Wait

a minute. You think Morgan did this to him? To his own nephew?"

"We went into Houston one afternoon. We brought back some kind of cylinder containing cryogenic material. Right after that he was gone for two days. That's when they must have put it in him. Christ. He nearly killed a guy to keep it from being stolen. Do you believe that?"

"You can treat it," Lena said. "Stellazine or Thorazine or any of the anti-psychotics. It's clinically similar to schizophrenia."

"What I want to know," Molly said, "is what it's doing to him. What's it telling him? What's it trying to make him do?" She glanced to her left, saw Takahashi leaning against one wall, his eyes narrowed as he watched the CRT display.

He knows, she thought. Takahashi had said he was a vice president, and she suspected he was more than that. Pulsystems had always had major Japanese funding, and she had a suspicion that it had been a large infusion of New Yen that had held the company together through the collapse of the U.S. government. Was Takahashi the watchdog for the Japanese faction? Just how important was he?

Reese must have been thinking the same thing. "Okay, Takahashi. It's too late to make any difference to anybody. What did Morgan do to him?"

"Why are you asking me?" Takahashi said.

"He wouldn't risk sending Kane up here with an implant unless one of us knew about it. It's not me and it's not Lena. You might as well tell us."

Takahashi sighed. "All right. It's pretty much the way Lena guessed it. But it was necessary.

Morgan tried the new techniques on Kane to save his life. His skull was fractured in Luxor, not just cracked, but sliced wide open. Without the operation he would have been dead, at best a vegetable."

"What is that . . . thing?" Molly asked. "That yellow box?"

"That's the processor," Takahashi said. "The programs are interchangeable. The first software they came up with was crude, barely let him function. When they get a more sophisticated implant, they can change it out, almost like changing a diskette. That's what you saw Kane bringing from Houston. Just the latest update."

"That doesn't make sense," Lena said. "What do they need to put software in there for? That area has nothing to do with his motor control, or his language, or his memory, or anything."

"You're asking the wrong person," Takahashi said. "If you want to know that you'd better ask Morgan."

"Speaking of which," Reese said. "Did you get through to him?"

"I told him about the colony. He said to rest up and just play it as it comes."

"That's it?" Lena asked. "Wasn't he even surprised?"

"Didn't seem to be."

" 'Play it as it comes?' " Reese said. "That doesn't sound like Morgan."

"Now what?" Takahashi said, flushing. "Do you think I'm lying about it, for christ's sake?"

"Why not?" Lena said. "You didn't say anything about Kane all this time. That doesn't really inspire a lot of trust."

"If you'd known Kane had a brain implant there would have been even more tension on the flight out than there already was. Weren't things bad enough as they were?"

Lena walked out and Molly turned back to the scanner. She cut the power to both it and the blood processor and waited for the tubes to turn white before she pulled them from Kane's leg. A single drop of dark red swelled up at the arterial puncture and she pressed a piece of gauze against it, feeling the tension in his sartoris muscle as his body resisted the Valium, aware of the heat of his half-erect penis, only a few centimeters away.

"Takahashi?" she said, and he helped her move Kane back onto the gurney and from there back onto his cot. Most of the other patients in the sickbay had fallen back into sedated oblivion, but two of them were still awake, awake and staring with confusion and fear at the aliens from Earth.

"Go to sleep," she said to them, and the eyes closed. She turned back to Lena and said, "I'll get you some Stellazine. In case he wakes up again."

Reese followed her back to the pharmaceutical closet and blocked the doorway. In his black clothes he looked like an overgrown teenage thug, threatening but anachronistic, out of place.

"We need to talk," he said.

"I know."

"What about Sarah? Is she . . .?"

"Still alive? Yeah, she's alive." Molly took a vial of Stellazine off the shelf and turned around. "It's strange, Reese. It's stranger than you can imagine."

"It's not my fault," Reese said. "I was coming

back. You know I was. It just took me this long to
get here. That's all."

"I know," she said. "It's not like there's anything you could have done." Her throat ached with
an inappropriate desire to cry. "I didn't mean it to
sound like I was blaming you for anything."

"I want to see her."

"I know you do." She'd expected this to happen,
still had no easy answer for him. "I'm just not sure
if it's a good idea, that's all. It's like there's nothing in her universe but physics. She won't even let
us call her Sarah anymore, did you know that? Of
course you didn't, how could ... but ... I mean,
it's all of them. All the ... different ones, it's like a
badge or something. If you've got an extra finger
or there's a hole in your liver then you get to have
a new name and then you're in the club, and you
get to live—" She broke off before she gave too
much away.

"Easy," Reese said, putting a hand behind her
neck and squeezing gently. The familiar gesture,
taking her back to her childhood, made her feel
instantly calm.

"I'm okay," she said. "Really. I need to talk to
you, too. There's just been so much ..." She was
suddenly aware of the open door, of the others
waiting outside it. "Tomorrow," she said. "When
you're rested. We'll talk some more."

"And Sarah?"

"I'll see. I'll talk to her."

She pushed past him, handed the Stellazine to
Lena, locked the closet and put the key away.
"Tomorrow," she said to Reese again, and then
she walked back out into the fluorescent night of

the dome. A sudden, powerful urge to see the stars
sent her past the animal pens and into an observation bubble in the side wall. Here, in the shadows,
she could see the lifeless plains outside and the
deeper, colder darkness above them. This was
normal. This was the way things were. How could
she put that into words that Reese would understand? Because until he understood that much he
had no hope of understanding Verb, or Zeet, or
Pen-of-my-Uncle, or any of the others. Having been
the first man to set foot here wasn't enough, the
few months he'd spent in the dome weren't enough,
not even sympathy and love and gallows humor
were enough.

The lights were off in their surreal, high-tensile
styrofoam cottage. She undressed and got into bed,
hoping that Curtis was already asleep. He let her
get settled and comfortable and then he said,
"Well?"

She jumped a little, in spite of herself. "We sedated him," she said.

"That's all? I mean, you were gone a long time
to just administer a sedative."

"For god's sake, Curtis, I'm fully grown. I don't
have to account to you for everything I do."

"I guess that depends on what you were doing. I
mean, if you found out something that was important to the future of the colony, that would be my
business, wouldn't it?"

"You were listening, weren't you?"

"Not me personally. But I suppose it comes down
to the same thing."

"So what do you want? A tribunal? Shoot me at
dawn?"

He came up on one elbow and dug his fingers into her arm. "Do you have the slightest fucking idea of what's going on around here or not? Are you actually pretending you don't know why those people are here?"

"I know what they told me. But I suppose that's not germane."

He let her go and rolled onto his back. "There's a leak, Molly. We have to assume they know everything. Everything. And you know what pisses me off? What pisses me off is that I don't think *I* know everything. I don't even think I know as much as Morgan's stooges about what those kids of yours and Dian's are up to. Now isn't that a kick in the ass?"

"Theoretical physics," Molly said. "I could write some of the equations out for you. Would that make you feel better? Because you wouldn't get anything out of them."

"Quantum mechanics was a physical theory and it wiped out Hiroshima and Nagasaki. What are they doing out there? What are they building?" When she didn't answer he sighed dramatically. "You really see me as some petty little Hitler, don't you? Power-crazy. You can't even trust me with the discoveries those kids are making right under my nose."

Yes, she thought, that's true. That just about sums it up. But she didn't let the words out, afraid they might take on a life of their own, that they might betray her too, just as Curtis had.

"You're wrong," he said. "You're more wrong than you know. I still love you. Did you know that? You've made it where it's almost impossible to get those words out without choking on them. But they're true. And I care about this colony. The lives of everyone here are my responsibility."

Was it possible? she wondered. Could it be that he did still love her, that this was all her fault somehow?

Then she remembered Curtis in the sickbay, his hand just millimeters from Lena's, the sick knowledge that the new woman had aroused his curiosity, that he would pursue her and have her if he could, the way he'd pursued and had the others.

Not for the first time she wondered what the word love meant to him, if it had a one-to-one semantic correspondence to a repeatable phenomenon, mental or physical, or if the word itself was everything, a self-defining verbal gesture. In physics, she thought, the first test is falsifiability. If you can't prove it wrong, you can't prove it right, either.

If he could write out the math for her, she thought, then she'd know.

"I believe," she said slowly, "that you mean what you're saying. But it's going to take more than words to convince me."

"You don't understand me at all, do you? You've got all your feelings so pushed back and under control that you think everybody else is the same way. Well, we're not. What do you think it's like for me? Eight years ago we pulled ourselves back from the edge of something that would have killed us all, and the only way we did it was by believing we could be more than some dying ghost town on the edge of space. The next two years were the best years of my life, and yours too, if you had the heart to admit it. Everybody's. We were all working hard, and we could see the results right in front of us, hold them in our hands. To see those first crops coming in, the kids being born . . ."

"Yeah, okay. I was there."

"Yeah. Well, I was there too. Do you think I haven't noticed how different it is now? Alcohol consumption up about 50 percent every year, every year more Thorazine cases out in the fields, people late to work, people not coming to work at all, almost half the female kids showing some symptoms of anorexia—"

"Right," Molly said, wanting to hurt him, "and then there's the ones that spend all their time in the isolation tanks, tripping out, running away from the things that scare them."

"Okay," Curtis said, "I'm not going to argue that right now. Maybe all this is just inevitable. Maybe it's the human condition. But that doesn't make it hurt me any less, make me feel any less responsible for it."

"Look," Molly said, "we may be close to something, okay? But we don't have it yet. It's going to take a few more months."

"We haven't got a few more months. They're here, it's happening now."

"We can handle them," Molly said. "It's going to work out." Come on, she told herself. Can't you be any more convincing than that? Even if you don't believe it yourself?

"It had better," Curtis said. He turned away from her and was asleep in seconds.

She wished she could escape into sleep that easily, the way she had all through adolescence. But more and more she was turning into her mother, who had roamed the house late at night and then been up again before dawn, always, in Molly's memory, dressed in a faded blue cotton kimono and clumsy houseshoes. Heredity, Molly thought. It's not even the anger and frustration keeping me up, it's simple heredity.

She slept fitfully until dawn and then came finally, violently awake as the east mirror rumbled open. Her heart pounded, the noise of the hydraulics sounding this morning like the crack of literal doom, like the shattering of the plastic sky overhead, the end of the world.

She hunched fetally under the sheet, her back to Curtis, telling herself it wasn't really that bad. But her arguments lacked force. The order of her existence *was* collapsing—Kane hallucinating and under Morgan's control, Reese evasive and cold, Curtis convinced of betrayal.

Not to mention the second ship from Earth, a further, unknown disaster, still waiting in the wings.

It's bad, she thought. Genuinely bad.

She put on a tattered NASA Constant Wear Garment and went into the kitchen, shutting Curtis behind the bedroom door. The light over the counter was on, silhouetting Verb and one of her friends as they ate breakfast.

Empathy again? Molly wondered. Or one of those synchronistic events that her physics is supposed to predict?

"Good morning," Molly said. The boy was about eleven, apparently normal, just sociopathic enough to prefer living in the cave with the more visibly strange. He was obsessed with electronics, and Molly and Dian used him in the construction of

Verb's devices. E17, she remembered, was what he was calling himself this week.

"Is he all right?" Verb asked.

"Reese, you mean?" Molly said, and the girl nodded. "He's okay. They used aerobraking instead of rockets, and it was hard on him, but he'll get over it."

"I want to see him."

"He wants to see you, too," Molly said. Was something up? The boy stared down into a bowl of cereal and goat's milk, pretending to ignore them. She had Verb's promise not to talk about her work, and she had to trust her. There simply wasn't anything else she could do. "Why is it so important to you? You weren't but two years old when he left. I don't see how you can even remember him."

She had wanted to tell Verb that she was related to Reese, but Curtis had opposed it. There was enough gossip, he said, without dragging his own family through it. Molly hadn't understood why it was so important to him, but she'd given in. She'd spent so much of her life keeping the secret that it had become second nature to her anyway.

"But I do remember him," Verb was saying. "I remember stuff you wouldn't even believe. Sometimes I even think I remember being born, just the colors. Is that too weird? But that's not the important thing. It's the connections. The connections, don't you see? That's what the physics is all about."

Molly mixed a cup of instant coffee from the hot water dispenser. "And physics," she said, "is everything. Right?"

When she turned around the boy was staring at

her, spoon poised halfway to his mouth. "Well?" Verb said. "Isn't it?"

They were scaring her, but only, she told herself, because she was letting them. The coffee seemed raw and bloody, as if she could taste her own nerve endings in it. "Forget it," she said, pouring the coffee down the recycler. "Forget I said anything. Let's get out of here."

In the fields outside, the first of the farm teams was already at work, six women, four men, two older children. Two of the women and one of the men were chemical lobotomies, apt to forget what they were doing and stand staring into the dazzling reflections in the mirror overhead. All of them wore goggles as well as the usual oxygen masks to cut the sting of the ammonia fertilizer they sprayed.

From a light pole overhead they were being recorded by a video camera, one of thirty or more that Curtis had salvaged from various early probes or converted from the home units of his subordinates. They fed a control room in the Center, the heart of Curtis's "electronic democracy."

As they passed the farmers, one of their children looked up and muttered, "Hey, freak."

"Hush!" one of the women scolded, but there were no apologies, no other reprimands, and Molly just let it pass. Verb went on talking about some new mathematical model as if she'd never heard.

It was all so fragile, the human chemistry as well as the inorganic. The ammonia, for example, came from Haber-Bosch catalysis of nitrogen and hydrogen that had been compressed, condensed, and filtered out of the martian atmosphere. The same process gave them their oxygen and the nitrogen/argon buffer they breathed with it, and squeezed almost a pound of water out of 30 cubic meters of martian air. Each piece fit snugly into place, endlessly recycled, without waste or inefficiency.

Their society had worked that way too, at least for a while. The first hard years had provided the heat to fuse them all together, Russians, Americans, Japanese, in a proton-proton reaction that kept them all alive. It was only now that the energy of that fusion was burning out, leaving collapsing factions behind that could flare into violence at any moment.

Through it all Curtis had kept his iron control, obsessed with his vision of a terraformed Mars, even after it became obvious that they just didn't have the resources to do it on their own. They needed help from Earth, the ships, the material to make huge solar mirrors, the mass drivers to bring them ice and asteroids.

Curtis had been right the night before, of course. He *didn't* know what Verb's physics was capable of, or he would have moved in and taken it for himself long before.

Because the new physics meant energy virtually without a price tag, energy for the taking, enough to make Curtis's dreams into reality and solidify his vision of Mars forever. And no matter how much she wanted to see Mars bloom, she couldn't let Curtis twist that garden into his own rigid image.

She stopped outside the Center. "Stay here," she said to the children. "If he's up to it, I'll send him out in a little bit."

All four of the astronauts were sleeping and for

just an instant, barely long enough for the thought to register at all, it occurred to her how easy it would be to get rid of them now, to inject air bubbles into their veins or move them into the surgery and quietly gas them.

Then Kane turned over, making a soft noise in his sleep, and she was back to normal.

She knelt beside Reese's cot, touching his forehead and testing the pulse in his carotid artery. He woke under her hand and said, "Hello," his voice still thick with sleep.

"How do you feel?"

"Hungry," he said, sitting up cautiously. "Hungry and . . . sort of stupid."

"Sarah's outside," she said. "Verb is what they call her now."

"What?"

"I told you, they have their own names for each other. Verb is what they call her now."

"Verb. No kidding."

"What's the matter?"

"Nothing. Go on."

"She's outside now. She'll take you to breakfast, if you want."

"Yeah."

"She's not beautiful, Reese. I just want you to be prepared for that. There's not anything beautiful about her. I don't even know if there's anything there to love. Okay?"

"Okay."

He stood up and she helped him as far as the sick bay door, and then she handed him an oxygen mask from the rack on the wall. He put it on and walked out of the Center on his own, Molly just behind him.

He stood there for a long moment, and Molly watched him take it all in, knowing that as sick as she was of this fishbowl city, as much as she missed the luxuries of Earth, as much as she wanted even more to be further, deeper, faster, that she would be homesick for this place if she'd been stranded the way Reese had, not knowing if he would ever get even this far again.

Then Verb came up to them, leaving E17 sitting a dozen meters away with his back to them. She took Reese's left arm in both her hands and quietly said, "Grandpa?"

● ● ●

The night before, after Molly had left, Reese had lain in the darkness, trying to second-guess Morgan's plan.

He tried to leave his emotions out of it. That he'd been swindled was no surprise, set up for some kind of complicated snatch-and-run by Morgan's promises of new frontiers; what hurt was the knowledge that it might all end here, not just for himself but for the entire human race, as if the only fish ever to crawl onto land had lasted ten years and then died with no offspring.

And surely he was not exaggerating. Whatever Morgan had programmed Kane to do would be devastating, might bring the entire colony down in the process.

Don't kid yourself, he thought. You know what Morgan wants. The transporter, the one that's good for ten or twenty light-years.

The very thing you want for yourself.

Someone at the far end of the sickbay groaned in her sleep, the whimper of the fly being sucked dry by the spider, a tiny, apologetic cry for help when there was no help to be given.

He knew his odds: his father had died of cancer, he himself had made two round trips to Mars and then this last run, had poisoned his body with alcohol and drugs. Given enough time, cancer was a virtual certainty.

Not me, Reese thought. Not that way.

He thought about Sarah.

She was alive, Molly had said, alive but strange, stranger than he would be able to imagine. Strange enough, he wondered, to build a matter transporter? The voice on the tape had said it was a kid, female, and then Molly had told him they had new names now. He remembered the last time he'd seen her, only two years old, already pacing herself through the elementary math and logic tutorials on Molly's computer, sketching from memory a diagram of a hypercube.

If it *was* Sarah, and it almost had to be, the irony was compelling, the grandchild become mother to the man. . . .

The sight of her the next morning was more than he could have prepared himself for: her pale flabbiness, her stringy hair and lopsided eyes. And then she called him grandfather.

"Molly?" he said. "You told her?"

"No. I had no idea she even knew. Not until now."

"It's no big deal," the girl said, turning her oversized head at an angle to look at Molly, as if it weighed too much even for her thick, wrinkled neck. "I can use a computer, you know. I've looked up your genetics and they're a lot closer to Reese's than to the guy that was supposed to be your father."

"Jesus," Molly said. "She was talking about connections this morning. I should have seen this coming."

"I don't suppose it matters," Reese said. "Not any more."

"It shouldn't," Molly said. "Not to any rational person. But it's liable to put Curtis over the edge. It's not like you guys are Damon and Pythias to start with."

"I never told anybody," the girl said. "I don't have to tell anybody now."

Reese looked at her again, tried to see past the distorted body to something more spiritual, and failed. "Molly said you might take me to breakfast," he said at last.

Sarah—Verb—nodded, and Molly said, "I'll catch up to you later. Be careful, will you? And keep a low profile. Curtis isn't going to want you walking around."

"Okay," he said. "What about Kane and the others? What happens to them?"

"I don't know," she said, and walked away.

It was morning under the dome. To his left, high up on the open expanse of plastic, Reese could see a suited figure, hanging on the outside of the cylinder, polishing away the minute scratches left by windblown dust, scratches that could eventually turn the dome opaque. Beyond, the pale green of the sky shaded upward to a blue flecked with stars and lit by the bright point of Deimos.

In front of him the fields and houses alternated in a checkerboard that covered more than three acres of land between the Center and the south wall. Reese remembered the work that had gone into making that soil arable, filtering out the salt and sulphur and lime, enriching it with treated sewage and nitrogen wrung out of the thin martian air, remembered the first crops, the endless radishes.

Then everything had been new, bright, and hard-edged, a planned subdivision just poured out of the developer's truck. In twelve years it had already passed into middle age, a martian equivalent of rocking chairs on the porches and weeds in the yards, only here the faces sat behind pressurized windows, without even a highway to focus their attention on.

"Are you hungry?" Verb asked, and Reese nodded. "We can go to his place," she said, and pointed to the boy sitting on a concrete bench a few yards away. "His mother's working." In the sudden awkwardness of her hands he saw unspoken messages, a need to communicate something whose words were denied her. He knew then intuitively what his rational brain had already determined. She was the one with the answers.

She called the boy over and introduced him. Reese shook his hand, wondering where the boy had unearthed the cliche of eyeglasses with electrician's tape wound over the bridge, an obvious affectation when surgery or contact lenses were so easily available.

The three of them followed the red gravel walkway around the Center. Reese stopped at the east animal pen and stared through the pressurized plastic bubble at the goats, their brown eyes shifting past him with animal indifference. Beyond them were the crowded chicken cages, and Reese could almost smell their sour odor through the double insulation of the plastic and his own oxygen mask.

"How many goats are there now?" he asked.

"Goats?" The girl looked at him as if he'd asked her about dinosaurs. "I don't do goats."

"It's not important," Reese said, remembering Molly's warning. *Stranger than you can imagine.* Not so strange, really, he thought. More as if they belonged here, as if Reese were the alien and they were the wise and mysterious lost race that everyone had dreamed of finding.

They led Reese across a newly mown alfalfa field and up to a pale yellow box, its durofoam shaped into ridges simulating clapboard, and through a swinging door with wire mesh set into its clear plastic panels. What a waste of ingenuity, he thought, to imitate a screen door between hundreds of millibars difference in air pressure.

He sat at a green Formica table in the kitchen, suddenly grateful to be off his feet. They felt swollen and undoubtedly were.

"There's not a lot of stuff," the boy said. "Eggs all right?"

"Eggs would be great," Reese said. "You want me to fix them?"

"Maybe you better."

Reese scrambled three eggs in a frictionless electric pan, keeping Verb in his peripheral vision. "Do you guys go to school or anything?"

After an awkward silence Verb said, "Not exactly. We study with the computers and stuff like that."

"What are you interested in? Physics? Your mom was always into physics."

"Lots of stuff."

"You ever . . . build things? Like maybe some kind of transporter that could move things around over really large distances? Like light-year distances?"

The girl's voice dropped to a whisper. "How much do you know?"

"Verb?" the boy said. "Hey, Verb, man, you said we weren't supposed to talk about any of this."

"I know what I said. Shut up, will you?" She looked back at Reese. "I made a promise, you understand? I promised I wouldn't leak it to anybody."

"It's already leaked," Reese said. "It's too late to stop it now. Dian radioed stuff about it to Morgan, back on Earth, and that's why he sent us here. I think Kane and maybe Takahashi know about it too. And I don't know for sure whose side they're on. But I don't like Morgan and I'm not going to help him."

"I don't know. Maybe I should talk to Mom first."

"Look," Reese said. He could feel the desperation building up inside him, wanted to keep the girl from seeing it. "You care about physics, right? I mean, it's the most important thing in your life."

"What are you trying to say?"

"Suppose they took that away from you. Took your computers away and made you do something else." The girl stared at him, blinking, and didn't answer. "That's what it's like for me. I put a U.S. flag into the ground here twenty years ago, and that was the high point of my life. Back then we thought we'd be going on to Ganymede and Titan at least, and all of us deep down thought somebody would come up with an antimatter drive or *something*, something that would get us out of this one crummy system and into the galaxy.

"But instead everything just fell apart. It's like . . . it's like somebody locked you in a closet in this big, beautiful house, and outside the house there's trees and hills and rivers and cities and the rest of the world, and you can't get to it."

"You're gonna burn those eggs," the boy said.

Reese put the food on a plate and forced himself to take a bite, even though his stomach was roller-coastering. You didn't waste anything on Mars, especially real food.

He looked up at Verb. She was combing through her dirty, tangled hair with the fingers of one hand. "Well," she said, "somebody did come up with an antimatter drive. We'll have it, anyway, in a couple of years."

"But there's more, isn't there?"

"The transporter, you mean. It's a toy. It may not even work. We can't be sure."

"I can't wait for an antimatter drive," Reese said. His chest felt cold and the words came out without his thinking about them, because if he stopped to think he wouldn't let them out at all. "If anything ever starts up again, I'm going to be too old. I'm already too old. If Morgan wasn't desperate he wouldn't have let me on *this* flight."

"What do you want? What are you asking me?"

"I want to keep going," Reese said. "A one-way ticket out."

"We sent a couple of mice," Verb said. "We sent them from . . . from where the machine is to my bedroom. One came through. The other one didn't. Everything was the same both times. We don't know what happened. We don't know why. We're out on the edge here, do you understand? This is crazy stuff, like part physics and part zen philosophy. Do you know anything about quantum theory?"

"A little, I guess."

"Well, there's stuff in it that doesn't work. There's the EPR experiment and Bell's Theorum that seem to imply action at a distance, and there's nothing in quantum mechanics to explain it. It's mechanics, see? It requires a mechanism."

"And your physics doesn't?"

"Mechanism is an assumption. So is cause and effect. People believe in them because they can explain most things that way and the things they can't explain they can forget about. We've got different assumptions. Quantum field theories get imbalanced at high momentum levels. They have to 'renormalize' the equations to get them to work. I don't, because I've added another variable that they didn't have. The objectivists used to believe there could be a 'hidden variable' that would complete quantum mechanics, and it turned out there was. A fourth-dimensional one."

"Like time, you mean?"

"Not necessarily. It's perpendicular to everything, that's all. Time is *a* dimension, not necessarily the *fourth* one. Do you see?"

Reese shook his head.

"It would be easier to show you the math," Verb went on, "but for sure you wouldn't understand that. Parts of it *I* don't understand. But I can *see* it sometimes, like a flickering just at the corner of my eyes, like I could almost see curves and angles where the desert out there is intersecting with fourth-dimensional space . . . I mean, if you had to use a word, it would be . . . synchronicity."

Sometimes, Reese thought, she looked like an old man, or maybe the words coming out of her just made it seem that way. She's twelve? he asked himself. At first she sounded merely brilliant, precocious, but then he began to see hints of an alien, frightening perspective that twisted his understanding of reality. He didn't know whether to just let her talk, or make a real attempt to understand her.

"Coincidence," he said.

"Pavel—he's one of the Russians—he gave me this book when I was eight. *Tertium Organum*, by this Russian Ouspensky from the early nineteen hundreds. He quotes Hinton in there, saying, 'the laws of our universe are the surface tensions of a higher universe.' I just read that, and I mean, there it was, you know? I mean, that's like a gauge field theory, except it comes out of philosophy, and everything just clicked."

"You're losing me," Reese said.

"Okay, an example. In a vacuum you get spontaneous pair production, a particle and an antiparticle. Like an electron and a positron. Virtual quanta, they're called. Happens at random, they annihilate each other, and that's it. But what if it's *not random*? What if there's a pattern, but it's fourth-dimensional? What if you could quantify that pattern? Then chance is working for you, making random antimatter, but it's not random to you anymore. It's all the antimatter you need, free energy."

"What about conservation laws?"

"I'm a conservation lawyer," she said. Reese attempted a smile, but her humor only made him more uncomfortable. "It's like potential and kinetic energy," she said, "everything evens out when you annihilate the stuff again."

Reese badly wanted to go somewhere and think this out. Did Morgan know what Verb had found up here? Dian's taped messages hadn't really talked about the antimatter, but Morgan had obviously seen the implications. Why else risk millions on a flimsy one-shot mission, plant weird circuitry in Kane's skull, rush the project into such a tight schedule? What had Morgan said? Something about Aeroflot wanting Mars as well?

Of course the Russians would want in. If their espionage was even mediocre they would know, and they had probably decoded and translated the same radio messages Morgan had gotten. So how far ahead of the Russians were they? Months? Days? Hours?

Reese took the diskette out from under his shirt, where he'd been hiding it since they'd landed. "What I heard is that your transporter needs information. It has to know exactly where it's supposed to send something."

"How did—"

He waved his hand at her. "Never mind how. I told you, the leak has already happened. The information is out there. Now. This is the map from the telescope on Deimos. It has the state vectors for every celestial object within a five-parsec radius, accurate within a couple of kilometers."

Verb took the diskette, turned it so the light glinted dully on its black surface. "What do you want me to do with it?"

"Send me to Barnard's Star."

Kane could feel the lingering caress of the Valium in his veins, the long half-life of the drug still whispering assurances to his jangled nerves.

He sat up in bed, relishing the pain in his chest, pushing back the skin of his face with both hands until his eyes burned and his cheekbones ached.

The air was charged with information. A faint, hazy loop of melody seemed to be coming from somewhere to his left, high voices in a minor key, without words that he could decipher. He turned his head and the music moved with him.

He was still confused, weak and disoriented. But his sense of purpose had reawakened, and for the first time since North Africa he felt he had a simple, straightforward series of actions to perform. The first was to find this woman, Dian, and make her tell him what she knew. Then he had to find the . . . the . . .

He shook his head. The magic sword. The grail. The *object*, whatever it was. That was the Pattern. The woman would make it all clearer.

Reese was gone. The others were asleep or sedated, except for a young Japanese woman in a chair by the door. A guard, Kane thought. He slumped down in the bed and carefully took the pistol out of the mattress and hid it in the back waistband of his trousers, pulling his hipari closed over it and tying the belt in a loose knot. Then he swung his legs over the side of the cot and sat up.

"*Ohayō gozaimasu*," the woman said.

"Yeah," Kane said. "Good morning." So, he wondered, how's it going to be? Is Curtis going to drop the pretenses and hold us under guard, or is he going to be subtle? "Do you think I could get something to eat? I'm starving."

"Sure. You're Kane, right?"

"Right."

"I'm Hanai." She was thin, with the sort of round face that was more prized by Eastern aesthetics than Western. Kane returned her short, stiff bow, conscious of the pistol moving against his waist. "Let me get somebody else in here and we'll find you some food." She punched a four-digit number on the wall phone and said, "I'm taking Kane to breakfast." She got some sort of answer and hung up. "Come on," she said to Kane.

He followed her into a hallway, admiring the graceful economy of her walk but unable to duplicate it. She led him into a wide, circular dining room supported by arching precast members along the walls. At one time it had been meant as some sort of communal gathering place; obviously the need no longer existed. The space had been broken down with Japanese screens or telescoping plastic baffles, isolating the areas around individual wide-screen video monitors mounted into the walls. Most of them were in use, filling the air with the clash of old-fashioned orchestrated cartoon music, synthesizers, droning voices.

The stucco walls between the columns, what Kane could see of them through the tangle of dividers, alternated neutral colors with bright oranges, yellows, and blues, the paint now chipped and beginning to fade. The ceiling was rendered in a Maxfield Parrish cloudscape, depressing Kane with its transparent and rather pathetic nostalgia for Earth.

"Communal kitchen through there," Hanai said. "There's usually plenty of eggs and vegetables. The good stuff people tend to keep at home."

Kane nodded. After nine months of solitary, introverted free fall, he found himself intimidated by the social normalcy of the three occupied tables in the middle of the room, by the seven or eight colonists drinking coffee and juice, lingering over their eggs and toast. He would have to walk past them, to pretend he belonged here, when in fact he felt hideously out of place.

Fuck it, he thought. I didn't ask for this. He walked into the kitchen, aware of eyes following him across the room, and put together a bowl of cereal, fruit, and goat's milk. Then he went back and sat down across from Hanai at an unused table.

She didn't say anything as he began to eat. He was having trouble reading her attitude; she was polite enough, but at the same time she seemed intent on demonstrating the imposition he was putting on both her and the colony.

Between bites he asked, "Do you know a woman named Dian?"

"The physicist?"

Kane nodded. A physicist? It made as much sense as anything, he supposed.

"Sure. Everybody knows everybody around here. Why?"

Earlier he had thought through a number of excuses, but he didn't know enough about Dian to lie convincingly. He ignored the question and asked, "Could I talk to her?"

Apparently she was not ready to abandon her ruthless sort of politeness. "I don't see why not. I can take you to her."

That would have to do, Kane thought. He had no doubt that Hanai reported directly to Curtis, but even so he could learn where Dian lived, find out something about her, maybe set up a meeting for later on. "What about these?" Kane asked, pointing to his empty dishes.

"In the vats beside the sink," Hanai said.

When he came back from the kitchen Hanai was standing by another of the wall phones. "You're in luck," she said. "She's usually working with Molly but this is her menials week and she's farming up in the Bronx."

"Sorry?"

"The northeast section. I'll take you over there."

At the outer door Hanai handed him an oxygen mask without explanation and he watched her to see what she did with the straps and valves. Then she opened the door and motioned him out.

He'd been nearly unconscious when they brought him from the ship to the infirmary, and now, stepping out under the dome for his first real look at the colony, Kane felt only dismay. He'd expected something that looked like the future, and what he saw reminded him of a shopping mall in decay: cramped, faded, lived-in.

"Is there someplace we can see out?" he asked Hanai.

"Over there."

It was getting easier to move around. His ribs hurt, but the ache was constant, controllable. The only problem came if he moved his head too quickly, baffling his inner ear and making his stomach lurch with vertigo.

Hanai led him on a curving path around the central building, past two long structures near the edge of the dome. Through dull plastic windows, bowed outward slightly from positive pressure, he could see a small herd of goats, the females diapered to conserve their milk. The animals didn't seem to mind the crowded conditions, bumping into each other, stumbling through the marble-sized pellets of their own dung.

"There it is," Hanai said.

Kane caught up to her, stood beside her in an oversized window box built out between two of the bulkheads that supported the dome. Concrete benches had been set up along the sides and the ground was planted in flowering cactus and yucca. Beyond the window Kane could see huge chunks of ice, wrapped in green plastic and shaded by aluminum *ramadas*: the colony's water supply. And beyond that lay the vast zen rock garden of Mars.

The land was more subtly alien than the cold white dust of Deimos, warmer, more like the deserts of northern New Mexico or Arizona. But the sand was too red, the rocks too dark and porous, the horizon closer but without promise, a desolation that went on endlessly beyond the reach of his eyes.

For the first time he understood, not just intellectually, but viscerally, that this was all there was. No ancient races and lost civilizations, no canals, no hidden valleys with jungles and perpetual clouds. Just the dry, empty husk of a planet and the few fragile lives clustered under the dome.

A gust of wind wrinkled the nearest plastic sheet and Kane, warmed by second-hand sunlight in the still air of the dome, shivered.

"A little bleak for you?" Hanai asked. "There's more interesting places. Like the Valles Marineris. But you wouldn't want to live there."

"No," Kane said. "I guess you wouldn't."

He turned away and followed Hanai through the zigzagged paths between the fields. As they came up on a strip planted in beans, about a dozen workers straightened up and stared at Kane, some with a distant, dreamy expression, others with obvious recognition.

They know who I am, Kane thought.

"Where's Dian?" Hanai asked.

The woman who answered her was short and thick-waisted, with limp brown hair cut to her jawline. "She didn't show this morning." The woman never took her eyes off Kane, even when talking to Hanai.

"Goddammit," Hanai said. "Why didn't you report it?"

Slowly the woman turned to face Hanai. "Hey, bag it, will you? I don't give a fuck why she ain't here. You want to phone it in to Curtis, you can fucking phone it in." She bent over and jerked a clump of grass from between the orderly rows.

The underbelly of Utopia, Kane thought. One or two of the others went back to work, but most of them stood and stared at Kane. Hanai blinked, twice, and said, "Okay, Kane, let's go." She broke into her smooth, gliding walk again, and this time Kane couldn't keep up.

In less than a minute she gained a dozen yards on him and Kane stopped, the pain in his chest glowing brighter like a coal under the bellows. "Hey," he shouted, the amplifier chip in his mask clipping the high end from his voice. "I thought you were supposed to be watching me."

Hanai looked back and said, "If you can't keep up, just wait there for me."

"What's the matter with you all of a sudden? A little backtalk from one of the peasants and you come flying off the handle."

"Look, Kane, I'm not here to argue politics with you, okay? Just mind your own business and everything will go a lot better for you."

"What's politics got to do with anything?" Kane said. And then he answered himself. "Curtis. You think he did something to her."

Hanai was already moving again, ignoring him. She ran up to the front steps of one of the maddeningly identical houses between the fields and pounded on the door. As Kane caught up with her he heard a low whistling noise, realized that it came from the edges of the door, which were bowing inward.

"Look out!" Kane shouted as Hanai reached for the handle of the door. "It's going to—"

The door seemed to leap backward, jerking Hanai with it. Air rushed into the vacuum of the house with a roar that numbed Kane's ears. The mask was nearly pulled from his face and he fell to his knees, hunching over to protect himself.

He knew then what they were going to find, but he wasn't prepared for the sheer quantity of blood.

It had pooled around Dian's head as she lay in bed, face down, dead in the act of trying to crawl toward the floor. The inrush of air had blown crusts and spatters of it onto the far wall in a complex pointillist pattern, and in it Kane could read the message that Curtis had left for him.

There were other ways that Curtis could have killed her. He could have poisoned her, could have stabbed her, clubbed her, dissected her with a laser. Instead he'd given her a uniquely martian death, a death that showed Kane that even the air he breathed was under Curtis's command.

"Okay," Kane said out loud. He folded his hands into tight hammers, the first two knuckles standing out in high, calloused relief.

Hanai turned Dian onto her back, exposing runnels of dried blood that met at her lips and spread in a chocolate smear across one cheek. "What?" Hanai asked belligerently. "You say something?" Her eyes locked on Kane's tightly clenched hands.

Kane straightened his fingers and brushed them against his thighs. "This was meant for me," he said.

"Was it? Well I hope to hell you got the point, whatever it was. I hope it was worth it to you. Because it's not worth it to me. I didn't know her, not that well, but she was one of us and you're not. It's because of you she's dead, you say. Well, that's great. As far as I'm concerned that's the same thing as if you killed her with your own hands. We don't want you here, none of us do. We don't need you, we don't need anything you could possibly give us. All we want is for you to go away and stay the hell away."

She was close to tears or violence, Kane saw, and she could go either way. This too was Curtis's fault, like the tension between Hanai and the farmer. "It's not up to me," Kane said, aware of too many levels in what he was saying.

"I don't want your excuses, either. What good are excuses to her?"

"Stop it," Kane said. "Wake up. Curtis killed her, not me. He's trying to protect something, and I don't even—"

"Kane?" Takahashi stood in the open doorway, his eyes narrowed against the shadows.

Hanai turned on him fiercely. "What are you doing here?" she demanded in Japanese. "Why are you by yourself?"

"I followed you," Takahashi said in English, with an innocence that failed to convince Kane. "No one stopped me." He looked at the dead woman and then back at Kane, nodding slightly. He recognizes her, Kane realized. He must have seen her last night. Just how much did Takahashi know?

"Aren't you going to call somebody?" Kane asked Hanai. "Or are you just going to leave her there?"

Hanai glared at him, then snatched the phone from the wall. She listened for a second and then dropped it in disgust. The receiver battered the wall and then spun on the tightly coiled cord. "Come on," she said. "I'll have to find another phone."

"No," Kane said.

"What?"

"I'm not coming," Kane said. "Are you going to

force me? Do your orders go that far? I don't think so."

"You're a visitor here," Hanai said, the words squeezed flat by the pressure of her teeth. "There are courtesies . . ."

"Fuck it," Kane said. "I'm walking out." From the way she moved he knew she could handle him easily if she chose to, would probably have been dangerous even if he'd been in peak condition and used to the lighter gravity. He was conscious once again of the weight of the gun in the back of his trousers, even though he dared not use it. He walked toward the door.

"Kane . . ." Hanai's voice was indecisive and Kane kept walking.

A few seconds later Takahashi caught up with him. "You took a big risk."

"You don't approve, of course."

"Maybe I just don't understand."

"It's the way of the warrior, Takahashi. When there's a choice, you choose death. You should know that. It's *bushido*."

"Is that supposed to be a joke? You're a two-bit mercenary and a corporate flunky, not without your uses, perhaps, but you're no *samurai*."

"If that's all you see, then that's all my uncle has let you see. The view's not that good when you spend your life behind a desk, anyway."

"You're in over your head," Takahashi said. "I wonder if you're going to find your way back out?"

"So that's the way it is," Kane said. "How much *do* you know about what's going on? How deep are you?"

Takahashi shook his head. It could have meant anything.

"I had to get away from there," Kane said. "Curtis is hiding something and I want to know what it is."

"And you think he'll tell you?"

"I don't know. But I have to try."

They were back at the central complex. Kane stopped a boy of about ten and said, "Curtis. Where is he? Has he got an office?"

"Upstairs," the boy said. The pressure of Kane's fingers seemed to frighten the boy more than hurt him, as if the mere threat of physical injury was shattering, unheard of.

Kane was beyond local taboos. He climbed the stairs inside the center and opened a door labeled "Governor" in English, Russian, and Japanese. A man behind a desk looked up from his bank of monitors.

"I'm looking for Curtis," Kane said. "Is he here?"

The man shook his head. Again Kane saw recognition and curiosity, tinged with fear. "I haven't seen him. You could try him at home . . ."

"Where's that?"

"Center house, first row south of here." The man's eyes swept over the dozens of screens, as if for some kind of reassurance. Kane left without shutting the door, taking the stairs two at a time, barely in control of his balance. Takahashi stepped out of his way at the bottom and Kane steadied himself against the braised aluminum railing. "Not there," Kane said. "You coming?"

"No," Takahashi said. "I don't think you're going to find him until he's ready for you to. Besides,

I've got some work to do in there." He pointed his thumb back toward the sick bay. "I can get into the main computer from there, I think."

"Okay," Kane said, and took hold of the door. The air pressure inside the center was Earth normal, 1000 millibars, three times the pressure outside, and he could feel the differential in his arms as he leaned back to pull it open. He could feel exhaustion eating into his anger, but beyond the adrenaline and fatigue poisons he could still hear those faint, high voices, urging him on.

He pulled up his mask and stepped into the sunlight. Curtis's house was just ahead of him, at the end of a short path.

He felt a powerful sense of imminence, of some kind of storm about to break. The air, he realized. It was the wrong color. It reminded him of the greenish skies in Texas before tornadoes or floods, provoking the same subconscious responses.

He pressed the button next to the door of Curtis's house and watched the camera mounted in the eaves turn automatically to focus on him. A few seconds later Molly's voice came through the speaker grille.

With one hand on the doorframe to steady himself he said, "I'm looking for Curtis."

"Come on inside," she said.

He nearly asked for Curtis again, hearing in her voice that Curtis was not there, but instead he let another awareness move through him, a memory of her touch and scent that brought a dizzying sense of lightness to his groin.

His sudden erection seemed the focal point of a binding force, pulling him inevitably, inexorably,

toward Molly. He pushed his way inside, let the
pressure suck the door shut behind him.

Molly stood on the far side of the living room,
retreating from Kane's presence. The thin white
cotton of her NASA undersuit revealed her body
clearly; her nipples were slack, her muscles relaxed.
"Sit down," she said, and Kane sat on the edge of
a long, low sofa. "Do want something? Coffee? A
drink?"

"No," he said. She could feel it too, he saw, the
sexual symbolism of his having penetrated her
house; she revealed it in the quick, nervous gestures of her hands. "Where's Curtis?" he said.

"Out," she said, holding his eyes for a moment,
and then suddenly turning away. The room was
crowded with plants: bamboo, palms, grasses, and
ferns. The air smelled rich, primordial.

"Out where? I have to see him."

"I'm afraid," she said, her voice strained, unnatural, "he can't be disturbed right now."

Kane moved to his feet, took her by one wrist.
"What are you saying? Where is he?" He felt as if
he were reading the words; he was only aware of the
nearness of her body, the heat of it.

"He . . . he keeps one of the abandoned houses
with power and air. He's there right now with Lena."

Kane let go of her wrist. "I'm sorry," he said.
She took another step deeper into the hallway.

Lamps over the plants carved the curtained
halflight into spaces that excluded Kane. He moved
toward Molly again, drawn by her electric field,
sensing their exchange of quanta as a tingling along
his skin. As he touched her lightly on one arm, her
current surged low in his spine.

"Kane . . ." she said, almost a plea, but he wasn't sure for what. He sensed her uncertainty and fear, but they broke harmlessly over the momentum of his need.

She turned to face him. His palms followed the sides of her breasts to the long, smooth latissimus muscles along her sides. She gripped his elbows, her eyes losing focus.

In her bedroom the smell of her was stronger, warm and sweet. She turned and faced him again, tearing loose the velcro fastners and exposing her breasts almost defiantly, pulling her arms free of the sleeves. Kane tugged at the knot in his belt, unwilling for just that instant to go on with it, the inevitable coupling and climax, preferring instead the complex emotional ambience of the seduction itself, the currents of power tinged with weakness and guilt, the hesitation, the surrender.

Molly kicked her clothes away and Kane shed his hipari, reaching back to push the revolver into the heap of olive drab material as he slid his trousers to the floor.

She sat on the edge of the bed, spine curved, breasts pointing downward, her nervousness aging her prematurely. Kane put one knee on the sheet next to her and pushed her gently by the shoulders until she lay on her back, arms extended behind her. He gripped her waist, just above the hips, where he could feel the primal power of her sexuality. Her legs opened to him and he could smell the heat and darkness of her, the scent turning sharp as she became aroused. He spread her labia with his thumbs and flicked his tongue into her cleft to get the taste of her.

Her hips moved slowly against the mattress. Her eyes were open, her teeth pinning her lower lip. Kane wondered what she saw.

He raised her knees until her heels sank into the bed, and then, left hand under her buttocks, he guided himself into her with the other.

His hands moved up her body, fingertips just brushing her fragrant skin, his weight shifting forward to rest on his left elbow and right palm. He held himself rigid, motionless, feeling the tension coiling in his spine. His breath began to come more quickly as the pleasure burned through his groin, across his hips and down into the contractions of his toes.

Then, slowly, he began to move in and out of her, lowering himself until he could feel the mass of her breasts against his damaged ribs. Her hands tangled themselves in the sheet behind her head, clawing at it in rhythmic contractions. Her excitement built slowly, seemingly against her will, until her jaw and shoulders were tight with it.

A ringing split the silence.

Kane looked up, saw the bedside phone flashing red. Molly seemed oblivious, introverted, locked into a divergent, subjective reality. The sudden, convulsive pressure of her pubic ridge confused and disoriented him; then he realized she was approaching orgasm.

He touched the hard point of her left nipple and she rolled him over onto his back, both her hands on the bandages of his chest, rocking hard until her entire body shook. Kane held her hips and thrust against her, not letting her finish. His throat muscles went tight. He felt his eyes roll back in his head and his leg muscles spasm as he pumped his climax into her, and when it was finished they lay without moving, her head and breasts resting on his chest, his hot fluid turning cool as it flowed back down his shaft and pooled on the sheet under him, the red light of the phone still flashing, silently now, at the far end of the bed.

They had reached the neutrality of afternoon.

Molly rolled onto her back. After a time she said, "When you find him, what happens then?"

"I don't know," Kane told her. "Does it matter to you? How much do you care what happens to him?"

"Once upon a time," she said, "everything in the universe was in one great, huge ball of fire. All the bits and pieces were controlled by the same interactions. Everything was symmetrical."

Kane turned on his side to look at her.

"Then things started to cool down," she said. "The symmetry broke down. One by one the different interactions turned into different things. Gravity, strong, weak, electromagnetic forces. Particles formed atoms and molecules and stars and planets and people. At every step the symmetrical patterns had to break down to become more complex. But without that symmetry breaking, there could never have been any life or intelligence in the universe."

"I don't get it," Kane said. "What are you saying?"

"Things break up. Marriages break up. But they were once together. Everything in the universe still has that memory of having been part of the same thing. Everything is still connected."

"Like you and Curtis, is that it? Still connected?"

She didn't answer him. She lay for another moment, totally relaxed, and then suddenly swung around to the end of the bed and snatched the telephone receiver. She keyed four digits, waited, then said, "Molly."

Kane propped his head on one hand to watch her. She had eluded him somehow, despite the intensity of their physical coupling.

"Yes," she said to the phone. "All right. I'll be there." She hung up, then stared at the floor, as if trying to focus her energies.

"Curtis?" Kane asked.

"No," she said. "It's the Russian ship. They're coming in."

• • •

She went to her closet and looked for something dignified to wear to meet the Russians. The best she could find was a sort of orange padded cape and trousers.

Her own calmness surprised her, even frightened her a little. She'd just been unfaithful, for the first time in thirteen years of marriage, and it was like nothing had happened at all.

No, she thought. Something had happened. Nothing as melodramatic as the end of her marriage; that had been over for years in any real sense. Something had changed inside her, not a sudden rush of guilt or desolation, but instead a growing sense of her own strength and power.

It had come from Kane. She remembered something Verb had said to her months ago, one of her feeble attempts at humor, when she was talking about her new physics as "quantified destiny." She made some joke about "destinons," quantum particles of fate that bound people and events through the fourth dimension.

For Molly there was more truth in the idea than even Verb would admit; she knew that she and Kane had exchanged more than bodily fluids and neural release.

Kane frightened her. He was quirky, nervous, with the dark flitting eyes of a bird and an aura of suppressed violence that seemed detached from his intellect. But it wasn't fear that had opened her so completely to him, and now, as she felt his fingers close on her arm, she promised herself that she would not be physically intimidated by him.

"You'd better get dressed," she said.

"You've known about this," he said. "How long?"

"They launched within a couple of days of your ship. They weren't firing messages off at us like you guys were, but we picked up some of their signals back to Moscow. Morgan must have known. Didn't he say anything to you?"

Kane took his hand away. "No. Of course not. What did you get from their signals?"

"Nothing. What's there to say? They're here for the same reason you are. Obviously." In saying it she had identified Kane as her enemy, or at least her rival, but Kane seemed to miss the implicit threat.

"Good," Kane said. "If I can find out what the Russians want, then maybe I'll know something."

Is he joking? she wondered. She took her clothes into the bathroom, and when she came back Kane had dressed.

"What about Curtis?" Kane asked. "Is he going to be there?"

"There's no telling. If he wants to know about it, then he knows."

Kane said, "I don't see the two of you together, somehow."

Molly shrugged. "He's changed. You want to see the landing?"

"Why not?"

"Walk with me."

They masked and went outside. Kane looked

even more predatory in his mask, Molly thought. It left nothing to focus on but those black, shark-like eyes.

"I don't know," she said. "Maybe he hasn't changed, not really. It's so easy to talk about power corrupting and all that kind of shit. But which came first, the idealism, or the lust for power? I mean, maybe all the ideals were just a means to an end."

"What kind of ideals are we talking about?"

"Nine years ago, when everything had turned to shit, Curtis saved this place." She moved her hand and the circle took in the dome over their heads, the orange grove around them, two teenaged girls leaning against one of the living modules, wires leading from their temples to a small metal box. "He did it just about singlehandedly. All anybody cared about was getting through from one day to the next, and it wasn't enough. Then Curtis comes along and starts talking about twenty, thirty, fifty years ahead.

"I think it was the first time any of us con-fronted the fact that we'd given up, we'd all de-cided there wasn't going to *be* a twenty years from now. Curtis changed that. He said we didn't need Earth, that we could make our own Earth, only better; shit, it sounds trite and stupid when I say it, but Curtis painted it, he sold it, until we could all feel it and smell it and taste it. Just the idea, just the *hope* that you could look at the sky with-out having a sheet of plastic between you and it."

"Terraforming," Kane said.

"Then you've heard all this."

"Just the word, is all."

"Curtis believed in the 'pressure point' approach, that you can change a few little things and get big results. Like if you dumped some dust on the poles, the heat absorption would melt the ice and increase the atmospheric pressure which would start a greenhouse effect which would melt more ice. There's supposed to be enough frozen junk at the poles and around here on the Tharsis ridge to bring us up to a full bar of pressure, same as Earth."

"That's a lot to happen in twenty or thirty years."

"Sure, but in the meantime you've got oases. Drop some ring ice from Jupiter or Saturn, say, into a nice low area and blow out a crater ten kilometers deep. You've got heat and gasses from the impact and the crater will hold the higher air pressure."

Kane stopped, put his hands in his trouser pockets. "What are you, crazy? 'Drop some ring ice.' Fucking fantastic. How the fuck are you going to go get this ice? With a leftover MEM and some ice water for propellant?"

He really doesn't know, she thought. About the physics, the transporter, the antimatter, none of it.

"It's not impossible," she said. "We have to make everything here. The air you're breathing out of that tank is manufactured. We can make rocket fuel, we can make stages, we can fix the ships still in orbit. We could do it."

"So why didn't you?"

"It . . . I don't know. It was just too hard, I guess. It would take sacrifices. There'd be less booze, less energy for Curtis and his pals to go riding around in the jeeps. By the time we'd sacrificed long enough that we could actually talk about building the ships, everybody was tired of sacrifices."

"Even you?"

"Maybe even me, a little. But I could stand it, if it would give us ships. And if we had ships I wouldn't just go to Saturn and turn back. You know? I mean, sure, build the oases, but don't stop there. Not with the rest of the universe out there, waiting."

"You sound like Reese."

With good reason, she thought, but she said, "Yeah, I suppose I do." She looked back and saw Blok hurrying toward them. She had a moment of panic: Blok would be able to tell at a glance that she and Kane had been to bed, he would tell Curtis—but it passed as quickly as it came. It was the same as with the Russians. If Curtis wanted to know he probably already knew. She didn't doubt for a nanosecond that he had his own bedroom as thoroughly wired as the rest of the dome.

She started walking again, pulling Kane along with her voice. "I suppose Curtis is as bad as any of them. He could have pushed harder, but I think it would have lost him his popularity. He's smart enough to know that. But I think he really bought the dream. He wouldn't want to admit it, but I think it's really been eating at him the last five or six years, knowing that we could be trying for something better and we aren't."

She opened the hatch to the suit room and started down the line of Rigid Experimental suits, looking for her favorite. From the corner of her eye she saw Kane peel off his hipari and clumsily stuff it into one of the lockers. She'd seen the same awkwardness when he'd undressed in her bedroom, and she suddenly understood that he was hiding something in the jacket. A weapon? she wondered. What in god's name for, if he had no idea of what was happening?

To hell with it, she thought. Let Curtis sort it out.

But the idea terrified her nonetheless. If it *was* a handgun, it was a threat to all of them, a lighted match in a room flooded with oxygen, where even steel would burn. Only a fool, or a lunatic, would have one. She was afraid Kane might be a little of both.

Blok came in while she was helping Kane into his suit. He stared at them for a second or two, his eyes half closed in what Molly thought of as his "inscrutable Russian" look. Then he introduced himself to Kane.

"So," he said. "What should I expect from my former countrymen?" he asked. "Rumor has it the Supreme Soviet is no more."

Molly felt protective toward Kane, responsible, at least, for her attraction to him. She tried to will him into politeness, if only for her sake.

"To be honest," Kane said affably, "we don't hear much. The government went under, some kind of Army coup. And then the Army just kind of went to pieces. The Kazakhs against the Uzbeks against the Byelorussians and so on."

"Tipich," Blok said. "Typical. Naturally the Army had to get rid of the KGB, so when the Army went there was nothing."

"Just the *obshchestvy*, like Aeroflot, and a few of the stronger labor unions, the steelworkers and the miners. And they ended up incorporating."

"Ah," Blok said. "How Russians love a purge. *Chistka*, they call it. The cleaning. Out with socialism, the god that failed! In with western corporations! Blue jeans! Rock and roll!" He seemed genuinely happy, his irony buried so deeply that it, or any of his other true political feelings, would never betray him.

She twisted the clumsy, oblong helmet of her suit into place and switched on the PLSS. The suit had an external microphone and speaker that allowed her a direct link to the outside world; she used the speaker to tell Blok and Kane to hurry up.

As she stood outside, watching the growing point of brightness in the sky, she found herself impatient to get the spacecraft on the ground, to get the last of the waiting over with. Once I know it all, she thought, once all the bad news is in, then we can start deciding what to do about it.

The Russian ship, visible only as a shadowy sphere-and-cylinder through the dust, hovered longer than it had to, touching down as gently as a pebble on a riverbottom. And why not? Molly thought. They'd been perfecting their soft landings while the U.S. was still dropping their Geminis and Apollos in the ocean—even if some of those landings had been blatant fiascos, like the Voskhod-2 mission where Leonov and Belyayev sat all night in their dead spacecraft, two thousand miles off course, fighting wolves and snow.

As the dust settled Molly could make out the hideous pale green of the ship's hull—"landlord green" Blok had once called it—and see where the CCCP and red rectangle had been clumsily painted out and replaced with the Aeroflot logo. The paint had blistered and flaked so badly in the heat of re-entry that most of the lettering was gone.

Kane, beside her, was visibly unsteady. His ragged breathing hissed through the comm channel like a distant waterfall. He should be in sickbay, she thought, but there was no time to do anything for him now.

The hatch of the lander swung open.

Blok and two of the others ran forward to help. Molly watched as the first of the white-suited figures climbed down the ladder, and Blok reached a hand to help. The figure rested its weight on Blok's shoulder, nodded, and walked away without help.

A second cosmonaut came out of the hatch and started down the ladder, then did something that Molly found odd. The Russian shut the hatch and punched a series of numbers into a ten-key pad in a recessed panel.

Locking it? Molly thought. What were they afraid of, thieves? She didn't like the implied mistrust and secrecy. Was there some kind of weapon on the ship that they needed to protect?

"*Zdrastvetyeh, tovarishch*—" Blok said as the Russian reached the ground, but his arm was pushed away. The figure straightened and stood on its own, glancing first at the crowd near the airlock, then once again at Blok.

"Hello, Blok," said a woman's voice, her English flavored with a sort of dry, European rasp.

"Colonel Mayakenska?" Blok seemed awed, even a little frightened. Molly recognized the name; Mayakenska had been one of the higher-ups in the Institute for Medium Machine Building, the Russian equivalent of NASA, but the Soviets had man-

aged to keep her exact position obscured by dis-
information.

"So you haven't forgotten me."

"Of course not, how could—"

She waved him silent. "I'm afraid it's only Mademoiselle Mayakenska now." She caught up with
her fellow cosmonaut and the two of them walked
away from the ship with their heads up, their
steps even and nearly in rhythm.

Molly knew the effort it cost them to put on such
a show of strength and it made her uncomfortable.
She also didn't like the fact that Mayakenska
insisted on speaking English, an attitude that struck
her as both condescending and overly theatrical.

Blok introduced her to Mayakenska, and Mayakenska in turn introduced Valentin, the other
crewman. Neither of them offered to shake hands
and Molly contented herself with a formal nod to
each of them, a gesture nearly imperceptible outside her RX suit.

"Are you in command, then?" Mayakenska asked,
and the choice of words and the tone told her that
this was as bad as it could be, that this was where
the end truly began.

"My husband is," she said. A cold lump lay in
her stomach; she suddenly hated the inhuman taste
of the compressed air she breathed. "If you'll come
inside—"

The airlock door opened behind her and she
heard Curtis's voice. "Okay, Molly, I've got it." He
stepped out and stood in front of the Russians,
blocking, as if by accident, their way into the dome.
"My name is Curtis," he said. "I'm governor here.
Welcome to Frontera Base."

Kane came back to life. He shifted away from her, legs spread, and through the tinted visor of his helmet she could see his black eyes focus on Curtis.

Christ, she thought, I want away from here. She tried to visualize herself in a sleek ship, headed out toward Titan, Mars shrinking to a point-source in the screens, the stars closing in around her. It was a vision that had eased her before, but now she could no longer believe in it. Three heavy cables were looped over the fins of the ship, dragging it back, and on the ends of the cables were Curtis, Kane, and Mayakenska.

"We have a good deal to talk about," Mayakenska said. The light was wrong for Molly to see into Curtis's visor but she could imagine how sexy he would find the Russian's voice, imagine the slow, predatory smile spreading across his face.

"I'm sure we do," he said. "Blok will see to whatever you need for the moment—food, a change of clothes, whatever—and we'll meet a little later at the Center. Blok will show you."

And that, Molly thought, is what he does so well: strut, posture, and maneuver. I would only have tried to be polite.

Curtis stood aside and let Blok and the two Russians go through the lock first.

"Kane," Curtis said as the door hissed shut. Molly realized Curtis had switched over the external speaker on his suit, cutting the Russians out of the circuit. She snapped her own switch to EXT and saw Kane and the three others do the same. "I see you're up and around."

The other three, she suddenly realized, were all Curtis's people.

"What happened to Dian?" Kane said.

"Dian?" Molly said. "Curtis, what's he talking about?"

"I don't have the foggiest notion," Curtis said.

"You killed her," Kane said. "You pumped the air out of her house and let her hemorrhage her lungs all over the walls and floor. Because you were afraid she was going to talk to me about something."

"Oh jesus," Molly said. The edges of her helmet seemed to be closing down into a tunnel, as if she were accelerating away at some phenomenal speed.

"Why was that, Curtis? What is it you're trying to hide?"

"You're obviously upset," Curtis said. "Let's go inside and we'll get you some help."

"Curtis." Molly's voice sounded distant and faint to her own ears; she still seemed to be falling away from the dome, from Kane, from her husband, even though she could see that she'd hardly moved at all. "Is. Dian. Dead."

"I doubt it, sweetheart. I don't think Kane is in any condition to tell what's real at the moment."

"Hanai saw it," Kane said. "She's one of yours. Takahashi, too. For christ's sake, man, this isn't New York. You can't just throw the body in some alley and pretend it didn't happen."

"Inside," Curtis said. Molly saw, numbly, that the airlock telltale had flashed green. Curtis was in first, followed by Kane. As soon as she was through the door Molly slapped the mushroom-shaped button to seal them in, isolating Curtis from his henchmen. The gesture was thoughtless, impulsive, but Curtis turned on her in a rage.

"You traitorous little bitch," he said, or at least

that seemed to be the gist of it. He was still patched through EXT and his voice was lost in the roar of compressed air.

Kane pulled his helmet off. The lock was small, less than a meter and a half on a side, and one elbow thumped against the plating of Molly's suit. He's crazy, she thought. His eyes were ringed with purple so dark the skin appeared contused, and a wide, white band of sclera showed under his irises.

He shifted nervously from one foot to the other until the inner door opened, and then he shoved past Curtis and ducked through the hatchway. Molly took her own helmet off and followed him, with Curtis right behind her.

The Russians were still getting out of their gear; Blok was handing them oxygen masks and explaining how to use them. Molly began to strip off the clumsy RX suit, her back to the airlock. When she turned around, orange padded cape in hand, she saw Kane standing by the controls, the inner door locked open, the lower half of his body still armored in jointed beige plastic.

"Don't push it, Kane," Curtis said. "Shut the door and let the others in." He hung his suit on the wall and belted on a pair of slacks. Blok, glancing nervously at Kane, hurried the Russians out into the dome.

"Not until I get some answers," Kane said. Molly suddenly remembered the bundle Kane had hidden in one of the lockers. The thought grew into a bright spot of panic. Could Kane have murdered Dian? Was he going to start shooting now, punching holes through this fragile box of air? She took a small, sideways step toward the locker.

"What am I supposed to tell you?" Curtis said. "We've found the lost city of Mars, and we've got the martians in an all-night poker game in a tool shed somewhere? That all those things that look like glaciers up there on Arsia Mons are really single-crystal silicon ribbons? What do you want to hear?"

"Just the truth, man. Everybody's been lying to me since I got involved in this fucking mission and I'm sick of it!" He threw his helmet aside and Molly saw him wince at the answering pain in his ribs. The helmet bounced off the wall of lockers with a booming crash and buried itself in the rack of suits.

"You stupid little punk," Curtis said.

Kane moved on him.

Turn around, Molly told herself. Walk away. You don't want to see this, don't want to have to deal with any more of this goddamned macho bullshit. But she couldn't make herself go.

Kane's attack was oriental, his legs bent and center of gravity low, his body twisting and turning as he covered the distance between Curtis and himself in two long strides. Even to Molly's inexperienced eyes he looked weak, off-balance, and she was surprised when he feinted a spin kick, turned in close, and caught Curtis with a fist under the heart.

Curtis stepped back, hurt and out of breath, but he was ready when Kane came at him again. He reached overhead for the long metal bar of the suit rack, levered himself into the air and drove both legs at Kane's injured chest, spilling a dozen suits off their hangers.

Kane saw it coming and tried to cover up, succeeded only in getting his own fists and elbows driven into his face and stomach. Curtis stepped away long enough to slam the inner door of the airlock and to make sure the light above it clicked to red. Then he finished Kane with a wide, looping punch that caught him just inside the cheekbone and stretched him across the floor.

Molly had no way of knowing how much more damage had been done to Kane's ribs. He was alive, and lucky for that much; what had he thought he was going to prove?

"You did kill her, didn't you?" Molly said to Curtis. "She must have been the leak you were talking about. She told Morgan about the new physics, and so you killed her."

"Don't start, Molly."

"Start? Me, start? Dian was my friend. She was part of the project, she was fucking integral, you asshole. You kill her and then you tell *me* not to *start?*"

"This is more trouble than you can handle, Molly. I sincerely advise you to butt out of this."

"Are you threatening me? Are you threatening me, you son of a bitch? Are you going to kill me next?"

The airlock light flashed green in her peripheral vision and the rest of Curtis's people came through. One of them went to Kane's body and dumped him out of the lower half of his suit, leaving him lying on the rough concrete in his black drawstring trousers. A second moved next to Curtis and a third stayed by the door.

Like little robots, Molly thought. Her hands shook with rage and frustration. It's out of control, she thought. There's not a fucking thing I can do to stop it.

"What about this one?" asked the woman standing over Kane.

"Put him in Little Juarez," Curtis said. "Lock him in and dope him to the gills, I don't care with what. Something to keep him out of the way until I make up my mind about him."

Little Juarez, Molly thought. So that's what he calls it, his little pleasure cabin. How demeaning. Did he tell all his conquests about the nickname? Had he told Lena, that morning?

He crossed the room to stand in front of her, massaging his right hand with his left.

"Don't touch me," she said quietly.

"I'm not going to," Curtis said. "I'm just going to ask you to do what I tell you, just for now. At least until we find out what the Russian position is. Okay? Can you handle that? Because everything is falling apart right now and my hands are full."

"You know what they want. They want the fucking project, same as Morgan does."

"And I'm not going to give it to them. Okay? That's what we both want, it's what we both know is right. So all you have to do is walk in and sit down at the table with me and listen to what the Russians have to say. Okay?"

"Okay," Molly said, looking away from the pained sincerity on his face. "Okay."

● ● ●

He'd been through it all those last nights in Houston. For nine months he'd locked himself away from the rest of the crew and stared at the possibilities, testing himself against them, the way a suicide would test the bite of the razor on his hands.

But now, now that he had committed himself, Reese was afraid.

Verb had left with the diskette. It had taken her only a few seconds with her eyes closed to tell him when Barnard's Star would be in optimum position for the run: at about nine that night. Her freakish abilities had begun to frighten him more than they impressed him, provoking some kind of instinctive xenophobia.

"Be there by eight-thirty or so," she told him, and gave him directions to the cave. Had she sensed his distaste? Did it matter? His sudden desire to hug her was as selfish and guilt-ridden as it was artificial. He suppressed it and nodded instead.

"Thank you," he said.

"Sure."

Molly would want him to report back to sickbay; Curtis would be even less happy about his wandering around without a watchdog. And then, like the bolt of a rifle sliding home, came the thought: this is it. These are the last hours I'm going to have with other human beings, maybe the last, period.

I ought to get laid, he thought, anyway. But he recognized the impulse as no more than a galvanic response, the frog's leg of his sexuality twitching under the applied current of some leftover, obsolete sensibilities.

His second thought was that he needed a drink.

He started back toward the Center, depressed by the uniformity and orderliness of the houses around him. In the first season under the dome, nicknames and handpainted signs had proliferated: "Tharsis Hilton" for the Center, "South Hell" for the unheated garages, "the Blister" for the dome itself. Now, in spite of the red-and-blue neon "Frontera Bar and Grille" sign outside the north entrance to the Center, Reese sensed that things had changed. Curtis's regime reflected the man's personal sterility and lack of humor. Reese had seen the cameras that tracked him as he walked, the sort of obsessive power icons that became venerated when true power was slipping away.

He went in under the glowing sign and turned left into the wardroom. In the tradition of American bars the lighting was minimal, despite the fact that it was barely after noon. He'd brought his Mars Identification and Credit Authority with him from Earth on a sentimental impulse; the MICA card fit into a slot on the far wall and allowed Reese to select a gimlet from the menu. A sentimental drink, he thought, appropriate to the occasion.

As his eyes adjusted he noticed someone else in the room. "Hello?" he said.

"You're Reese, aren't you?" The voice belonged to a young woman, Oriental, slim, attractive.

"That's right."

"Hanai. Do you want to sit down?" She was clearly upset about something; she was on her third drink, and she still had to steady the glass with both hands.

He took his drink and card and sat down at her table. The room was antiseptic as a hospital automat. He could remember when the walls had been covered with handwritten messages: want ads, poems, kids' art work. Now, from what he'd seen, people did their drinking at home, sometimes even in the fields outside, pulling their masks just far enough from their faces to accommodate the neck of a bottle or the end of a straw.

"Shouldn't you be with somebody?" Hanai asked.

For an instant Reese thought she was propositioning him, then understood she was talking about security. "Not me," he said. "I used to live here." He wished, for a second, that she had been coming on to him. Her lips were shallow, but exquisitely formed, and he watched with longing as they moved softly against the edge of her glass.

Stop it, he told himself. You're just trying to bail out, to load yourself down with some low-grade sexual *karma* so you won't go through the gate.

"Something's wrong," he said to her. "Do you want to talk about it?"

She shook her head. Then, as if changing the subject, she said, "The Russian ship is landing. Did you know?"

"Russian ship?"

"The one from Earth. It's probably already here. I'll be on duty again tonight because of it, I shouldn't be drinking." She made no move to put the glass down.

Already here, Reese thought. Of course. That was why Morgan had left him so little time. It was no vague threat but an actual mission, one that Morgan had known about even then.

"Do you know what they want?" he asked Hanai.

She shook her head. "It's funny. We went so long, thinking we would never see anybody from Earth again. Now all of a sudden you're all over the place, and we realize we really didn't miss you at all. You know? Only now it's too late."

Reese downed the gimlet, the sour lime juice burning more than the gin. "Are they taking them to sickbay?" he asked, standing up.

"Sickbay's full. I don't know what they're doing with them." Her eyes stared down into her glass, telling Reese she didn't particularly care, either.

He reached across the table and gently touched her hair. She jerked her head away, startled. Reese wanted to console her somehow but all he could find to say was, "I'm sorry."

He turned left on his way out, intending to cut through the main dining hall to sickbay. Instead he heard familiar voices from one of the meeting rooms off the hallway. The door was open and he could see Molly and Curtis at the far side of the room, their backs toward him. Across the table from them sat three others: Blok, the senior survivor of the Marsgrad disaster, and another woman and man. The woman saw Reese and stood up.

"Reese! Come over here."

He stood behind Molly and reached across the table to shake her hand. "Colonel Mayakenska.

They finally let you fly one." He'd only met her in person once before, but her photograph was well known at NASA. She was a very well preserved fifty, tall and thin, each small muscle perfectly defined. She had been a body builder, Reese remembered, and evidently she'd kept it up. Even her face showed the effects of exercise, her cheeks hollow and her chin firm, despite the months of free-fall. Her brown, Mongol eyes had only a trace of puffiness and she'd left her khaki-colored hair long enough to curl under her chin.

It was intimidating, Reese thought, to have somebody get off a spacecraft looking that good. He had no doubt she'd intended it just that way.

"Why don't you sit with us," she said. "What we're talking about concerns you, too."

Reese sat next to Molly, trying to pick up the mood of the table. Mayakenska exuded calm authority; Curtis and Molly seemed withdrawn and frightened, waiting for some figurative axe to fall. Blok was openly nervous, and Reese could feel the unspoken pressure the Russians were exerting on his loyalties.

"I don't see any need to talk around the edges of this thing," Mayakenska said. "We know of your discoveries, at least some of them. Unfortunately, your political position is somewhat ... tenuous. Neither the U.S. nor the Soviet Union, um, I believe the exact language was, 'makes or recognizes any claims' on other planets of the solar system. Since the population here is a mixture of Russian, Japanese and American—"

Curtis cleared his throat. "Is there a point to this?"

"These discoveries," Mayakenska went on, "are clearly the property of all humankind. Therefore we have come to participate in a joint endeavor to develop and exploit this new technology."

"So," Curtis said, "you're a scientific expedition, then."

"In a manner of speaking, yes."

"And you thought you'd just drop in, like this was some kind of Video Expo, and take a look at the new gear? Come on. Let's just move on along to the next tissue of lies."

"Do I understand," Mayakenska said, "that you are refusing to share your knowledge?"

"One," Curtis said, "I don't even know what knowledge it is that you're so eager to get your hands on, and two—"

"You know perfectly well what it is," Mayakenska said. "Even Reese knows, don't you Reese?"

"*Two*," Curtis said, nearly shouting now, "nobody asked you here. Where were you when your own people were hiking across the Sinai Planum in *shuttle* suits, for christ's sake? Where were you when we were trying to squeeze nitrogen out of a vacuum? Sorry, Mayakenska, I don't buy it. I can't believe for an instant you thought I *would* buy it."

"I don't suppose I did," Mayakenska said. "Okay, let's try it this way." She brought her wrist up dramatically and looked at her watch. "We all have these nice Seikos that keep time in sols rather than days." Reese had one himself; the electronics of the watch allocated the extra 7 minutes of the martian day over a twenty-four-hour period, lengthening each second by a factor of .0257. "Right now mine says it's 13:52 and a few seconds. Our ship is in synchronous orbit overhead, in continous radio contact with us. They're expecting to get a coded signal from us each hour. If they don't get it, or if we don't send another, very specific coded signal tonight at midnight, they're going to open up with a narrow-beam heat laser. If you want a demonstration we can set one up for you."

She leaned back in her chair. The plastic creaked. Reese could hear his own breathing.

He felt his fear as a hollow ache near his stomach, almost like hunger, except that it was vibrating, and the vibration was moving into his hands.

When his brain began to function again, his first thought was: I was right. I was right to find a way out of this. This is a sickness, and now that there aren't any countries to blow each other up the corporations have caught it and now they're going to finish the job.

Mayakenska stood up. "You'll need some time. Blok tells me there's an empty house, S-23. We'll be there when you're ready to talk about this."

For a second Blok was the focus of Curtis's hatred, and Reese wondered that the weight of it didn't crush him flat. Then Blok got jerkily to his feet and followed Mayakenska and her silent countryman out of the room.

Molly's head sank onto her folded arms. "It's all over," she said, rubbing her forehead against the spherical bones of her wrist. "Fuck it. It's finished. Let them have the goddamned thing. It's not worth it."

"Right," Curtis said, barely louder than a whisper. Against the darkness of his five o'clock shadow, his puffy lips were turning up at the ends. A stranger,

Reese thought, might innocently mistake that look for a smile. "Then they'll just go away and leave us alone. Right? Sure they will." His arm blurred as he spun around and hurled the chair next to him the length of the room. It slid across a table-top and banged into the wall with maniac force. The violence of it had brought him to his feet, but only a tiny tic in his left eye betrayed his emotions. "You just bet they will," he said in the same even tone, and then he walked away.

"I'm sorry," Reese said to Molly.

"I know you are," she said. She sat up, brushed ineffectually at the tangles in her hair. There were fine, brittle lines of white now, Reese noticed, in the straw-colored mass. "It wasn't your idea. Maybe it wasn't anybody's idea. Maybe it's just the semiotics, you know? Once Verb built the machine, it changed our own ways of thinking about it."

"You can look at it that way," Reese said. "If it's easier."

"I don't think it is." She put her hands in her lap, as if they needed protective custody. "It's Curtis I'm worried about. He's not just going to lie down, and . . ." She trailed off into a shrug.

"Fight him, then," Reese said, feeling like a hypocrite. "You've fought for things before. You fought to get a place on the colony ships."

"Yeah, right. And look how that ended up."

"Would you rather have been stuck on Earth? Maybe gotten killed in the riots or spent three years in the breadlines like Lena did, because there wasn't any work?"

"Okay," she said, letting her head fall back, taking in a noisy breath. "Things are tough all over.

And what am I talking to you for, anyway? You're the enemy too."

"I'm not the enemy."

"Aren't you? Then what are you here for?"

"For myself," Reese said. "I'm neutral. I'm a bystander."

"There aren't any bystanders," Molly said. "What was it your father used to say? 'If you're not part of the solution you're part of the problem?' "

"That was a long time ago."

"I guess it was."

Reese started for the door.

"Reese?" She was standing up, arms at her sides.

He walked back to her and she put her arms around his chest. "You're getting fat," she said.

"I'm getting old."

"I'm sorry. I'm sorry for what I said. I guess . . . I guess I just needed somebody to tell me everything's going to be all right. It's a father's job, you know."

Reese smoothed back her hair.

"Goddamn you," she said. "Couldn't you lie about it? Just this once?"

●　　●　　●

Leaving Blok and Valentin in the kitchen, Mayakenska closed herself in the rear bedroom and unfolded her keyboard.

The few pieces of yellow plastic furniture in the
house were coated with dust. The air, newly
pumped in on Blok's instructions, had the metallic
tang of the chemistry labs at the university. The
keyboard hung over both sides of the flimsy desk
and she had to perch on a corner of the bed to
play.

Her brief spasms of guilt had given way to a
sense of mortality. If the dome was destroyed she
would die with it, probably in a flash of light and
pain as an expanding embolus of nitrogen tore
out a piece of her brain. Was that an excuse for her
part in it?

She plugged in her headphones and tried to cap-
ture the cool discipline of Brubeck's "Picking Up
Sticks."

A perfect world would not demand such decisions;
but then, a perfect world would have given her
longer fingers, a better ear, an earlier start, would
have made her a real pianist instead of a clumsy
imposter.

When the second revolution came to Russia,
Mayakenska had been in bed with Valentin, her
cosmonaut lover. She had brought him to her
Zhukovka *dacha* for the weekend, despite gossip

that she was taking advantage of her position to prey on the young, politically susceptible men of the space program she controlled.

The gossip failed to annoy her. There was nothing so sincere, she believed, as a fully erect penis.

The first time the phone rang she was preoccupied by the delicious anguish of Valentin's teeth on her nipple. When it rang a second time, waking Valentin from a vodka stupor, she knew it had to be serious. Hardly anyone used the phone in Soviet Russia; because it was so little used it was low on the government's priority for repairs, perpetuating a vicious circle.

She pushed Valentin aside and got to the phone by the fourth ring. "*Allo?*" she said, and a male voice at the other end echoed her, "*Allo?*"

Fear of telephones, Mayakenska thought, will one day destroy us. "This is Mayakenska," she said tiredly. "What do you want?"

"Petrov here," the voice said. "Listen, I thought you should know. Everything is . . . it's crazy here. Novikov is dead."

"Dead?" she repeated. He'd been premier less than three weeks, not even long enough to solidify his power. "Assassinated?"

"Arrested."

"You've got to be joking. Arrested by whom?"

"The Army. He was charged with sedition and, uh, 'shot while trying to escape' or something. We think there was meant to be a trial and somebody just screwed it up. Everything's changing so fast . . ."

"What about the *cheka?*" Mayakenska asked. It was unthinkable that the KGB could have allowed Novikov to be taken so easily.

"Don't you get it? There is no more *cheka*. The Army is in. The Party is out. Everything is upside down. I just wanted you to know. Be ready for anything." The line went dead.

Outside the open window she could see a jay, shifting from one leg to the other on a narrow branch. She could smell pine needles and spring grasses and the cool dampness of the Moscow River, just beyond the edge of the woods.

And yet, she thought, less than 40 kilometers away, the entire world is coming apart.

Just the day before she had been reading an article on Novikov in *Literaturka*. The illustration showed Novikov's bald head and hollow cheeks defaced by a staff artist, with Stalinesque eyebrows, mustache, and monolithic hair crudely penciled in. The masses, *Literaturka* said, remembered Stalin only as the *krepki khozyain*, the firm master who brought discipline to the young and efficiency to the factories. Novikov had first called attention to himself with his zeal in exceeding the government's Plan, in one case doubling December production in his entire district.

The Army had been alarmed by his belligerence toward China, although the quantum leaps the Chinese had taken in biotechnology had frightened and embarrassed all the world powers. *Literaturka* had made cautious references to Stalin's decimation of the military high command; the censors had passed them, probably because Novikov appreciated the importance of a well-placed threat.

And so, Mayakenska thought, forcing a glass of hot tea into Valentin's hand, the Army had taken Novikov seriously. Between Chinese threats of aggression in North Africa and the ongoing collapse of the Americans there were ample opportunities for a war, but it was clearly a war the Army did not want to fight. Nothing had been said in the press about the mass desertions, mutinies, and racial tensions, but they were common knowledge among the military elite, even for someone like Mayakenska, whose rank was purely honorary.

She had no way of judging what the news would mean to her career, but it would doubtless mean shortages and total confusion in her personal life.

She hurried Valentin into his clothes, keeping the keys to his Zhiguli for herself. She forced herself not to hurry as she led Valentin, cursing and befuddled, out to the car; forced herself not to spray gravel as she pulled out of the driveway.

At the cinderblock village store, called the Krushchev store as long as Mayakenska could remember, the black Zils and Zhigulis already filled the parking lot. The store was reserved for the *nomenklatura*, and access to information was the most valued privilege of the elite.

I should have answered the phone, she thought, the first time it rang.

In the end she did come away with some cheese, bread, and canned meat, but the news she'd learned was more important than steaks or vegetables.

"Have you heard the latest?" someone she knew only vaguely asked her as they waited in the long queue at the cashier.

"Which latest?"

"The mutinies." It was the first time Mayakenska had seen him in anything but a dark suit and tie. Rumor had it he was highly placed in the *cheka*, and his sudden casual clothing seemed to confirm it. "All the non-Russians—the Uzbeks, the Yakuts, the Lithuanians, draftees, all of them—they're refusing to fight."

Back in the car, Mayakenska let her head fall forward onto the wheel, unwilling even to start the car until she could make a decision.

"What's going on?" Valentin asked.

"It's over," she said. "It's all over. All that's left is to save what we can. Whatever we think is important enough." That put it in focus for her. She turned east, toward Moscow.

"Where are you going? Are you crazy? Aren't you going back to the *dacha?*"

"No time," Mayakenska said. "We're going to Zvezdagrad."

"And we're going to *drive* there? You *are* crazy." The Russian secret launch complex was in Kazakhstan, thousands of kilometers from Moscow.

"No," Mayakenska said. "We'll take a helicopter from Kaliningrad."

"That's on the other side of Moscow. We don't know how bad it is in the city. They could be rioting there."

In Valentin's groping for excuses she saw the weakness of the age. It was the legacy of the west, this loss of moral certainty. Mayakenska had never understood it or had any patience with it. For her the difficulty lay in finding the correct path to follow. Once the choice was made, the required actions were mindless and simple. What difference did a little hardship make if hardship was what was required?

"Rioting?" she teased him. "Are you implying the masses are not happy with the socialist state?"

Valentin stared at her for an instant with bloodshot eyes, then turned away to watch the thick pine forest whip past the car. "That's really funny," he said, eventually. "Sometimes you really make me laugh."

He was married, Mayakenska suddenly remembered. No children, she was fairly sure, and he'd never mentioned his wife, but it was possible he was concerned for her.

"I can let you off in the city," she told him, "if you want. Otherwise I'll go around, stay off the highways."

He was silent so long she thought he might not have heard her at all. Then, finally, he shook his head. "Go on. I'm with you."

Once they left the main highway they were confined to dirt and gravel roads. A month before they would have been axle-deep in red mud, but spring was giving way to summer, the roads were dry, and the entire countryside was in flower. This is what it's like, Mayakenska thought, to truly be Russian; even now, with chaos closing in, she wanted to stop the car and bury her face in the sweet, fertile earth of *rodina*, Mother Russia. It was a love that never conflicted with her other single greatest desire: to touch the red soil of Russia's furthest colony.

She was too valuable, the Party had told her, to be risked in the cosmonaut program. There were simply not enough high-ranking women to serve as examples of the Party's mythical lack of sexism, and far too many disasters in space. They didn't care that the promise of Mars had lured her into the Army from her engineering career in the first place; they assumed a promotion and authority over the program would be enough.

What the Party didn't know was that she had trained alongside the cosmonauts, studied all their textbooks, sat through all their lectures, sculpted her body into better condition than those of women half her age. It brought her the respect of her students, and when her moment came, she knew she would be ready.

She never got the chance. By the time the Americans sent their last expedition to shut down the Frontera base, the Soviet Union was overextended at home. Crop failures and famine were more important than prestige in space, and Marsgrad was left to find its own way.

That had been five years ago. Mayakenska had not even heard of the Marsgrad fire from her own people, but read about it in the New York *Times*. Her friends, cosmonauts she had trained, had been abandoned there; she had no way of knowing which of them had survived the fire and made it to the American base. Not that it mattered, for surely the Americans were dead now as well.

So why was Zvezdagrad so important to her? It was a question she hardly needed to ask herself. Without Zvezdagrad, Russia would not go into space again, not within her lifetime. And if she didn't save it, no one would.

She parked the Zhiguli outside Mission Control in Kaliningrad as the sun was beginning to set. The base was an anthill that had been kicked to pieces: abandoned vehicles blocked the streets, civilians and soldiers swarmed over the grounds without apparent purpose. Holding her embossed red work pass in front of her, Mayakenska began shouting orders to anyone who would listen. Within minutes she had the base sealed off; by the time it was fully dark she and Valentin were on a helicopter headed for Tyuratam. On her instructions the big Kama trucks were already carrying every piece of space hardware she had been able to locate toward the Central Asian steppes.

If nothing else, she thought, watching the endless miles of empty land unroll into the night, she had gained an appreciation of the way Novikov had risen so quickly. The workers at Kaliningrad, even the officers, had seemed absurdly grateful for any voice of authority. The dissidents who wanted a truly democratic society in Russia had no idea of the enormity of what they were asking.

"So," Valentin said, his blond good looks even more wasted and sickly-looking in the green light of the control panel, "now we will have Zvezdagrad. What are we going to do with it?"

"Hold it," Mayakenska said. "Hold it and wait."

She held Zvezdagrad for seven months, the longest seven months of her life. She took cows and goats and chickens from the nearby village of Tyuratam at gunpoint, then offered the villagers sanctuary within her walls. They refused, of course; from the outside the space center looked depressingly like a Gulag, with its miles of barbed wire and its grim cinderblock buildings.

Most of the villagers died a few weeks later when the People's Independent Army of Kazakhstan swept through the steppes like a modern Mongol horde, on the backs of jeeps and dune buggies and balloon-tired motorcycles, armed with Kalishnikov machine guns and towing what appeared to be a tactical nuclear ground-to-ground missile.

Mayakenska let them pass. They in turn seemed to feel the center wasn't worth the trouble of getting past the fortifications. The surviving villagers didn't agree. They attacked Zvezdagrad with the puny weapons they had available, and Mayakenska saw no way to reason with them. She ordered her people to fire on them, and they lived with the stench of decaying bodies for the next two weeks.

The radio, when it worked, brought news of the capital. The *chekists* had been the first to try to fill the power vacuum. While their communication lines were second to none, the apex of their power structure had been amputated in the Army coup. Without experienced leadership their authority never solidified. Looters began shooting anyone in KGB gray uniforms and the rape of Moscow went on.

In the end it was the unions that began to organize the pieces. Under the old order they had been just another arm of the state, responsible for morale and unemployment benefits, but when the first cases of cholera appeared on the streets, they extended their responsibilities. Mayakenska began to hear words like "corporate infrastructure" and "bottom line" on the radio. Using the *zaibatsus* and the multinationals for models, the unions put together a new, decentralized society.

On New Year's Eve she put the traditional three pieces of paper under her pillow and went to sleep, alone, sober, and aching with hunger. In the morning she pulled out one of the pieces, unfolded it, saw the words "Good Year."

"Please," she said, sitting on the edge of the bed, glad there was no one to see her crying. "Please."

She sent a cable to the old Aeroflot address in Moscow that afternoon. Within a week the first company representatives had flown out to see what could be done with several square kilometers of vintage space hardware. Mayakenska was awarded the honorary rank of vice president and all her loyal supporters were hired by the company.

"There is one condition," she said, staring at the fine, meaningless print of the "contract" they wanted her to sign. "If there is another mission to Mars, I will be on it."

"No problem," said one of the other vice presidents. He was western educated, and wore glasses with colored frames, a silk shirt and tie, and *dzhinsy* pants.

"Write it down," she said. "Write it in your contract."

The company representatives looked at each other, and then they shrugged. The vice president with the colored glasses amended the contract and Mayakenska signed it and they all shook hands. And then, because they were Russians, the vodka bottle finally appeared and they drank to the dawn of a new age.

They seemed to expect her to retire to her *dacha* and her pension, but instead she brought her cosmonauts back to Kaliningrad and the training facilities at Zvezdny Gorodok. For three years she put up with the bemused acceptance of her new superiors. She would have put up with it for another ten, but she didn't have to. Word had come from one of the moles buried deep within Pul-systems of the incredible discoveries at Frontera base.

"We are ready," she told her board of directors, and less than three months later she was back at Zvezdagrad, strapped into a modified Soyuz, pointed at Mars.

For Mayakenska, history was the irrelevant process by which a present moment was constructed. By extension, the present was no more than a tool for shaping the future. And this, she told herself, thinking of the laser orbiting over her head, is what I have to do.

She shifted into the slow arpeggios of Max Middleton's solo from "Diamond Dust." From countless listenings she could recreate the string section in her mind, lacing their minor chords through the notes of the piano. Jazz music, for Mayakenska, was the only thing of value ever to come from the moral and spiritual desert of American culture. It was a music untainted by capitalist values, at least the best of it was, played only for the joy of the music itself.

The piece worked itself to the finish, climbing to the final B above high C. She loved that note, the way it floated above the rest of the music, the sense of completion it gave to the whole. At last she brought her hands away, unplugged the head-phones, and folded the keyboard again.

She'd slept well before the landing, in order to be strong and alert, and though the martian grav-ity had tired her she could not imagine trying to sleep again. Still not reconciled? she wondered.

Still waiting to find that perfect note, the one that would make sense of this undeniably brutal and imperialistic mission?

After nine months she had been unable to find any answers. The transport device and, more importantly, the antimatter generator, must not become the exclusive property of Pulsystems. It would mean not only the end of Aeroflot, but the end of Russia as any sort of world power.

There was a knock at the door and she said, "Come in."

"Valentin is asleep," Blok said. "Are you all right? Can I get you anything?"

They were questions, she thought, he should be asking himself. His eyes seemed to vibrate with nervousness. "Relax," she said. "There's nothing to worry about. I think Curtis will accept the political realities of his situation."

This was her fault, she knew. She had played Curtis off against Blok at their meeting, polarizing him before he was truly ready to make a choice. But she needed him, needed an inside man to take the load off of herself and Valentin.

"Do you?" Blok said. "I'm not so sure."

He had been one of her most difficult students, a true political, a *Komsomol* member since his teens, with high marks in leadership and poor physical condition. She had done well, she thought, toughened him up enough that he had survived.

"It's out of our hands, in any case," she told him. Blok nodded, started to turn away, and then she had a thought. "Just a second. If you really want to do something for me, you could. Stay and watch things for a few minutes."

"Of course. Get some sleep. You must be worn out."

"No," she said, "I'm fine. I just want to . . . to go outside. Just for a couple of minutes. I don't think anything's going to come up, but if it does you can radio me."

"Let me come with you."

"No. I'll be fine." She reached for her radio and called the orbiter. "This is Mayakenska at 15 hundred hours. Code Dniepr. Repeat, code Dniepr."

"Okay, we have you," said Chaadayev, the command pilot. *"How did they take it?"*

"Not too well. What did you expect?"

"I guess I hadn't really thought about it. Listen, you may be getting some weather down there. Everything's gotten really hazy-looking down to the south."

"Any idea when it's going to get here?"

"Are you kidding? I'm from Moscow. I don't know anything about this shit. But it's heading right for you and it seems to be moving pretty fast. Maybe in a few minutes."

"Okay," Mayakenska said. "We'll call back in an hour." She threw the radio on the bed and stood up.

"Be careful," Blok said. "If that's a sandstorm you don't want to be out in it."

She hugged him. "You always worried too much," she said.

In the changing room she tried on one of the American rigid suits. It fit well, but didn't seem as solid and trustworthy as the Soviet model. She strapped on a life support pack and cycled through the lock.

For the first minute or so she was distracted by

the unfamiliar suit, by the vertiginous pull of gravity, by the rasping sound of her own breath. She had to pick her way through the jetsam of the dome, the ice bags and abandoned science experments, and rows upon rows of solar collectors.

And then she reached the top of a low rise and for the first time she could see a horizon that had no human mark on it, an expanse of orange sand and dark brown rock and hazy, gray-green sky. She sat in the dirt like a child and ran some of it through her gloved fingers.

"Hello, Mars," she said.

The wind swirled around her and tiny grains of sand began to ping against her helmet.

• • •

Kane dreamed of an ocean full of colors, crystalline turquoise over shallow sand, purple where the sluggish living rock of the reefs grew toward the sun, dark, cold blue over the depths.

Ahead was Mount Arganthon, its hollow peak veiled in thin sheets of cloud; off to port he could see the powdery soil and dark green brush of the Cianian coast. The wind was freshening, finally, now that his fifty oarsmen were exhausted and the sun was within a hand's width of the horizon. A gust puffed out the single massive sail in the center of the penteconter and he gave the command to ship oars.

They rode the breeze into the port of Mysia, rich smells of frying oil, ripe fruit, and mingled sweat and perfume drifting across the water of the harbor to meet them. They tied the *Argo* at the dock and climbed into the city by torchlight, the Mysians in crudely dyed *chitons* and *pepla* swarming around them, desperate for news.

Over dinner he stared hungrily at the dark-eyed woman across from him, steam from the charred sheep carcass in the center of the table rising between them. Afterwards, the grease from the meal still smearing his mouth, his nose full of her thick perfume, he plunged his swollen, aching penis into her, holding her wrists against the rocky soil of the hillside, her heavy breasts lolling in the night air, her linen clothes scattered behind them like the wake of the *Argo*, her mouth open in a silent scream of protest or perhaps even pleasure.

When he finished he rocked back onto his knees, sniffing the air. Someone was moving below, on the path that led to the village spring. He let his chiton fall over his loins and crept barefoot down the slope for a better look.

It was Hylas, Herakles' lover, done up in full *kosmētikos*, hair and cheeks dyed red, face blanched, eyebrows painted in, his hair full of flowers. He carried a bronze pitcher over one shoulder.

Kane followed him, irritated that the boy was wandering around unarmed. Hylas was enough trouble as it was, stirring up the other men, afraid to brutalize his hands with an oar, toying with Herakles' unstable emotions. But he was the price that went with Herakles' services.

Kane stood behind a thicket while Hylas bent over the still surface of the water. The moon was high and Kane could see that they were alone, but his calf muscles were jumping and the air smelled wrong, smelled like rain though the sky was clear.

The water of the spring began to move.

Ripples Kane could have understood, but what he saw was the entire surface tilting and swaying. At the same time it began to glow, an oily sheen like glistening fat, but with rainbow colors melting and turning inside. The air began to hum and Kane felt the hairs on his legs and arms stand straight away from his body. The Gods, he thought, they're moving . . .

Hylas disappeared.

"Hylas!" The scream came from Herakles, trampling the path like an entire army.

Kane stepped out in front of him, said, "Reese, stop!" not knowing why he used the strange-sounding name.

Herakles knocked him aside. As he tumbled into the dirt Kane saw Herakles circled with a light like the phantom fire that danced from the masts of ships. And then Herakles was gone.

The water shimmered and heaved, and before it went still again Kane saw the image of a cup, and a strange, curved sword, and finally the Fleece itself, the wool heavy with glittering particles of gold.

"Kane?"

The voice came from the spring, a woman's voice, stirring something just out of the reach of his consciousness.

"Kane, snap out of it!"

He crawled toward the water, feeling the sand soften and pucker under him, light flooding his eyes, blinding him . . .

"Jesus, I thought I'd lost you for a moment there. What the hell happened to you?"

Kane focused, saw a woman with a dark, sculpted face looming over him. Fragments of the ancient sailor's personality still clung to his own, making him feel drugged, dissociated from himself. Gradually he recognized Lena, remembered having brawled with Curtis in the airlock.

"Kane? Are you all right? Can you talk at all?"

He had trouble hearing her. The voices were filling all the unused spaces in his brain, had moved smoothly from the dream into this other reality with their echoing harmony. "What did you give me?" he asked, feeling a sudden wash of chemical energy shoot through his spine.

"Adrenogen," Lena said. Kane nodded. He'd heard rumors of the stuff from his uncle's chemists, supposedly some kind of synthetic hormone that forced the body to produce massive quantities of adrenaline. He felt light-headed and barely in control of his emotions, alternately terrified, enraged, and moved nearly to tears by the music in his brain.

"You pulled me out of this," he said. "Why? I thought you were with Curtis . . ."

"Yeah," she said. "I was with him. He's a sick fuck, Kane. Full of power—political, personal, sexual, you name it. But he's hooked on it, and now his whole midway ride is starting to come apart on him."

"The Russians," Kane said, remembering.

"Yeah, the Russians. They're going to laser this whole place into a junkyard at midnight. That's like three hours from now. Maybe sooner if somebody panics. It's time for us to get the hell out of here."

"No," Kane said.

"Listen, man, there's stuff you don't know about. Your uncle fucked with your head. I'm not talking about brainwashing here, I mean some really serious shit, some kind of implant wetware that we don't even *know* what it's doing."

"Implant," Kane said. "Jesus."

"Something about North Africa, Takahashi said. They had to put it in to get your brain to function at all, or something. He said they can swap programs in and out of it like changing cassettes in a tape player."

The sequences began to click into place for him: the years of stunted ambition, the phantom voices distracting him; the cryogenics briefcase with a new module to be installed, the subliminals to activate it, the headaches, the dreams, the music. "How long have you known about it?"

"Me? Just since last night. But Takahashi's known all along, him and your uncle both."

"Yeah, sure he would. But he'd have to. It's just part of the Pattern, see?"

"See what?"

"My father died on the Gulf Freeway, an axle broke or something and he went into a concrete embankment. I was seven, I was in the car, and I got thrown clear. I was wearing those Mexican sandals, *huaraches*, and one of them got blown away. When my uncle came to get me at the hospital, I was just wearing *one sandal*."

Lena stared at him as if he were raving.

"Don't you see?" Kane said. "That's how Pelias was supposed to recognize the man that was going to kill him. Which was Jason. So Pelias sent him after the Fleece, thinking he would never make it back."

"Greek mythology," Lena said. "Do you know where you are? Do you understand what's happening?"

"I'm on Mars. Where my uncle sent me to die. But that's only a piece of it. It's the entire Pattern that's important. Separation, initiation, and return. Where we are now is the Penetration to the Source of Power." Kane sat up, saw that he was on a bare, stained mattress in a deserted living module. Empty bottles, hypos, and various plastic wrappers littered the floor. "Where is this place?"

"Curtis calls it 'Little Juarez.' Charming, isn't it?"

"We're looking for a cave. That's where it is, usually, like where Orpheus goes into hell to rescue Eurydice."

"Curtis's kid is in a cave," Lena said.

"What?"

She looked startled, as if she hadn't meant to say it out loud. "There's some kind of a cave out on the slope of the volcano. A bunch of the kids moved out there, including Curtis's little girl."

"Why? What are they doing out there?"

"I kind of got the impression there's something wrong with them. Birth defects, genetic damage, like that. Jesus. There's a couple of lifetimes' worth of work up here and they won't even let me *see* those kids."

"Then that must be where it is."

"Where what is?"

"The source of power. Like the Fleece, or the Grail, or Susa-no-wo's sword."

"Kane, man, this is not a *myth*. This is happening. Real Russians, real lasers, real corpses, real soon."

"But what if the other was real, too? Like some kind of *tension* in the universe, and it has to keep happening over and over again until somebody gets it right. See, because Jason got the Fleece but he didn't do it right and ended up all alone, an outcast. Percival gets to see the grail, but he doesn't get to keep it. Yamato-Takeru was a great warrior but his spirit was weak and that was what killed him."

"And now it's your turn? Is that it?"

"Maybe."

"I've got a better idea. All this mythology shit, that's what you did in college, right? So your uncle puts this implant in your skull because there's something up here he wants you to do for him and he doesn't trust you to do what you're told. Only the biotic circuit isn't quite hooked up right, or maybe it is but you're fighting it too hard, and as a result all his orders are getting filtered through a layer of intellectual bullshit, and it comes out in these crazy fantasies of yours."

"This isn't just some intellectual exercise. I've been *seeing* all this shit, reliving it."

"Those dreams, you mean. Where you woke up screaming."

"More than dreams. It was like I was really *there*."

"Yeah, okay, that's fine, but none of that is any reason for *us* staying *here*. As soon as I can get Takahashi off the computer in the sick bay we should get the hell off this planet."

"Computer? He said something about that. What's he doing?"

"It looks innocent enough but apparently he's shuttling all the scientific data from their computer into a blind file where it's being transmitted to the ship."

"Doesn't he need some kind of access codes to get into their files?"

"He's got all the overrides. Who do you think built their computer?"

"Oh," Kane said. "Yeah. Morgan. Does everybody but me know what's going on around here?"

"Morgan had this all planned. Haven't you got that figured out yet? He can trust Takahashi because Takahashi's loyal to the company. You he doesn't have to trust. He's got you wired. He owns you."

"And you?"

"I'm just desperate," Lena said. "I don't know enough to hurt him and I don't have anyplace else to go."

"And Reese? What about him?"

"Reese is out of it."

Out of it, Kane thought. There had been something in that last dream, something about Reese. He'd called Reese's name . . . His stomach squirmed with unease and the adrenaline amplified it toward panic. "I have to find him," he said. "Where is he?"

"I haven't seen him all day. I can't tell you. But I think you should let him go. He's off on some private trip of his own. Just let him play it out, and you and me and Takahashi will save ourselves."

Kane stood up. The adrenaline leveled the room and kept him on his feet. "We need him. Where's this cave you were talking about? Could you find it?"

"No way. And neither could you. There's a duststorm blowing up out there. If we launch right now, we should still be okay. If we wait around we're going to get stuck here."

Kane pushed past her into the empty living room and started to open the front door. The resistance against his pull reminded him that he needed a mask and he looked around for one.

"Don't do this, Kane."

He saw the tank lying in a corner by the door and slung it under his arm. "I'll be back," he said.

Night had nearly fallen; a swollen, refracted sun oozed through a cloud that covered the horizon. Most of the window boxes along the west wall were occupied, but the colonists showed only a minimal interest in the approaching storm. They'd seen it all before, Kane thought. To them it would be as dull as rain in the tropics of Earth. At least half of them looked drunk or sedated, their faces slack and accepting. The adrenaline made Kane feel like a blur of light in a slow motion film.

He followed his voices to the south air lock, moved in a near frenzy through the neatly stacked helmets and life-support packs. That afternoon he thought he'd seen an infrared helmet, the only sure way he had of tracking Reese through the dust and darkness.

Assuming he was right, assuming Reese was with the kids in the cave. But he had to be. That was the Pattern.

Some of the RX suits still lay sprawled on the floor like blast victims; under one of them Kane found the helmet. He slipped it over his head and powered up. The room shifted into cool yellows and greens, Kane's handprints showing like orange bruises on the suit he'd just turned over.

He took off the helmet and suited up, the dexterity of his fingers unable to keep up with the urgency screaming in his brain. Finally, almost as an afterthought, he opened the locker where he'd left his hipari and took out the Colt .38.

A gift from Morgan, he now realized. With a hypnotic—or implanted—instruction to forget it until the subliminals had turned on his software in Deimos space. He still wasn't quite sure what he was to do with it, but that too, he felt confident, would come to him.

This time he thought to check the cylinder of the gun; dull brass showed in five of the chambers, with the last, under the hammer, empty. Kane threw out a can of emergency rations and fitted the pistol into his chest-pack, barely getting the velcro fasteners closed over it.

He was raising the helmet into place when he saw the blood.

Three coin-sized splatters lay on the floor under the airlock controls; a long smear, carrying a single thumbprint, stretched across the edge of the airlock door. Kane did not doubt for an instant that it was Reese's.

He sealed the O-rings on his helmet and crossed through the airlock into the desert. Heat puffed out in yellow clouds around him as he stepped out onto the dark green regolith. Arsia Mons was preternaturally clear in the infrared screen of the helmet, sharply profiled in shades of yellow-green. As he moved toward the mountain he began to see Reese's footprints as faintly lighter splotches on the cold green ground. Then, behind a tall vertical outcrop, he saw the edges of a metal airlock, glowing an inviting red.

The wind around him was strong enough to lift particles of sand, meaning a wind velocity of close to a hundred miles an hour, but the air itself was so thin that he could barely feel its resistance. The electronics of his helmet divided the last blue-white light of the sunset into quantified brightness bands, the pattern distorted by the turbulence of the upper atmosphere.

The eerie, digitally-processed beauty of the night had only a peripheral effect on Kane; it was a stage set, a cyclorama, for a play in which he had been completely consumed by his role.

His voices sang to him as he climbed the shining mountain.

• • •

His last throw of the *I Ching* had given Reese hexagram 56, *Lü*, the Wanderer. "Strange lands and separation are the wanderer's lot." "Fire on the mountain" was the image, and Reese pictured Arsia Mons blazing in volcanic splendor, the way it must have looked hundreds of thousands of years ago.

He put the coins in the pocket of his pants, a final, sentimental gesture, and put the book into the duffel under his bed. He could not seem to get warm. He knew it was the hypothermia of dread, his central nervous system desensitizing him for imminent disaster.

Takahashi sat in the next room, programming some complex swindle into the main computer. Reese didn't want to interrupt, but time was running out.

He stood behind Takahashi's chair and watched the cursor shooting across lines of programming. "Listen, man," he said. "There's trouble."

"What kind?" Takahashi's concentration did not waver; his fingers rattled the keyboard like a maraca.

"Russians."

"Have they landed yet?"

I shouldn't be surprised, Reese thought. He's known everything else. "Half of them here, half still in orbit, with a laser."

Takahashi nodded and fed his program to the compiler. "Are they going to use it, you think?"

"Yeah," Reese said. "I think they are. They gave Curtis until midnight, but I don't think Curtis is going to play."

"Curtis is an asshole. What does this do to your plans?"

"My plans?" Reese said.

"I'm not stupid, Reese. I know what those kids have. I heard the same tape you did, and others besides. I know what was in that base camp on Deimos—an astrometry unit. I could see the diskette under your shirt yesterday and today it's gone."

"Don't try to stop me, Takahashi."

"I wouldn't dream of it," he said, turning back to scan for errors.

"I don't get you. If Morgan knew—"

"Morgan doesn't know. I didn't send him any message last night. The last he heard we were heading down toward the surface yesterday morning." Takahashi almost smiled. "I expect he's half out of his mind."

"What kind of game are you playing? I thought you were Morgan's man, all the way."

"I'm a company man," Takahashi said. "There's a difference. But none of that is important now. You get on out of here and I'll do what I can about the Russians."

"Takahashi, I—"

Takahashi shook his head. "Good luck," he said.

Reese took his hand. "Thanks," he said, and left him there.

In the long afternoon under the dome the martians were carrying on with their fishbowl lives.

By now Molly would be huddled with Curtis, no doubt trying to talk him out of some desperate cowboy-and-indian shoot-out with the Russians. He'd already said goodbye to her anyway, as best he could. He would have liked to have seen Kane one more time, to somehow divest himself of the responsibility he felt for Kane's being here, to shed the paternal role he'd never wanted.

But maybe it would be easier this way.

He recognized the dark clouds boiling out of the south and thought they could only make it easier for him to get away from the dome. He could feel his emotions pulling back deeper inside him, the way the heat of his body had pulled back toward the core, cutting him off from the rest of the world, severing the connections. Soon, he thought, he would look like one of the zombie farmers, with no recognition left in his eyes.

He fought not to respond to the colors of the evening, so rich that he could almost smell them through his oxygen mask: the damp ground of the fields, the sharp yellows and browns of pineapples, the soft pinks of flowering cacti. *All things are full of weariness*, he told himself, *a man cannot utter it*. He thought instead of the narrow, filmy rings of Uranus, of the green, staring eye of the planetary nebula in Lyra.

He went into the south changing room and closed the door.

Something had happened here earlier today; the suits and helmets had been badly knocked around. Reese ignored the damage, took an extra large suit from the far end of the rack and started to take his shoes off.

"Reese."

He turned, saw Blok standing in the doorway.

"What are you doing?" Blok said, his nervousness driving his voice even lower than its normal slavic pitch.

"I'm going up to the cave, Blok." He wasn't sure why the words came out. It seemed to him he might just as easily have said nothing at all.

"I can't let you do that," Blok said. Reese looked up again, and this time Blok was holding a 7mm Luger.

"So," Reese said. "It's Russia again. I thought you were beyond that. I thought you were part of the colony now."

"Don't patronize me, Reese. What do you know about loyalties? Who do you have to be loyal to? Your fellow astronauts? Your family?"

Reese flinched, his guilt feelings at abandoning Jenny to her husband suddenly fresh in his mind again. He could have tried harder to get through to her, maybe won her away, and saved her life. . . .

Stop it, he told himself. There's no point in torturing yourself. It's too late for any of that.

"You can't even understand how I think," Blok went on. "You can't understand what *rodina* means to a Russian. You don't even have the word in your language, just ghosts of it. 'Homeland.' What does that mean? You can't even translate the idea."

"This isn't to do with you," Reese said. "It doesn't have anything to do with Russia or America or Frontera or anything else. This is just for me."

"That's naive, Reese. You know better. There is no such thing as a non-political act. Everything is political. And I cannot let you leave. Nobody leaves until this whole thing is sorted out."

Reese stood up. "You can't use the gun in here, Blok. It's too dangerous."

Blok steadied his right hand with his left. "Then don't force me."

Reese took a step toward him, but Blok stood his ground.

"Put it away," Reese said. "Please. This is something I have to do."

They were less than six feet apart. Reese stared at the distorted proportions of the Luger, the swollen barrel, the arms stretching away forever behind it. It seemed to Reese that Blok would probably use the gun. It was like poker, he thought. There were times you paid to see the hole card, even when you already knew what it was going to be. Because, he thought, there were just certain hands you had to pay for.

He took another step and Blok fired.

For a second Reese could not connect the loud, sharp snap of the pistol with the shove that rocked him back on his feet, with the point of heat in his left shoulder that was at the same time numbingly cold. Then his forebrain put it into one-syllable words for him: *I've been shot.*

Before Blok could fire again Reese stepped in and put his own, larger hands around the gun. His left arm was nearly useless, but with the strength of his right he began to crush Blok's fingers, pushing the barrel of the gun up and back, until Blok whimpered and tried to let go, and Reese pushed the gun back hard, catching Blok across the bridge of his nose and down one cheek with the barrel.

Blok slipped to his knees and Reese pulled the gun away with his left hand, the fingers stiff and desensitized, swinging his right fist around, trying for the jaw but bouncing painfully off the cheekbone instead. He stood back, breathing hard, and watched Blok sway for a second, then topple slowly forward onto his face.

The bullet had torn through the trapezius muscle of Reese's shoulder and dimpled the durofoam behind him, lodging in the structural plastic of the wall without cracking it. A good thing, he thought, I was there to slow it down.

There was a good deal of blood. He touched the hole in his shoulder and had to steady himself against the doorframe, leaving a trail on the enameled metal. He found a first aid kit and sprayed both sides of the wound with K platelets, feeling the skin prickle and tighten as the tangle of fibrin formed quickly into a scab.

He had to put the Luger down to get into the gloves of the suit; when he was finished, he fitted the gun back into the limp fingers, not knowing what else to do with it. A sizzling ache spread through the muscles of his back, making his throat tighten and his eyes water. The first aid kit contained a vial of Butorphanol, but Reese closed the cover before the temptation got the better of him. He was not going to stagger through this in an analgesic haze.

He had to start moving. He cycled through the lock and walked toward the setting sun, watching the south wind pump billows of dust into the twilight. The kids' cave had been the first permanent outpost on Mars; his feet knew the way, even if shock had left him a little faint and clumsy. He crawled into the airlock and lay still as the atmosphere blew in around him, reality flickering on and off as he fought to get his breath.

"He's hurt," somebody said, and the helmet came off his head. Somebody else handed him a dish of beet sugar and a glass of water and he lapped up the sugar with his tongue, the taste of it alternating between nauseating sweetness and the bitterness of sand.

"How bad is it?" Verb asked, squatting in front of him.

He blinked. He sat propped against one wall, looking out on a room of endless darkness, punctuated by cones of intense white light. Under two of the cones he could see children typing rapidly into CRT's; under a third, a Rhesus monkey ate popcorn out of a wastebasket. Verb's slightly pop-eyed stare was centered on the blood at the edge of his neck.

"Not . . . serious," he said. "Just let me get my wind back, I'll be okay." He saw the gun still clinging to his useless left hand and shook it loose, pushing it away from him across the floor.

"You're bleeding," Verb said. "You don't look good."

"It's superficial," Reese said. "I sprayed it, it's okay. Really."

"Don't fool around with me," Verb said. "Okay? Because this is important to me, too. I can't have you dying on me."

"I wouldn't dream of it."

"Okay, then. Because it looks good. It looks really good." Her face shone with a thin film of sweat and her body gave off a sharp odor of excitement. "Crunch, do the lights, okay?" One by one the spots blinked off, and Reese felt his pulse skittering away from the totality of the darkness, the darkness like a sensory dep tank, like blindness, like death.

"Crunch has got a program," Verb said. "You run that map you gave us through a hologram projector, and set it for a very small scale . . ."

Pinpoints of light appeared in the darkness, not giving off enough illumination to locate the walls or floor, instead creating the illusion of stars in infinite space. And then, gradually, they began to move. A trinary system spun past his face, and below his legs he could see the dense, exploding gas at the heart of the galaxy. In the distance floated the purple smears of the great nebulas, and beyond them tiny quasars spat high-intensity radiation out through the tornadoes at their poles. All of them visible at once, crammed together, blazing with life.

Reese felt the hard, hot kernel of despair that had brought him this far begin to melt, to transform itself back into its original components of wonder, awe, and burning ambition.

"You'll go through in your suit," Verb said. "We've got a parachute and some survival gear just in case, including some food and water and extra air. There's a transmitter that will let us know if you made it. Eventually, that is. About twelve years from now, for the round trip."

"Okay," Reese said.

"We're shooting for a kilometer above what we think is the surface of an Earth-size planet. We could screw up and put you underground, in which case you explode, or we may put you so far out you'll burn up on the way down. There may not be any air for the chute to grab. It could be a gas planet in which case none of this matters anyway. Okay?"

"Okay," Reese said.

"It may not work at all."

"Do it," Reese said. "Let's go." He didn't know if it was the sugar, the aftereffects of circulatory shock, or Verb's dazzling light show, but he was euphoric, nearly manic. He got to his feet, felt like he was flying through the universe without a ship.

"Crunch!"

In the darkness between two arms of the galaxy a cold, cloudy rectangle began to glow, then shimmered and fluoresced into an oily rainbow of colors. Reese took a halting step toward it, disoriented by the invisibility of the physical room. Large, soft hands moved over his injured arm, attaching the parachute and some kind of knapsack. He shrugged into the harness, wincing at the pressure over the wound, and tightened all the straps. He pushed his helmet back into place and switched the radio to EXT.

"What do I do?" he asked, his mouth dry again.

"You just walk through. The next thing you know you'll be there. Even if you were conscious, which you won't be, there's no such thing as time when you're moving that fast."

Reese felt himself nodding. He slid one foot forward and his ankle brushed the edge of a desk; he felt his way around it with his good hand, never taking his eyes from the glistening doorway. He could see the hard metal edges now, could almost reach it if he stretched out his hand.

The room flooded with light.

He turned, saw a suited figure crawling out of the lock.

"Reese," said a droning, mechanical voice from the suit. "Reese, stop."

"Kane?"

Kane pulled the helmet off. "Reese! For god's sake, man, get away from there!" In the harsh light of the airlock Kane's face was lunar white, his eyes luminous craters. Reese could read comprehension in his expression, but no understanding. Their eyes locked, and Reese felt the anguish of Kane's rootlessness, the depth of his betrayal.

Explain it to him, Reese thought. Tell him that you're not some Greek hero, noble, selfless, dealing justice with swift, righteous arrows. Tell him he's on his own. Tell him.

The biggest of the children, a giant with the distorted jaw and fingers of acromegaly, put a hand against Kane's chest, and Reese saw him flinch from the pain in his ribs.

"I'm sorry," Reese whispered, his suit radio turning the words flat and metallic. "I'm sorry, Kane. But you don't need me anymore." As he heard his own words, Reese realized they were true. "You never did," he said.

He raised one hand, the cold in his chest and testicles consuming him, robbing him of his voice. He turned away from Kane and walked slowly through the shimmering doorway.

● ● ●

"Three hours," Curtis said, "seven minutes, and about fifteen seconds left."

"Maybe they're bluffing," Molly said.

She'd been through too much too quickly, she thought: Dian's murder, Kane's arrest, the Russian threat, and now this, her first sight of Curtis's inner sanctum. She'd seen the bank of monitors at his secretary's desk, but nothing had prepared her for this, another entire room that opened out of the back of his office, lined on both sides with monitor screens.

At the far end of the room sat one of Curtis's lieutenants, a bearded, good-looking Brazilian named Alonzo who'd once made a rather blatant and unsuccessful pass at her. He'd been carrying on an obvious attempt to ignore her bickering with Curtis for over fifteen minutes now.

"Russian technology, you know," Molly went on. "It's not exactly dependable."

Unlike this stuff, she thought. The cameras could be operated by remote control and each held up to three hours of continuous updated information that could be replayed in programmable sequences. It shocked and frightened Molly that so many of the colony's resources could have been diverted into such a comprehensive and insidious program of surveillance. They had let it happen, all of them had, and she was just as guilty as anyone else.

"They offered us a demonstration," Curtis said nastily. "You want to take them up on it? What would you like to lose? The ice reservoirs, maybe? How about the cave, and all the kids up there, and that goddamned secret project of yours? All we have to do is ask."

It seemed to Molly that he had been walking for some time now along the cliff-edge of some kind of epiphany, a revelation that would fuse the disparate aspects of his personality into a single, unified whole. Maybe, she thought, it would turn out to be a true apotheosis, that he would somehow save Frontera in a bare-chested act of heroism. More likely it would be a spectacular, shattering collapse. He was coming unraveled at an ever-increasing rate, caught in some kind of runaway neurogenic disaster.

"Okay," she said. "Okay. They're not bluffing. So how much longer are you going to just sit here?" His cameras had followed Mayakenska as she'd taken her walk, then followed her back to her room. The house was dark now, Valentin sitting on a spotlit stool in the kitchen to phone in the hourly codes. They now had three of those calls on tape.

"Until I think of something," Curtis said. "Like figure out the codes, or *something*."

"They're using mission designations from the Salyut program," Molly said. "I saw them in a book once. They probably have to be in chronological order or something. But I don't see what that gives us."

Curtis looked startled, then embarrassed. "You're

probably right. It's not much, but it's a start. If we have to, now we can—"

"Curtis," Alonzo said. "You'd better look at this."

Molly spun around in her chair and followed his pointing finger. All she could see was an ordinary star field.

"Christ!" Curtis shouted. "That's the camera in the cave! Are they jamming us?"

"I don't think so," Alonzo said. His nerves, Molly thought, were suffering too; she could see nasty red discolorations through the beard on the underside of his chin. "I think it's some kind of holo projection in the cave itself."

"Back up the memory," Curtis ordered, "and put it on another unit." Molly watched as a second screen filled with the star field. Then the stars winked out and she could see Verb bent over a suited figure.

"Reese!" she shouted. Her chair shot away as she came to her feet. "He's hurt. Back up the camera at the south lock, catch him on the way out."

Alonzo glanced at Curtis, who nodded. "Do it."

On a third screen Molly watched Reese move backward in time, backing out of the airlock, turning, lurching into Blok's unconscious body as it rose from the floor. She watched a bullet dig itself out of the wall and suck a thin line of smoke into the barrel of Blok's gun.

"Oh my christ," Molly said.

On the real-time screen an oily pool of light had formed in the center of the cave. A shadow moved across it: Reese, in his suit, silhouetted against the opalescent field of energy.

"Stop him!" Molly shouted. "For god's sake, somebody stop him!" She lunged for the microphone to radio the cave, but Curtis wrenched her away by one arm.

"No," he said. His head shone in the dim, flickering light of the screens, reflected images distorting his features. "I want to see this."

"He can't . . . they can't let him go through there! It isn't tested! He . . ."

The milky glow touched the edges of Reese's suit, flared, and consumed him.

Curtis let go of her arm, and Molly sank into one of the chairs, feeling betrayed, frightened, on the verge of hysteria.

"Well," Curtis said. "This is getting really interesting. Do you want to tell me some more about how those kids are just playing around with theoretical physics? About how we should just let the Russians have anything they want? Jesus, Molly, I can't believe you let things get this far without telling me."

My father, she thought. The words carried an eerie emotional weight. She'd always called him Reese, never Father, never Daddy. Daddy was the stranger who had lived with her mother, and died with her on the *Gerard K. O'Neill*. There were no precut words that fit Reese and what he meant to her.

What could have been so important to him that he thought he had to risk that weird machine? Where had Verb sent him? Not back to Earth, that made no sense at all.

Outward, then. Like father, like daughter, both obsessed with the outward urge.

Not that it mattered, because now he was dead. Probably dead the instant he stepped into the energy field, but if not, then he'd be dead at the other end, was now only a probability wave whose value was death, death by explosion, by fire, cold, or vacuum.

She tried to picture it, to use the pain to cauterize the wound.

"Alonzo," Curtis said. "Get three or four of your people, whoever you can find, and get them to the south airlock. We'll meet you there."

Alonzo squeezed between Molly's chair and the console, his eyes moving expressionlessly past her face.

"Come on," Curtis said. He pulled at her arm, trying to make her stand up. She stared at him blankly. "Come on!" he repeated.

She got to her feet. "Where . . . ?"

"I've had it. Okay? I've had it. I'm through fucking around. It's answer time."

"What do you mean? What are you doing?"

She followed him down the stairs, stumbling a little in trying to match his pace. It wasn't until they passed the last row of living modules that she realized where he was taking her.

"We can't go out there," she said. "The storm—"

"Fuck the storm," Curtis said. "We know the way."

Molly didn't answer. The danger was not in getting lost, and certainly not in being blown around by the wind, which didn't have the friction velocity to lift anything larger than a pebble. The danger came from the sheer quantity of fine particles in the air, particles that could clog or abrade the worn, delicate mechanisms of their suits.

Molly stripped off her foolish orange suit and put on a pair of recycled cotton pants and a T-shirt from her locker. As she was getting into the bottom half of the suit, Alonzo came in with three reinforcements: a young woman named Hanai, one of Curtis's sapping partners named Ian, and Lena.

"She was wandering around downstairs," Alonzo said. "She wanted to come."

"Fine," Curtis said.

Molly watched the thin black woman get into a suit. Kane *had* slept with her, she decided, feeling a morbid sort of curiosity about it, a slight, illogical pang of jealousy.

They dressed in silence, Curtis ready before any of the others and pacing out his anger in front of the lockers. Then they crowded into the airlock and passed through into the night. Molly kept her head down as they crossed the plains to the cave, seeing only the swirling dust and the rise and fall of Curtis's boots in the circle of light in front of her.

The cave was spotlit again as they slithered in, two at a time. The vivid, dizzying hologram starfields had disappeared. At the dim edge of one cone of brightness she could see Verb's transporter gate, a steel door frame connected to kilometers of fiber optic cables. Depression spread through her like a cloud of ink and only then did she realize that she'd still been hoping to find Reese alive, saved by a blown fuse or a last-second failure of nerve.

No, she thought, not a failure of nerve. Not Reese.

Curtis stripped off his suit as he waited for the others, but Molly left hers on. Insulation, she thought, against the unpleasantness to come. When the last of his people came through Curtis locked the hatch open to keep anyone else from using it.

"Spread out," he told them. "Just stay out of the way for right now." Molly noticed a look passing between Curtis and Lena, Lena questioning, Curtis distracted and vaguely irritated. Lena moved off with the others.

"Verb?" Molly said. "Verb, where are you?"

Finally she saw the girl coming toward her out of the shadows, her eyes shining with a joy that was still not enough to transform her face. "I did it, mother, I sent him. He already knew about the machine, I wasn't the one who told him about it. I didn't break my promise."

"I know you didn't," Molly said.

"He wanted it, he wanted it so much, and so I sent him."

"I know," Molly said. She reached out a hand and Verb took it, carefully, and held on to it.

Then Curtis moved into the light and Verb pulled away. "So he *is* here," she said, as if some dire prediction had just come true. "What does he want?"

"I want to talk to you," Curtis said.

"No," Verb said. Her massive head, on its trunk-like neck, rolled back and forth. "No."

"You've really got yourselves quite a setup here," Curtis said, ignoring her. "It's been a long time since I've been up here. Too long. How about a little light, and then you can show me around."

Verb stared at him in rigid defiance.

"I know where the controls are," Curtis said. "Either you can do it yourself, or I'll go over there and do it for you."

"Crunch, turn on the lights," she said, and Molly

saw that the girl had taken her first step backward, that ultimately she would not be able to resist him.

The lights faded up to the level of a cloudy morning.

"Good. Now let's have a look at your machine, okay?"

"No," Verb said. "It's my machine. I don't have to show it to you."

"You're not a baby anymore," Curtis said. "Don't overplay the role, okay? You're a part of this society as long as you use up our resources, and you've used up a hell of a lot of them here. I represent that society and I have the right to know what you're doing."

Verb's head swiveled to face Molly.

Oh god, she thought, this is it. What in christ's name am I going to say to her? "He's right," she said hesitantly. "I mean, he's right that he represents the society, and you have to account to him for what you're doing." She took a breath and looked over at Curtis, who nodded with a smug self-assurance that infuriated her. She could see a thin, dark line where he'd cut himself shaving his head; he could have used a depilatory cream, she thought, it was crazy to shave your head with a blade . . .

She turned back to Verb. "But you also have to account to yourself. You're responsible for what you create, do you understand? If somebody is going to use what you've made for something bad—"

"That's enough, Molly," Curtis said.

"—that makes you responsible for what *they* do, too. You can't let your work be perverted—"

"Shut up!" He didn't need to raise his voice; the violence screamed from the angles of his wrists and legs. She let herself trail off.

Verb seemed to be physically shrinking, as if the psychological pressure were crushing her body as well. Dear god, Molly thought, the future of the human race may be riding on this little girl. And I think she knows it.

"Listen to me," Curtis said to the girl. "You care for your mother, don't you? When she talks about loyalty and betrayal and taking responsibility and that kind of thing, you believe her, don't you?"

Molly saw it coming and could not get out of the way, like an animal trapped in the lights of a car.

"You trust her, don't you? You want to believe she's noble and brave and loving, but suppose she knew something important, and didn't tell you about it, because she was afraid it might hurt this project?"

"She wouldn't do that," Verb said.

"I think she would. Suppose it was something about you that might upset you so much that you couldn't work anymore?"

"What?" Verb whispered. "Go on, say it."

"Ask your mother," Curtis said, and folded his arms in front of him.

"Well?" Verb said. "Is there something?"

"Yes," Molly said. Her throat was blocked and it came out as a glottal hiss.

"Then tell me now."

"We thought . . . oh god, we thought we could find something. We didn't want to frighten you . . ."

"You think this isn't frightening?"

"There's something called Turner's syndrome. It's not what you have, but it's similar. In Turner's you only have one X chromosome instead of two, and the ovaries never form."

"Are you saying I can't have any kids? Because I don't care about that. Why should *I* want to have kids?"

Molly shook her head. "No. You've got both X chromosomes, but they're full of what they call nonautonomous elements, that inactivate the genes. When you get to puberty—" Molly started to cry. She tried to make the words come out but they couldn't get past the blockage in her throat. I've been holding them back so long, she thought, and now they just won't come.

"Tell me," she said to Curtis.

"It's going to kill you," Curtis said. "High blood pressure, edema, protein in the urine. Convulsions. Coma. Death."

Verb nodded. She was still staring at Molly and Molly couldn't look away from her. React, she ordered her silently. Cry, hit me, for god's sake do something.

"We've known since you were three or four," Molly said. The tears ran down her face and neck, past the collar of her suit and down the channel between her breasts. "It's . . . it's like a part of whatever it was that gave you your intellect. It's like prodigy burnout or one of those things where . . . you just burn all of yourself up at once."

"You could have told me."

"I know," Molly said. "But there was nothing you could do . . ."

"What the hell," Verb said, her face suddenly red, her fists clenched, "does that have to do with it? I know it's hopeless, I've known for three years."

Molly looked at Curtis, whose expression seemed frozen in place. "You . . . knew?" she said.

"Of course I knew. I've been into all the medical records, even the ones you tried to hide. How do you think it felt to learn it that way, sitting alone up here, watching it come up in little green letters on a black screen? And then after I tried to give you chances to tell me, I did everything but bring it up myself, because I wanted to hear it from *you*.

"But you never told me, and you know why? Because you don't care about me. I'm not really human to you, I never have been. If your dog has a terminal disease, well, you just give her a warm place to sleep and all the food she wants and then you cry when she goes."

"Sarah . . ." Molly held out her hand but the girl looked at it with contempt. Was it true? Molly wondered. If Sarah had been more loving, more . . . . *normal* looking, would it have made a difference? Would she have fought harder when Curtis said not to tell her?

Verb turned her back on both of them, silent sobs moving through her curved back and wattled neck. Molly felt herself slipping into the mindset of despair: *if I ever get out of this* . . . She and Curtis were finished; the truce that had been in effect since that afternoon was over. She thought she could kill him now, if she had to.

At that moment Curtis stooped and picked something off the floor. It was the gun that Reese had been shot with, the one he'd brought with him from the dome. She saw how seductively the weapon fit into Curtis's hand.

Verb faced them again, her tears gone, her emotions back in harness. Her eyes registered the gun in Curtis's hand, then moved slowly back to his face.

"You won't need that," she said. "I'll tell you what you want to know."

• • •

"He says it's important," Valentin told her.

Mayakenska shook her head, trying to come completely awake. So, she thought, I could sleep after all. "All right," she said. "I'm coming."

She pulled on a pair of coveralls, wincing at their stale smell, and walked carefully into the living room. Her visitor was short, oriental, wearing a sleeveless shirt that showed off his physique. "Do I know you?" she asked.

"No," he said. "My name is Takahashi and I work for Chairman Morgan." He frowned and corrected himself. "For Pulsystems, I should say."

"And what do you want with me?"

"Curtis is not going to deal with you," Takahashi said. "If your threats are genuine, that means I am scheduled to die with the rest of this settlement at midnight tonight."

"I see news travels quickly here."

Takahashi shrugged. "We both want the same thing. I've spent most of the day inside the main computer, and I've located the main source of computer time usage. That means I know *what* the project is and *where* it is. On the other hand, you can call off that laser. What say we make our own deal and cut Curtis out entirely?"

She remembered who this Takahashi was, now. He didn't just *work* for Pulsystems, he was a junior vice president and sat on the Board, representing the interests of the *zaibatsu* that controlled Pul-systems Tokyo.

She distrusted him, in particular, and the Japanese in general. Ever since the Japanese sneak attack on Port Arthur in 1904, Russia and Japan had been enemies, Japan even choosing to side with America after World War II, despite the fact that American bombs had obliterated Hiroshima and Nagasaki.

"And your part in this would entitle you to a share in the knowledge, is that right?"

"Of course."

"I fail to see why we need you."

"*If* you could locate the equipment—and even that is not going to be as easy as you might think—you don't even know how to run it or what to do with it."

"And you do?"

"The answers I don't have, I can get."

The phone rang.

"It seems to me you are trying to sell me your self-confidence and little else." She held up her hand before Takahashi could answer her. "Excuse me."

She crossed the room and picked up the kitchen extension. "Mayakenska."

"This is Curtis. Can we talk?"

"Of course."

"Good. Let's get some basic terms squared away, then, okay? Because a lot of this is new to me, too. The machine you're interested in is a transporter, am I correct? Straight-line transmission and recovery of material at or near the speed of light?"

She felt the first tinglings of a flood of relief and

excitement. "Ah, yes, correct, that sounds like the equipment."

"Good. You should probably know that we also have the ability to produce rather large quantities of antimatter—in fact, the power for the machine in question comes from antimatter."

Mayakenska glanced over at Takahashi and repressed a smile. "Curtis, if you want, we can wait and go over this with my people . . ."

"I think you should hear me out. The antimatter is stored in Liedenfrost jars that use the energy of the antimatter decay to contain the antimatter itself. Are you with me so far?"

"Yes." She had to pull her right hand away from her mouth to answer him; she had found herself gnawing on the thumbnail without realizing it.

"This decay is mediated by an electromagnetic field. That field may be turned off as the container is sent through that matter transmitter that we were just talking about. In that case the material of the container will be quickly eaten away. An explosion is the result. The explosion can be quite large, as I'm sure you can imagine. Are you still with me?"

"Yes," she said.

"My first thought was that we would drop a canister of this stuff into your Salyut and blow them out of the sky. But it occurred to me that the message might not be clear enough if I did that. So what I'm going to do is send a rather larger cannister through the machine and deposit it in Red Square, just outside the walls of the Kremlin."

"No," Mayakenska whispered.

"I make it to be about ten minutes before ten,

let's see, that's 21 hours 50 minutes. Your deadline was midnight, so I'm going to make mine a half hour earlier. I want to see your Salyut performing a Transearth Injection burn by 23:30 hours or you lose Moscow."

"You're bluffing," Mayakenska said, though she didn't believe he was.

"Put on your mask," Curtis said. "Turn right as you walk out your front door, and walk clear out to the edge of the dome. There's a phone mounted on the wall there. I'll ring it in three minutes." The receiver went dead in her hand.

"Curtis?" Takahashi said politely. Of course he had heard.

She nodded. Her legs felt weak and she had to perch on the edge of a kitchen stool for a moment before she could walk. "You might as well come along," she said.

His eyebrows came together and he shook his head slightly, not understanding her.

"You'll want to see this," she said. "It's the beginning of the end."

It took a little over a minute to find the wall-mounted phone in one of the observation alcoves. It occupied one edge of a panel that included three shielded buttons labeled EMERGENCY, ABANDON, and SHUTDOWN. The sight filled her with anger and sadness. That's the enemy, she thought, looking out at the dimly floodlit martian night, at the ocean of blowing sand. And yet we persist in doing the enemy's work.

The directors should have known this would happen, should have forseen this contingency. It was too much like the way Kennedy had humiliated that peasant Krushchev. Brinksmanship and blackmail, weapons too powerful to be used, vicious circles of terror. Was there no way to break the pattern?

The phone rang and she snatched it up. "Go ahead."

"Tell me what you see outside the dome," Curtis said.

"Not much. There's a lot of dust. There's some good-sized rocks."

"Okay. Can you see four of them sort of together there?"

"Yes, okay."

"Pick one."

I hate this, Mayakenska thought. But what else am I supposed to do? "There's a low rock shelf about a hundred meters past those four . . ."

"Fine," Curtis said, and hung up on her again.

Maybe, she thought, it won't work. Maybe it will blow up in his face. *And maybe Uncle Lenin will come rescue us all.*

"We're going to get a demonstration, then," Takahashi said.

She turned, startled. He'd been so quiet she'd forgotten he was there. "Yes, I think so."

"Beating the proverbial plowshare into a sword?"

"Sorry?"

"It's not important," Takahashi said. "Will there be a flash? Should I be looking the other way?"

"Gamma rays, I think. This is outside my experience." She sat down on one of the cast concrete benches, then stood up again. "Maybe it's not—"

The flash was bright enough that she turned

instinctively away, covering her eyes with her hands. The sound followed instantaneously, rising with the shockwave through her feet, pitching her to her knees, a booming peal of thunder so loud she felt something tearing in her ears. She reached out for the bench and felt it shaking too, closed her eyes and bent her head to her knees, still hearing a ghostly feedback whine behind the thudding of rocks and dirt against the dome.

The phone began to ring.

"All right, I hear you," she said, crawling onto the bench. "*Yob tvayu mat*, I hear you." The explosion had torn dirty white chunks out of the dome's plastic, but had somehow not cracked it. Nothing remained of the shelf of land but a thickening in the cloud of red-brown dust.

She thought of the *importny* leather coats in the window of G.U.M.; the somber red granite of Lenin's mausoleum, just across the cobblestone street; the riotous colors of the domes of St. Basil's at the south end of the square; the contrived Byzantine opulence of the Historical Museum at the north end. In an hour and a half they too would be dust.

The phone kept ringing.

"Are you all right?" Takahashi asked her. A thin line of blood ran from one of his nostrils. She nodded at him, looked past him to the crowd that had come to stare at the dome.

"You," someone shouted, a woman's voice, the owner anonymous. "Is that your work?"

Mayakenska could only stare. Takahashi moved in front of her. "No," he said. "Curtis did that. Your own boy did it. But it's over now. Everything's okay."

"It's not over," Mayakensaka said, but no one heard her. When she looked up again the crowd had dissolved into confused, frightened individuals, moving randomly under the artificial twilight.

She stood up. "I've got to stop this. I'll call the ship."

"I'm going to the cave," Takahashi said.

"Cave?"

"Where Curtis is. The first settlement. The computer shows a phenomenal amount of usage up there. That's where they have to be."

Mayakenska looked at the phone, which had finally stopped ringing. "All right," she said. She stood up. Her legs were shaky, but she could walk. "I'm going to stop this," she said. "I promise."

The house—living module, the Americans called it—at S-23 looked like something out of one of their TV comedies from half a century ago, a "cottage in the suburbs," if she remembered the vocabulary. The front of the house was weakened by large panes of clear plastic, and the surrounding land was planted with useless, ornamental shrubs.

Lying next to one of the shrubs was a body.

"Blok?" she asked, approaching him cautiously.

"Yes," he said. "It's me." His mask was crooked and his eyes seemed swollen. "Reese is gone. He's gone up to the cave."

"The cave where the transporter is. You didn't tell me about that, Blok."

"Just . . . kids up there. Didn't want them hurt."

"Come on inside," she said. "There's not much time."

She helped him into the house and put him in one

of the bedrooms. He was bruised and embarrassed, but not critically hurt.

"Valentin?" He had been sitting in the living room watching her, wide-eyed, his right leg jiggling nervously. Amphetamines, Mayakenska thought. "Come with me. You need to hear this."

She called the orbiter from her bedroom. "Twenty-two hundred hours, code Pamir, repeat Pamir. Give me a relay to Dawn." Dawn was Mission Control at Kaliningrad, and now that Frontera Base had turned away from the sun she would have to bounce her signal off a worn American comsat orbiting the far side of Mars.

"Okay," Chaadayev said. *"What's going on down there? We saw some kind of explosion a few minutes ago. Is everything all right?"*

"No," she said. "Everything is wrong . . ."

• • •

Kane pulled free of the giant just as Reese flickered and vanished. He ran toward the glowing doorway, throwing away the infrared helmet as he ran. "No!" he screamed. He tripped over something in the darkness and lunged headlong toward the wall of incandescent particles.

His right hand stretched toward the fiery wall, came close enough for Kane to feel the hairs on the back of it tingle and flutter. Then he found himself sprawled across the spongy durofoam floor of the cave, the metal frame of the doorway arching over him, the power shut down.

Reese was gone.

Kane got onto all fours and looked around. Pockets of lights held various CRT's and scientific instruments; green digital readouts blinked at him from every corner of the room. The illusion of stars and infinite space that he'd seen from the airlock had disappeared, leaving no clue as to whether it had been a hologram or just another product of his implant.

Like the voices, whose high, pure harmony still rang in his skull.

Slowly the children moved out of the darkness, some in rags, some wearing braces on their limbs, some with the glittering eyes of fierce curiosity, some with the slack, moist lips of brain damage. One of them came to within a few feet of him and stopped, her heavy, malformed head turned on its side.

"Welcome to Synchron City," she said. Kane thought perhaps she was smiling. "Are you Kane?"

"Where's Reese?" Kane said. "What did you do to him?"

The hideous little girl leaned from side to side, almost dancing with pleasure and excitement. "We transcribed him," she said. "We transcribed him and then we broadcast him."

"Broadcast him?" Kane sat back on his heels, bringing himself further away from the girl. "You're crazy."

"Do you think so?" she said, and Kane saw that he had carelessly opened an old wound. "Well, I did broadcast him. I gave him the one thing he wanted in the entire universe."

"Where?" Kane said. "Where did you send him?"

"He brought me a data base that showed maybe a habitable planet around Barnard's Star. He should reassemble there, if everything works."

The diskette, Kane thought. So that's what it was for. That meant that Reese had known about all of this before they'd landed, probably known before they left Earth. One more betrayal. "Barnard's Star?"

"He'll know in about 5.868 years. Of course it won't be that long for him."

"Jesus," Kane said. This was it, then, the source of power, of more power than he had imagined. The electricity that had charged his hand at Reese's gateway was all around him; he stood in the Omphalos, the navel of this world. The roots of the tree of life grew under his feet, and from here the waters could be freed, releasing grace, nourishment, and light to transform the universe.

He stood and let the awareness electrify him like current charging a capacitor.

Suddenly the girl jerked her head around and Kane followed her gaze to the lights over the airlock, which had just shifted from green to red.

"Somebody's coming," Kane said.

"Curtis."

"How do you know?"

She shook her head and pointed to a ladder along the nearest wall. "There's a catwalk up there. You can watch without them seeing you." Kane hesitated and she said, "You'd better go."

Kane climbed, the strain on his arms sending waves of pain through his pectorals and deep into his chest. At the top he found a perforated aluminum walkway that circled the cave. It was barely a yard wide and less than six feet from the ceiling, forcing Kane to walk with bent legs and cling to the handrail.

He circled toward the front of the cave, then froze as his foot touched yielding flesh.

"Hello," said a voice. "Are you from Earth?"

Kane squinted. A boy of about eight or nine clung to the railing, staring intently back at him. A clumsily repaired cleft palate had left the boy with a scar that ran through his upper lip and along the entire left side of his nose.

"That's right. My name is Kane."

"*Avec plaisir.* I am Pen of My Uncle. Do you speak French?"

Fifteen feet below them the airlock door swung open and they began coming in, two at a time:

first Curtis and Molly, then Lena and Hanai, then two of Curtis's shock troops. Seeing Molly gave him a pang of lust and sorrow that quickly gave way to alarm. Something major, something pivotal was happening; Curtis was making his move. Kane could barely concentrate on what the boy was saying to him. "No," he said. "English, Japanese, a little Russian."

"Practical," the boy said. "French is stupid, nearly useless, except for the existentialists. Russians are good, though. Do you read Ouspensky?"

"I don't read much," Kane said. The girl with the swollen head was talking to Curtis and Molly now. The low air pressure kept the sound from reaching him and he could only tell that an emotional storm was building; tears ran from Molly's eyes.

"Ouspensky is Verb's favorite. That's where she got the idea for her physics." Overhead lights came on and Kane moved further into the shadows.

"Who's Verb?" he asked.

"That's her down there. Did you know she was Curtis and Molly's kid?"

Kane shook his head. "That's weird. It's like everything is tied to everything else, all these lines of force . . ."

"Ouspensky says, 'Every separate human life is a moment of the life of some *great being*, which lives *in us.*'"

The boy's words staggered Kane, parted for an instant the membrane that separated his dream personalities from his waking existence. He could feel them watching behind his eyes: Percival, maddened by his imperfection and loss of the Grail,

Yamato-Takeru of the shattered spirit, Jason, the fanatic sailor who had failed to intuit the Pattern.

"The Pattern . . ." Kane said.

"Sure, that's it, a pattern. That's all we are in space-time, you know. Just a pattern. In seven years you don't even have any of the same cells you used to have. There's only the pattern left. The pattern survives . . ."

"Yeah," Kane said. The fever swept over his brain like a brushfire. His neurons all seemed to be firing at once; he rode the tide of electric potential to a psychedelic level of consciousness. "The Pattern of the hero survives."

"Ouspensky says heroic characters are just 're-flexed images of human types which had existed ten thousand years before.' He says they're reproduced by 'mysterious powers controlling the destinies of our world. *That which has been will return again.*'"

On the floor below them Verb had led Curtis and Molly into a sudden cone of light. It revealed a wooden folding screen of Japanese design; the back had been fitted out with aluminum cages to hold circuit cards and ribbons of cable that led to disk drives and bubble storage.

Kane focused on one panel of the screen, on one 18- by 24-inch sheet of plastic, studded with chips and crowned with a dark blue ceramic box the size of his open hand.

He began to hallucinate in earnest.

From somewhere behind his eyes a ghostly schematic of the circuit card formed and began to spin into his field of vision, slowly turning through all its axes and dropping away from him, toward its physical counterpart below.

He shut his eyes and the glowing diagram remained, sketched in the visual purple pigment of his retina, still falling, spinning away from him.

He swayed queasily, opened his eyes, and grabbed for the railing. The phantom projection had aligned itself with the genuine board, and as Kane watched, awed and terrified, the image superimposed itself on the original.

For an instant the entire cave was suffused with brilliant, golden light and a spasm of pure pleasure arced through Kane's nervous system.

He dropped to his knees, shivering.

He had just seen his grail.

●   ●   ●

It seemed to Molly that she was watching a butterfly metamorphose into a worm. Ten years ago Curtis had seemed full of strength and beauty and grace; in the cocoon of the Center's isolation tanks he had become another personality: dry and bitter, erratic, amoral.

In the explosion of the rock ledge outside the dome his transformation became complete.

She hadn't believed it was really going to happen until the mountain trembled under her feet. There had been no single moment when Curtis had hesitated or lost momentum long enough for the weight of her fear to stop him, to push the balance away from the vision of doom that now obsessed him. And if she had seen her moment, she thought, Alonzo and the goon squad would have kept her from seizing it.

Curtis had sat through the preparations with a phone in one hand, giving orders to his henchmen back inside the dome. Molly could see that he missed his cameras; the explosion would not be completely real for him until he could replay it on the video screen.

It had shocked her to learn that Verb already had packets of antimatter whose retaining fields could be switched off. For experiments, Verb said, or for extending the cave. It was just something they'd made up, that they'd thought would be useful. To Molly it seemed hopelessly naive to have built something that could so easily be transformed into a weapon.

And now they were huddled together, father and distorted daughter, Curtis watching her program the coordinates for Moscow into the computer. Think, she told herself. You're not helpless. She knew the machine, knew its weaknesses well enough to disable it if she had a chance.

The power board, with its blue ceramic antimatter jar, was the most vulnerable point. From where she stood, behind Curtis, it was five or six meters away on the other side of the bank of CRT's, disk drives, and walls of folded program listings. If she could get at it, she could pull it completely free of the assembly, like pulling a giant plug out of a socket.

The problem was that Curtis still held the gun. She was not afraid to die, if it came to that, but she was afraid to die without stopping him, without even being able to get to the panel.

She pushed herself away from the desk she'd been leaning on and walked toward the front of the cave, keeping her distance from any of the critical parts of the transporter. All told the thing was nearly ten meters long and four or five wide, the oriental folding screen standing in the center like an oversized breadboard in a child's do-it-yourself electronic kit. The gateway itself was on the far side, out of Molly's reach, and none of the thick, black power cables led anywhere but to the main power panel.

She kept walking, noticing for the first time in a long while how large the cave actually was. Most of the time it was lighted with pin-spots or dim red floods, as if Verb resented the inflexibility of the raw rock walls. The general overhead lights, dim as they were, seemed like a violation, one more small brutality.

Something flashed at the front of the cave.

The airlock. Somebody wanted in.

Molly glanced back at Curtis; he hadn't seen. Alonzo was looking over Curtis's shoulder and the only one watching the airlock was Hanai. Molly started for the open hatch as quickly as she could without attracting Curtis's attention, but before she could get within ten meters Hanai blocked her way.

"Don't do it, Molly," she said.

"Do you know what's going on here? Do you know what Curtis is trying to do?"

Hanai shook her head. "That doesn't matter. Just stay away from that hatch."

"I'm not trying to get away. I'm just going to close it."

"I can see the signal as well as you can. You don't know who's out there. What if it's the Russians?"

"What if it *is* the fucking Russians?" Molly hissed. "Curtis is crazy. He's lost it. He's going to wipe out Moscow. Do you know what that means? Not just that we lose Frontera, which we will, but it means war, nuclear war, bombs dropping on cities, the end of everything. The Russians will have to retaliate, Morgan will get sucked in, and then it's the end. Everybody dies."

Before Hanai could answer Molly gently pushed her aside and crossed the open floor in front of the hatch, stepping over Curtis's empty suit and switching on the intercom mounted on the wall. She tuned it to the standard suit frequency and said, "This is Molly. Who's out there?"

"Takahashi. The inner door is jammed or something. Can you get it shut?"

Molly looked back at Hanai, who was still wavering. "Yeah, I'll shut it. But come in fast and get under cover as soon as you're inside. There's a world of shit going down in here."

"I already know."

She closed the hatch and stood with her back to it, watching Curtis at the far end of the cave. Keep your head down, she thought. Just don't look up. She heard the hatch open behind her and twisted her head to see Takahashi move into the shadows of a set of metal shelves.

Hanai moved slowly toward him, as if fighting her instincts. Takahashi pulled off his helmet and his eyes connected with Hanai's. She looked away quickly.

"Is she still with Curtis?" Takahashi asked Molly.

"I don't know. I think she's making up her mind. I take it you two know each other."

"This morning," Hanai said. "I found Dian—her body, I mean. I think Curtis killed her."

"Yeah," Molly said. "I think he did, too."

"Can we stop him?" Takahashi asked.

"I don't know," Molly said. "He's got a gun. He could kill us both. I think he'd kill any of us if we pushed him."

"What about Kane?" Takahashi asked.

"Kane?" Molly risked another look at Curtis; he still had his head down, but he could look up at any moment. Now Lena had noticed them and crossed over from the far wall.

"If Kane's here," Takahashi said, "we can use him. He can stop Curtis. It's what he was programmed for."

Molly turned slowly and looked at the shadows that clung to the walls of the cave, the clutter of equipment and furniture. The idea that Kane was out there somewhere, dazed, obsessive, a pawn to the biotechnology in his brain, gave her chills.

"Kane's programming is fucked," Lena said. "He's living out some kind of Greek mythology fantasy. We can't count on him."

"Can we count on *you?*" Takahashi asked.

"Depends on what you want," Lena said, and Molly could see the claustrophobic tension of the flight from Earth in her sudden anger. "I'm with you against Curtis."

"Then somebody," Molly said, "for christ's sake think of something. There's less than an hour left."

"What about her?" Takahashi asked, pointing at Hanai.

"I'll help," Hanai said. "But I want protection from Curtis. Whatever it takes, even if it means taking me back to Earth."

"You'll be okay," Molly said.

"That's not good enough. I want a promise."

"I promise," Molly said. "I'll do whatever I can to protect you from him."

"I want to know where Kane is," Takahashi said. "I still think he's our best chance."

"He's here," Lena said. "He was coming here, anyway."

"Then I'm going to look for him." Takahashi

pulled off his suit and moved quietly into the darkness.

"We better break this up," Hanai said. She was looking past Molly's left shoulder and Molly turned to see one of the other guards moving toward them. It was Ian—whose hero thing, Molly remembered, had been a solo rover expedition to the Mutch Memorial Station, site of the first Viking landing, where he'd snapped off the soil sampling arm and brought it back as a trophy.

"What's this about?" he said, and Molly shook her head at him.

"Nothing," she said.

"Let's just get away from this hatch, then, eh?" he said. "And you, Molly, come back with me. I want you where I can keep my eyes on you." He put one hand on Molly's arm and she shook him away fiercely.

"Don't touch me."

He held up both hands. "Right. Just let's move along, okay?"

She walked away from him, crossed the cluttered floor to stand next to Curtis. He and Alonzo were staring at an odd-shaped polygon on the CRT. The shape reminded her of an Apollo spacecraft for a second, the heat-shield pointed slightly up and to the right. Then she noticed the fainter lines surrounding it.

The Kremlin, then, and the upper right corner was Red Square.

"Phenomenal," Curtis said. "Un-fucking-believable."

"Curtis," Molly said.

"Don't start."

"Will you listen to me for just thirty seconds? Will you think about what you're doing? Do you think this is some kind of video game you're playing?"

Curtis glanced up from the screen, checking the disposition of his troops. "Ian," he said, "shut her up, will you?"

She glared at Ian, who shifted his feet uncomfortably. "What exactly do you want me to do with her?"

Curtis handed him the Luger. "Take her out of my way and watch her. Use the gun if you have to, but for christ's sake don't hit any of the equipment."

"That's right, Ian," Molly said. "You wouldn't want to damage anything valuable."

Curtis turned in his chair to stare at her with a look of angry impatience. "Shut up."

Above the CRT a digital display clock read 23:11.

Nineteen minutes left.

• • •

"Moscow coming in," Chaadayev said.

"All right," Mayakenska said into the radio. Her heart was pounding and she didn't know whether to be terrified or to try, somehow, to pray.

"Mademoiselle Mayakenska," the voice said. She recognized it as belonging to the vice president with the colored glasses and the *dzhinsy* pants. She nearly answered him, forgetting the eighteen minutes it would take her words to reach Earth.

"The committee—or rather, the Board—has decided not to take your advice. It is our conclusion that the mechanism is located somewhere within Frontera Base itself, and not in some distant cave. We find the idea that such a device could be the work of children to be preposterous."

"Idiots," Mayakenska said. Tears of anger ran down her face. "Idiots."

"Therefore your instructions are as follows. If Curtis seems set on his threat you will destroy Frontera Base with the laser. You will do so before the expiration of Curtis's deadline, and you will do so without telling anyone there on the ground. Also, from this moment forward I expect you to maintain a continuous radio link with Mission Control, detailing all your actions. I trust this is all sufficiently clear."

"Chaadayev?" Mayakenska said. He was the one

252

who would actually have to fire the laser. "Were you listening?"

"Yes," Chaadayev said.

"They're insane. You've seen what the weapon can do. I want you to make the ship ready to leave orbit."

"I'm sorry," Chaadayev said.

"What does that mean?"

"I agree with Moscow. Besides, it isn't my place to question orders. I suggest that you already be in your suit when you make your final communication with Curtis. Have Valentin in the ship, ready to go. We'll start with the north end of the dome at 23:25 exactly, which will give you time to get to the ship and rendezvous with us."

"Chaadayev, I order you to disable the weapon and lay in a course for home."

"I am genuinely sorry," Chaadayev said.

The radio went dead.

Mayakenska looked at her watch. Ten forty-five. The ship was locked, all systems powered up, ready for immediate launch in case of an emergency. With constant thrust and a low trajectory, she might make it.

The living room was still dark. Valentin paced the floor, pretending nonchalance. "I trust you overheard," she said to him.

He glared at her, then shrugged. "Only by accident."

She had no time to waste on this feinting for position. "Your opinion?"

"It's not my duty to have an opinion."

She nodded and went to Blok's room. He slept

with his mouth open, his face bruised and lined with pain. She shook him gently.

"Hmmm . . . what?"

"Blok, listen carefully. At eleven fifteen, that's just half an hour from now, I want you to go outside. Go to the nearest alarm and push the ABANDON button. Do you understand me?"

"Abandon?" he asked groggily. "What's happening? Why—"

"You must trust me. Do not let anyone or anything keep you from doing this."

He sat up, holding his neck and twisting his head to pop the vertebrae. "They're going to burn the dome, aren't they?"

"Don't ask questions. Be a soldier. Will you do this for me?"

"Yes, but—"

She touched his lips with one finger. "Once you've sounded the alarm, if you can . . . see that Valentin gets out alive. If you can."

"Your lover," Blok said.

Mayakenska shrugged.

"Ah, my colonel, you have such a weakness for lost children. I'll do what I can."

She left him.

"I'm going outside," she said to Valentin. "I want to take a closer look at that rock. There must be no possibility of a mistake."

"I'll go with you," he said, reaching for a mask.

"No," she said. "There's . . . another broadcast at 2300 hours."

"What difference does that make now?"

"Everything," she said, "must be as usual. Do you understand?"

"All right," he said.

"The call sign is Taymyr. 2300 hours."

She ran for the airlock. Her legs, swollen and aching from the blood that gravity had pulled into them, would not obey her brain. She tripped over nothing and rolled into a soggy field of young spinach. She came up with ammonia fertilizer soaked into her coveralls and one ankle painfully twisted.

She limped into the changing room, forcing herself into a suit and through the airlock. The wind was a genuine force now, buffeting her, throwing her weight onto the bad ankle. All she could smell inside the suit was the bitter tang of ammonia and the stink of her own fear.

She fell down twice in the darkness. She could still see the lights of Frontera behind her, keeping her from losing her direction, but she could not find her ship.

She bumped headlong into something metal, squinted and saw it was the American lander. Hers was not far away, then. She staggered on, and a moment later she saw the circle of light leaking from the porthole.

Clinging to the side of the spacecraft, the wind ripping silently at her arms and legs, she pried open the cover of the magnetic lock. Her fingers fumbled the combination, cleared the memory, tried again. Every second, she thought, every mistake, could be the one that lost her her chance.

The hatch opened and she climbed in, surrounded by swirling dust. She slammed the hatch and fell into the pilot's sling, her fingers already snapping switches on the panel above her.

Stop them, was all she could think. Further back in her mind she knew she might be too late, but she refused to deal with that thought until she had to. For now she only wanted to get to the Salyut, get on board, and stop them from firing the laser.

Any way she had to.

The computer released its hold on the count-down with 15 seconds left. She frantically punched in the parameters for the fastest possible ascent to the Salyut, stopping only to buckle her harness as the first jolt of acceleration shook the ship.

The winds boiled around her, hammering the shell of the ship with rocks and dirt, threatening to destroy the careful balance of the engines' thrust and send her tumbling out of control. She fought the T-shaped pitch and yaw control for stability, trusting her dangerously atrophied instincts to keep her right side up.

"Climb, you prick," she whispered.

The G forces leaned into her, sickening her, and within seconds she was out of the turbulence.

Gently she took her hands away from the controls and let the computer guide her in to a low, fast orbit. Lifeless, frozen wastes flew past the windows as she hurtled toward the sunrise, thinking, I did what I could.

She wished she could believe it would be enough.

· · ·

Kane ripped open the front of his chest pack and took out the Colt.

The boy who called himself Pen of My Uncle shrank against the wall of the cave. "Oh shit," he said.

Kane ignored him. The gun completed a neural circuit, and he could see one step further ahead. First the circuit board, and then, he knew, the rest would come to him.

He circled toward the ladder and the boy scurried away toward the opposite side of the cave.

Someone was already climbing toward him.

Kane eased back into the darkness, the gun in front of him, his gloved finger snug in the trigger guard.

"Kane?" said Takahashi. "Kane, are you up here?"

"Come on up," Kane said. "Move slowly and don't do anything to make me nervous."

Takahashi clambered up onto the catwalk and stood uneasily, keeping his hands away from his body. He was sweating and his nostrils flared with suppressed tension. Kane had never seen him so nearly out of control.

"You okay?" Takahashi said.

"Okay?" Kane asked. *"Okay? What the fuck do you think*, man? You and my uncle've been using me like I was one of the robots out of his factory. You move me around like a piece of furniture, you even try to reprogram my fucking brain, and you ask me if I'm *okay?*"

"Easy," Takahashi said. "You think *I* set you up for this?"

"You knew about it. You spent nine months in your goddamned rowing machine, knowing they were still alive up here, knowing about that goddamned circuit in my head, knowing about this machine that . . . that scrambled Reese and just blew him away. . . ." His metabolism was devouring itself. He mopped sweat from his forehead and wiped at his running nose.

Takahashi was not much better off. His eyes kept flickering toward the figures moving below them. "You were dying. The implant operation saved your life." His sincerity was urgent, frightened. "As to the programming that went in it, that's Morgan's doing."

"What's the difference? I've seen your file. That whole corporate loyalty thing. Morgan owns you just as much as he does me, only he doesn't need any chips in your brain to do it."

"Kane. There isn't much time . . ."

Kane turned the gun so that the dim light rolled and shimmered off the metal. "Right now all you've got is the time I let you have. I could kill you right now."

"I'm not your enemy, Kane. Neither is the company."

He had shifted into a sudden, intense calm that Kane found more frightening than his earlier display of nerves.

"In Japan," Takahashi said, "the company was my mother and father. You think Pulsystems is big in Houston, but that's nothing compared to Japan. It was the Japanese division that supported the entire corporation for the last ten years.

"And over there we didn't just work for a paycheck. The company fed me and gave me my house and clothes and car, and it gave me something to believe in and work for and devote myself to. Morgan doesn't do that. Morgan is an egotistical, devious incompetent."

Kane's gunhand began to tremble. Bright filaments of pain glowed inside his skull and sweat ran down the sides of his chest. "I don't understand."

"I'm loyal to the company, not to Morgan. There are factions that believe this transporter and this antimatter power grid are too valuable to let Morgan have. They got me onto this mission to protect them, and when I get back Morgan will be replaced. As soon as they can find a successor that the Board will accept."

"Successor?"

"Don't play coy with me. You know who I'm talking about."

"I don't . . ."

"You've wanted it all along. You've been maneuvering yourself toward it since your first summer job in the mail room. And Morgan knew it. He's used the implant to keep you down since North Africa, and he sent you up here because he didn't think you'd ever come back, or if you did you wouldn't be in any position to fight him."

"Maybe he's right. This thing in my head . . ."

"Once this is over with, once the program has terminated, it won't make any difference. You can just leave the current ROM in there, or you can make it work for you."

"How? What are you talking about?"

"You could set up a direct brain link to the Pulsystems computers, and access all their storage. You could expand your mental powers, your senses. The possibilities are endless."

Kane rubbed his sweaty, throbbing forehead with the glove of his left hand. "You're an optimist, Takahashi. First we have to live through tonight, and the Russians . . ."

"There's more than the Russians to worry about. Curtis is out of his mind and he's down there right now trying to start World War III."

"Curtis . . ." Kane said.

"With him out of the way, we can take the panel and get back to Houston. Then nothing can stop us."

"The Return," Kane said.

"What?"

"The Pattern, man, the life-enhancing Return . . ."

"Forget this pattern shit. There's no time." Takahashi's calm was visibly eroding. "Stop Curtis. Get the panel. You've got to be the one to do it. You've got the gun, the reflexes, all that berserker shit they taught you in the mercenaries. I'll tell the Russians we're ready to deal, stall them long enough for us to get to the ship and get out of here."

"That *is* the Pattern, man. Slay the monster and return with the Ultimate Boon. That *is* the Pattern."

Takahashi look as if he wanted to smash the wall with his fists. He's starting to believe what I said about the implant, Kane thought. He really is starting to believe I've lost it.

"I'm sorry, Kane," Takahashi said. "I didn't want it to be like this. But I can't take him all by myself. None of us can."

"What are you—" Kane said, but Takahashi had already closed his eyes and begun to recite.

" 'When I am grown to man's estate/I shall be very proud and great./And tell the other girls and boys/Not to meddle with my toys.' "

Kane was paralyzed. Part of his brain recognized the nursery rhyme his uncle had read to him as a child, before his father died, but another, distinct part read the words as a lock reads a key and opened under them.

He watched as his left hand wrapped around his right, steadying his grip on the pistol, both thumbs cocking the hammer, a shining, live cartridge moving into line with the barrel.

Program, he thought, watching helplessly as his feet took him toward the ladder. Last-ditch program. Takahashi. Bastard. Didn't believe I could do it.

He put one foot onto the ladder, carefully brought his left hand from the Colt to the railing.

He took a second step, and a third. His shoulders were level with the floor of the catwalk.

A blast of sound nearly blew him off the ladder. He jammed his hands over his ears and the revolver fell into a pile of plastic sheeting below him.

Alarms were going off all across the cave. Reese had drilled them on the three different sound patterns; this one, the shrill, one-note siren, was the signal to abandon the dome.

He could think again, had some voluntary control over his body. But the compulsion remained, the driving, overwhelming need to point the gun at Curtis's face, to squeeze the trigger, to watch him die.

The alarm shrieked at him from less than five feet away, from a metal horn mounted on the catwalk support, battering him with sound. Frenzied, disoriented, he thrashed from side to side on the ladder, trying to see where the gun had fallen.

He felt the slick plastic elbow joints of his suit begin to slide off the rung of the ladder and lunged for the handrail, but he was too late.

He tumbled backwards off the ladder, his scream of terror lost in the maelstrom of noise.

• • •

"That's it?" Curtis asked.

"That's it," Verb told him. "Type '.RUN XLAUNCH' and NEWLINE and the machine does the rest."

She looked eaten up inside, Molly thought, worse than she'd ever looked before. She stood near Curtis now, and refused to even look in Molly's direction.

Curtis turned away from the keyboard with a look of regret and picked up the phone. "You still have the Russians on the screen? . . . Yeah, fine . . . Oh really? What were they saying? . . . You what? Jesus christ, you asshole, why didn't you tell me you don't speak Russian! Get somebody in there who does, for christ's sake, and replay those goddamn radio signals!" He slammed the phone down and turned to Alonzo. "Those fucking morons—"

The ABANDON alarm cut him off.

Christ, Molly thought, momentarily stunned. They did it, they hit Frontera, they didn't even wait for the deadline. . . .

She saw Curtis lunge for the CRT and knew her options had run out.

Ian was half turned toward Curtis and didn't see her until she was already coming off the floor. Her first punch caught him in the throat and he went down choking.

She didn't have time to try for his gun.

Curtis stood in front of the keyboard, legs spread. He was typing, carefully, one letter at a time.

"Curtis!" she screamed, but her voice was drowned in the shrilling of the alarms.

Curtis reached for the NEWLINE key.

She had nothing to throw, no weapon to use but her body. She hurled herself at his legs, knocking him off balance, and as they fell over together she saw his right hand come down.

Curtis had fallen underneath her. She got to her hands and knees, saw green letters scrolling up the screen of the CRT.

XLAUNCH was running. The metal doorway began to swirl with color, washing out the dark blue of the ceramic canister that lay balanced inside it.

She got to her feet, felt Curtis's hands close around her left ankle. Her right leg was free and she pulled it back, then drove the point of her toe between his legs, using all her strength.

He must have screamed, but she couldn't hear it. He thrashed and shook like a drowning fish and she pulled her leg free and ran for the Japanese screen in the center of the room.

"Molly no!" Verb's voice, higher, louder than the sirens.

With her gloved hands she grabbed the power board and yanked it loose from its connections.

The voltage kicked her ten feet across the floor, sparks dancing in front of her eyes and smoke trickling from the forearms of her suit. She couldn't breathe, but air wasn't what she wanted. She wanted to *see* ...

She pulled herself up, literally crawling up the side of the wall.

The canister was still there.

Thank god, Molly thought. That much saved, that many more that didn't have to die.

The dome, she thought. Had the Russians really done it?

She couldn't stay on her feet. She slumped to the floor, one foot sending the power board skittering away across the durofoam.

The sirens wound down and the sudden silence hit Molly like a physical blow. She passed out for a moment, and when she forced her eyes open again she could see Curtis moving toward her.

"—the panel back in and we'll have another go," he was shouting to Alonzo. He had the gun again and now he was looking at her. "And you, bitch, are going to die."

She put out one hand, tried to lever herself up. Her muscles had no strength. As her fingers clutched uselessly at the durofoam floor she saw Verb, standing behind a row of machines, watching her.

Curtis picked up the panel and held it under one arm. He brought the gun up and Molly watched numbly as his elbow locked and his shoulder moved in toward his chin.

Somebody stepped in front of her and she couldn't see Curtis anymore.

"No, Curtis," Lena said. "It's over."

"Over?" Curtis said. "They destroyed the dome, they killed god knows how many people, and you say it's *over*?"

Molly felt a hand pulling at her and managed to stand up long enough to brace herself against the rear wall of the cave. The touch of the fingers was strange, hesitant, and Molly looked over into the face of her daughter.

"I'm sorry," Verb said. The girl's eyes were red, but she had stopped crying. "I screwed everything up. I just got so hurt and angry, and I . . ."

"It happens," Molly said, the words coming out a little breathlessly. "You're just human, that's all."

"I don't know if I like that," Verb said. There was a tension around her eyes, a distance that had never been there before. She's growing up, Molly thought. She hasn't got long now at all.

"I know," Molly said. "I know. And I'm sorry, too. I shouldn't have kept anything from you. Whatever . . . whatever time we have left, I'll try to do better."

"Okay," Verb said. The pressure of the girl's hand on her shoulder was strong, comforting. I can't remember the last time, Molly thought, she touched me on her own.

Curtis was staring at Alonzo. "Come put this panel back in," he said, "while I watch these assholes."

Alonzo stayed where he was, behind the CRT. Molly heard the beep as he switched it off. "They're right, Curtis. This is where it has to stop."

"I don't believe it," Curtis said. "I don't fucking believe it. You're going to just lie there and let this happen to you? I could kill you all."

"Not all of us," Hanai said, moving over to stand near Lena. "One or two of us, but not all of us."

Curtis began to back away, toward the airlock. "I know what you think, all of you. You think I'm the Fisher King or something, that I'm all dried up, that maybe you can sacrifice me and get a new king and everything will be okay again." He stepped into the bottom half of his suit, and then had to put the panel down to get into the upper half.

"It's easy to blame me," he went on. "But it wasn't my fault. I never lost my faith. I always believed we could change this place, and I still believe it." He picked up the panel again and held it over his head. "With this kind of power we could have started those changes months ago, maybe even years ago. But you kept it from me, you refused to trust me with it. But now I have it, and I'm going to build the new Mars I promised. And if you won't help me, I'll find somebody else who can."

"How many have to die first?" Molly said. She reached her right arm across and held onto Verb's hand for just a second, then took a couple of shaky steps away from her. "We can't build a new world and then turn it into Earth all over again, with factions and war and bombs . . ."

Curtis' expression was feral, crazed, a cornered animal's. He put on one glove at a time, keeping the gun up and trained on the room with the other hand.

"Even Morgan," he said, "even Morgan would not be this stupid. He'd know what to do with power like this." He grabbed a helmet and slid into the airlock feet first.

The ship, Molly thought. He was going to take Reese's ship.

He could do it, too—any of them could. In an emergency it would only take a single crewman to get the lander back up to Deimos, to refuel the

Mission Module, to pilot the big ship all the way back to Earth.

"Don't—" she said, but the hatch had already closed and the indicator over the door flashed red.

No one else seemed to understand what was happening. They stood frozen in place, their shoulders starting to relax, Frontera forgotten, Curtis dismissed.

Somewhere she found the strength to walk. She looked at the charred spots on her gloves, couldn't see any serious damage to the suit. She pushed a helmet over her head and got a green telltale on her chestpack at the same time she started the pumps to fill the airlock.

She looked back, saw the others starting to move, the fear taking hold in their faces, but she couldn't hear them in the sealed environment of the suit. The airlock light went green and she opened the hatch and got inside and slammed it shut again.

The wait seemed impossibly long, but there were no thoughts at all in her mind, just an agonizing awareness of how slowly time was moving. And then, finally, the outer hatch cycled open and she crawled out into a hell of blowing sand.

Hydraulics drew the hatch shut behind her. She took a few staggering steps into the night, unable to see anything but the billowing dust in the light of her helmet. She switched off the lamp and let the darkness close in around her.

There, in the distance, barely visible through the storm, were the lights of Frontera.

She dropped to her knees and held onto a chunk of frozen lava, weak with relief. There was time yet.

"Hello?" she said into her suit radio. "Hello, is anybody monitoring?" She fumbled with the switch on top of her chestpack and tried the emergency frequency. "Mayday, for christ's sake, somebody answer me!"

No one there. Of course not, the alarm had gone off, they had abandoned the dome. She tried the short-range frequency again. "This is Molly, I need to get through to Mayakenska, is she there? For god's sake, if you can hear me—"

"Mayakenska is gone," said a voice in her ear. She thought she recognized the voice of the other Russian, the tall blond.

"Gone?"

"It is too late," the voice said. "There is nothing you can do to stop it now."

"No," Molly said. She stood up again, lost her balance, and rolled four or five meters down the slope. "No, you have to stop them—"

She looked up to see a line of ruby light, narrow as a spotlight beam, connect Frontera to the sky overhead.

"No," she screamed, and then she screamed again, without words.

It was not a spectacular death. Where the laser cut through a living module there was a tiny burst of flame, barely visible from where Molly lay; before the fire could spread, the carbon dioxide smothered it. The beam moved steadily down the length of the dome, then crossed it from side to side.

Molly saw the Center explode, a brighter flare that sent glowing chunks of concrete into the dust and darkness. And finally, just before it disappeared, the creeping line of red touched the reserve oxygen tanks in the north wall and melted them in a hot, blue sphere of fire.

She hardly noticed when the airlock opened and a single, suited figure came out, wearing an infra-red helmet and carrying a gun in its hand. "Kane?" she said, but the helmet only paused for a second as its gaze swept past her, and no one answered. The figure bounded down the slope and disappeared into the swirling sand.

Molly leaned against the rock and closed her eyes. She was still there when the first of the survivors began to climb past her toward the cave.

• • •

Twenty miles from the Salyut, when it had just become a point light-source on her screens, Mayakenska fired her retros. ⸰

She wanted to keep the thrust at maximum, to ram them out of the sky, but her common sense held her back. And then she saw the hair-thin line of red wink into existence and she knew that it would not have made any difference, that nothing she could have done would have mattered.

They had been ignoring her signals but now she tried again. "This is Mayakenska. You must stop this attack. You must—" She broke off in rage and frustration, trying to slam her fist into the control panel. With no weight behind it the gesture was feeble and meaningless, serving only to wrench her shoulders off to the right and nearly spin her out of her chair.

She forced herself to lean back into the sling, tightening her straps against the negligible thrust of the retros, and concentrate on the upcoming rendezvous.

She'd swept across the daylight side of Mars, over the western edge of the Elysium Planitia and the Syrtis Major Planitia in twenty minutes, watching the digital propellant gauge counting backwards toward empty tanks and the various forms that disaster could take. One by one she watched the gruesome possibilities put to rest: not enough fuel to reach escape velocity, not enough height to reach the Salyut, not enough thrust for the retros.

Now she only had the docking to worry about, and that no longer mattered.

She had defied her superiors, gambled against time and lost. In the old days she would have become a non-person, pensioned out or even sent to a GULag as an example. She wondered what the current equivalent would be; a desk job in Yakutsk, or perhaps an auto accident on an empty stretch of road?

Gently she nosed the ship into a higher, slower orbit as she closed on the green, tapering cylinder of the Salyut. Once her greatest pleasure had been the hours she'd bought on the simulators with her position, her *blat*. Now she flew the actual ship with less feeling than she'd had on the dullest hour in training, as far beyond emotion as she was beyond fatigue.

With cautious puffs of hydrazine from her attitude jets, she brought the nose of the lander into the Salyut berth, feeling the latches click solidly into place.

She reached for the toggle switches that would pump air into the tunnel between the lander and the Salyut, and then stopped her hand halfway there.

What you're thinking, she told herself, is murder. Worse than murder, it's treason.

And what do you call the cold-blooded destruction of the dome? she asked. Russians died down there, not just Americans and Japanese.

She moved her arm back to her side. She felt the feverish chill of sweat drying on her forehead and cheeks. It's not something, she thought, that you talk yourself into. It's an emotional decision, and you know you're not going to do it now; you've lost the impulse. So go ahead and turn those switches, pump in the air, finish all the seals. Don't think about the other possibilities . . .

Her radio crackled. "Mademoiselle Mayakenska, please complete your seal on the tunnel. You are hereby ordered to place yourself under arrest and surrender the landing vehicle—"

In a rush of anger and despair, her hands shot to the console and typed in a series of numbers. Numbers Chaadayev would never have heard of, numbers known only to the most senior ground personnel. The computer asked her to verify the order and she did it.

The explosive bolts that held the airlock hatch in place blew off in silence, shaking the lander like a rabbit in the jaws of a dog. But the latches held her firmly to the Salyut and in a few seconds everything was still again.

Three men had died, the air sucked from their lungs, the moisture leached from their skin, their eyes nearly blown from their sockets.

Murdered.

She closed her eyes.

Go on, she thought. You can't stop here. It's too late to bring them back, to undo any of this. So take it one step at a time.

But finish it.

She removed the hatch from the nose of the lander and crawled through into the long, narrow hallway of the Salyut. The air of the ship seemed to be filled with stars, winking between the orbiting bodies of the three dead cosmonauts; after a second or two Mayakenska realized the lights were tiny, frozen crystals of blood.

She brushed past Chaadayev's corpse and patched her helmet radio into the transmitter. "Dawn, this is Zenith. Zenith calling Dawn. Mayakenska here. The American base is destroyed. I regret to report that our information was inaccurate, they—" She stopped, took her finger off the transmit button to get her breath, then started again.

"The transporter did not—does not exist. I . . . examined the rock which was supposedly destroyed by the antimatter. I found traces of plastic explosive and indications that others of the rocks had been similarly wired. It was . . . only a hoax."

She released the button again. And now what? The lander was out of fuel, but even if she could get back to the surface, what kind of life could she have there? Curtis would still be alive, sheltered by the rock walls of his cave, and he would hold her accountable.

For that matter, without the dome, what kind of life would any of them have?

Her eyes came to rest on the propellant gauge, reminding her that the outboard tanks had been filled at the Phobos station. She had more than enough fuel to get back to Earth, but that, she thought, watching the frozen corpses in their grisly *pas de trois*, was no longer an alternative.

She tried to remember. How big a crater would it take? Deep enough to hold in two or three hundred millibars of pressure, at least three or four kilometers deep. Would the fuel tanks, pushed by the mass of the Salyut, protected by the carbon-carbon heatshield of the lander, make that big an explosion?

She didn't know.

If not, she thought, then let it be a gesture. A first, halting step.

"Zenith to Dawn. We are preparing to leave orbit." She flicked the power switch on and off to create static in the transmission. "Dawn, there is a problem with our attitude control. Repeat, we are experiencing—"

She switched the radio off, then smashed it with a wrench. No backing out, she told herself. She would display no lack of moral certainty.

A little hardship would now be required.

She programmed the computer for a course that would take her into the Solis Planum, the frozen wasteland they used to call Solis Lacus, the Lake of the Sun. The buried ice there would melt and add to the explosion, releasing precious gasses into the air. For an instant its name would become the literal truth, and it would burn with the brightness and heat of a star.

If Blok had sounded the alarm, then there would be survivors. That cave was the original settlement; it had supported the colony before the dome was built, and it could support them again until they moved to their new home.

For one final time she felt the pull of gravity as the Salyut dove into the martian atmosphere, the thin air screaming against the lander's heat shield.

She listened as the long, high note climbed the scale and held at a perfect B above high C.

Kane felt the impact in his ribs and the muscles of his neck, no more, really, than a burst of light and a second of galvanic shock. He rolled onto his hands and knees and let the blood flow into his brain.

The noise of the alarms was so great that Kane could no longer hear the high harmony of his voices. For the first time since they'd touched down on Mars—had it been only a day and a half ago?—he had his mind to himself.

It made little difference. Even without the compulsion from the implant, his course was obvious: kill Curtis, steal the panel, return to Earth and bring justice to his uncle.

The sirens faltered for a second and Kane saw a vision of depthless crystal seas fouled with blood, of butchered flesh in the wake of the ship. He saw the dusty yard of a monastery and a filthy, bearded monk on his knees, praying for the waters to be released.

The sirens stopped and the compulsion seized him again with fierce inevitability. He burrowed through the sheets of black plastic, searching for his gun, hearing only the voices in his head and not the ones across the cave from him, muted indistinct noises with no semantic content.

The implant worked on his adrenal gland as well, renewing the effect of Lena's adrenogen. He felt the chill of norepinephrine constricting his blood vessels; his kidneys ached from the tension of the surrounding musculature.

He saw the gun.

His hand closed around it and he stood up, dizzy, edgy, barely in control. He saw Curtis by the airlock, putting on a helmet, and he raised the Colt until the sight covered Curtis's neck. Before he could fire, Curtis had moved, turning and jackknifing into the lock.

He remembered the storm, though the image in his mind was muddled, confused with gray waves and clashing rocks. But he knew he needed the infrared helmet, could remember having thrown it somewhere near where he stood.

By the time he'd found the helmet Molly had gone through after Curtis. Kane ran for the hatch, pushing Hanai to one side. A voice behind him said, "He's got a gun!" as he slammed the helmet in place and dived into the airlock.

The inside of the lock was smeared with the heat of the bodies that had just passed through it. He tapped the butt of the gun against the curved metal floor of the cylinder, his right leg shaking to the rhythm.

The hatch opened. He slid out and stared toward Frontera, at the blinding column of white light that overloaded the contrast sensors of his helmet, reducing the rest of the planet to deep green.

"Son of a bitch," he said, only realizing he'd vocalized it when he saw the droplets of spittle on the inside of his helmet.

He turned his head downward, blocking the worst

of the light with his hands, and made out Curtis as a dull yellow blotch moving down the slope. A few yards away Molly lay with her knees drawn up almost to her chin, as close to a fetal position as the clumsy rigid suit would allow.

Kane moved down the side of the volcano, his feet turned sideways for better traction, each leap jolting his ribcage and firing off telegrams of pain. The laser had vanished and the ruins of the dome glittered in oily white heat, bringing the foreground back into focus, the cold lumps of rock, the molten patch where the Russian ship had been, the warm orange of Kane's own ship, the dull red of Curtis's suit and the brighter red of the panel under Curtis's arm.

He could hear Curtis's heavy breathing through the speakers in his helmet. It would be bad for Curtis, in the darkness and chaos of the storm, and Kane knew it was his one advantage. If he failed to catch Curtis before they got to the ruins of the dome . . .

No, he realized. It wasn't the dome Curtis wanted. It was the ship.

He forced himself into longer, more reckless leaps and he forgot the strength of the wind. It unbalanced him as his legs reached for an open square of ground and threw him too far forward, sent him falling endlessly toward the rocks, so slowly that he had time to wrap his arms around his chest before he hit. The rigid suit bounced and rolled, rattling him inside it like dice in a cup.

The lights on his chestpack still glowed, but his infrared scanner could not distinguish between red

and green. The suit was all right, he told himself.
If it was compromised, he would already know.

Get up, he told himself.

He got up.

Curtis was nearly to the ascent stage of the ship,
but Kane had picked up a few yards on him. He
could see the articulation of Curtis's suit in shades
of red, see the man's arms stretched blindly in
front of him.

And behind him came new shapes, a dozen or
more suited refugees from the dome, stumbling
toward Curtis, toward the ship, toward the mouth
of Kane's gun.

"Curtis!" Kane shouted.

Curtis stopped, turned halfway back toward the
cave.

Kane ran at him, holding the gun in front of
him. He was a hundred feet away, eighty, sixty. He
slowed himself, feet skidding in the dust, almost
falling again, and sighted down the barrel of the
Colt.

Now, he thought, now, quickly, before there are
too many others underfoot, now while you have a
clean shot.

Something was making his helmet vibrate.

He looked to his right, to the south and east, and
saw a tiny ball of flame rip through the sky. It
vanished into the horizon near the Syria Planum
and a moment later a perfect hemisphere of molten white rose like a new sun.

An asteroid? Kane wondered. If so it had been
enormous, and the impact must have been devastating. . . .

He whirled back to face Curtis and saw him climbing the side of the lander.

"Curtis!" he shouted again, and he fired the Colt, missing Curtis and leaving a white hot streak where the bullet had grazed the spacecraft. Before he could fire again Curtis dropped to the ground behind the ship and disappeared.

The radio band hissed and rattled with the frightened voices of the refugees; Kane switched his receiver off and ran after Curtis. He dodged between the stumbling automatons who'd been left night-blind and disoriented by the storm, following the retreating image of Curits's suit. The heat of the ruins was closer now; the analytical circuitry of the helmet dropped Curtis to a dull yellow in comparison. Kane yearned for another shot but had no chance in the milling crowd.

Curtis had broken for the eastern side of the dome, dodging through a gaping, melted wound in the wall. Kane slowed to walk, his lungs burning, his concentration breaking down.

The dome was ravaged, mangled beyond repair. Superheated gasses had blown globs and droplets of molten plastic for hundreds of yards in all directions, leaving only a few hundred square feet of limp, opaque plastic over the burned and frozen fields.

Something moved in a gap in the wall and Kane almost fired, then saw that it was a child in a low-pressure shuttle suit. From the obvious pain in her motion Kane could see that the four psi oxygen in the suit had left her with the bends, excruciating bubbles of nitrogen in the joints of her arms and legs.

There was nothing Kane could do for her; if she got to the cave in time, the pain would eventually go away.

There would only be worse inside the ruined dome.

The first thing he saw as he stepped through the wall was a corpse, embolized, nearly as cold as the ground beneath Kane's feet. A few yards away lay a hand, with no sign of the body it belonged to.

Kane was sweating heavily. He had no idea where Curtis was; at any moment the man could circle back and blend in with the others heading uphill toward the cave. Kane turned constantly to check his back, and at least once every minute he stumbled back outside to make sure the ship was still there.

When the rumbling started under his feet he thought it was a hallucination. Then he saw that the brown, spongy walls of the shattered living modules were quaking and that bits of congealed plastic were falling from overhead.

No one was left alive inside the dome. He saw a flash of heat and fired at it, then saw that it was only a jet of warm air escaping from a sealed room.

His knees shook from the vibration underfoot. A high-tensile aluminum strut tumbled gently to the ground just in front of him, shattering frozen stalks of corn as if they were stained glass sculptures.

He had to get out. He ran for the nearest break in the wall and saw a pane of plastic explode a few inches away from his head. Curtis, he thought, aiming at the noise Kane had made. He threw himself forward and rolled, bringing the gun up as he fell.

Nothing moved.

I can't stand this, Kane thought. The roaring was in his ears now, coming up through the soil and vibrating the air in his suit. He pushed himself up on his elbows and saw Curtis running for the ship.

The survivors, a few dozen of them at most, were bright dots on the slope leading up to the cave. No bystanders, Kane thought, no more mistakes.

The shockwave came up out of the southeast at the speed of sound, a white-hot tidal wave of dust and ash and volatile gasses ten miles high. It picked Kane up and flung him against the wall of the broken dome so hard that he blacked out for an instant, and when he came around he was stunned, overwhelmed by the deafening chorus of voices in his brain, hurting in at least a dozen parts of his body.

He saw the lander still, somehow, standing upright on the plain.

He saw Curtis get to his feet and run for the hatch of the lander, the panel still hanging from one arm.

He raised the gun and fired, saw Curtis clutch his leg and go down.

He pulled the hammer back, watching globular patterns of reflected heat crawl across the visor of Curtis's helmet.

He fired again, saw the visor split and the face behind it explode, spraying steam and tiny droplets of blood into the churning air.

The gun tumbled out of Kane's limp fingers. He pushed himself away from the wall, took one step, then another. He stumbled, went to his knees, got up and walked some more.

The first time he tried to pull the panel from Curtis's fingers he lost his balance and went down again, his knees hitting Curtis's chest in an accidental echo of his own broken ribs, his helmet thumping into the ruin of Curtis' face as his momentum carried him forward. He tugged again and the panel came free.

It's over, he thought. He stood on the threshold of the Return, the conceptual rebirth. He put one hand on the ladder, pulled one leg onto the bottom rung. Back to Earth with the panel. Kill the king, marry the princess.

He shook his head. There was no princess. What was he thinking of?

"Takahashi?" he said. His radio was off.

He pulled himself another step up the ladder. He thought of the curvature of the ship's orbit, a Hohmann elipse that would match the one that had brought him here and complete the circle, perfect the symmetry.

Curtis lay in the dust beneath him like the monk he'd seen in his dreams, desiccated, shattered, the promise of his Pattern betrayed.

The body in the wake of the ship, Medea's brother Aegialeus, butchered to delay Aeëtes' vengeance; the embolized victims inside the ruptured dome. Morgan owns you, Lena said. Symmetry breaking, the beginning of life. When I am grown to a man's estate.

He slammed his helmet into the side of the ship, waking himself up. Somewhere in the back of his skull the biological circuit whispered to him in neural languages that his conscious mind could not hear, sweet, irresistible voices that told him to take the panel, to lift the ship.

Yamato-Takeru knew, Kane thought; he'd felt his spirit stolen away from him, just like this.

Every separate human life, the boy had said. A moment of the life of some great being which lives in us.

The membrane parted again and Kane saw them all, Jason and Percival and the hundreds of other human lives and the single Pattern they formed, the single act they performed again and again, outside time, each of them with their own unique moment, their own contribution.

Kane knew what his had to be.

Molly was still sitting on the cliffside when Kane found her. He had remembered to turn his radio on again, but he couldn't find the words that he needed.

Takahashi stood next to her, with three or four others. In the aftermath of the shockwave the dust had settled and the night was turning clear.

"It was the Russian ship," Takahashi said. Kane looked at him with incomprehension. "Mayakenska. She crashed the Salyut in the Solis Planum. That was the explosion."

"The oasis," Kane said.

"The beginning of one, anyway. If the crater's not deep enough, some of Verb's antimatter can finish it up. I guess it was her way of trying to settle up."

"Not much . . . not much of a trade," Kane said, looking back at the ruins of Frontera, cooled now to within a few degrees of the plain around it.

"No," Takahashi said. "But it's a start."

Kane knelt in the dirt in front of Molly. "Take this," he said, and he put the panel in her hands. "Build ships."

"Kane . . ."

"Shut up, Takahashi," he said. There was more, but this was not the time for it. Later he would tell her about the rest of his plans, a full-fledged relief mission with food and medicine and whatever else they needed. A treaty with Aeroflot to keep them safe. But he would tell her later, by radio, once he was on his way back to Earth.

"Where's Lena?" he asked.

"Inside," Takahashi said. "She's staying. There's a lot of work for her here. They're all staying, even Hanai. That doesn't matter; the two of us can run the ship. But we have to have that panel. That's what we came for."

"Is it?" Kane said. "I don't think so."

"Kane . . ."

"We've got time," Kane said. "We need these people, they need us. We'll work it out." Even without eye contact Kane could feel Takahashi's will bending to the new order. "Go on ahead," he said. "Get the ship ready. I'll be there in a minute."

Takahashi turned and walked away.

"Curtis?" Molly said.

Kane leaned toward her, put both his hands on her helmet and held it facing his own.

"He's dead," Kane said.

Her hands closed around the panel and she seemed to nod; she got up and carried it toward the airlock.

Kane had a vision of her, standing under a green

martian sky, hair blowing in the wind, dressed in a heavy jacket and mask, but standing in the open air, thick, green shrubbery at her feet.

The vision was his own, not a product of the implant; his voices were silent. He wondered if Molly would hear them when her time came, if she would see the ghost of Odysseus in the video screens of the ships that would take her to Io and Titan and on to the stars.

The colors of the night began to shimmer and bleed until the martian landscape glowed like Reese's gateway. Only a force of will held Kane's perceptions together as he walked down the hillside that would lead him back to his ship, back to the Earth, back to his kingdom.

AUTHOR'S NOTE

Kane's Pattern is the Pattern of the Hero, detailed in Joseph Campbell's *Hero With A Thousand Faces* (Bollingen, 1968). Quotations from the *I Ching* are from the Wilhelm/Baynes version (Bollingen, 1967); quotations from Ouspensky's *Tertium Organum* are from the Bessaraboff/Bragdon translation (Vintage, 1970).

I would like to particularly acknowledge the superb nonfiction books of James E. Oberg, which were indispensible in the writing of this novel: *Red Star in Orbit* (Random House, 1981), *New Earths* (Stackpole, 1981), and *Mission to Mars* (Stackpole, 1982).